THE STORY
OF A
STRANGE TIME

THE STORY
OF A
STRANGE TIME

Leonid Borodin

*Translated from the Russian and with
a Foreword by Frank Williams*

COLLINS HARVILL
8 Grafton Street, London W1
1990

COLLINS HARVILL
William Collins Sons & Co. Ltd
London · Glasgow · Sydney · Auckland
Toronto · Johannesburg

BRITISH LIBRARY CATALOGUING IN PUBLICATION DATA

Borodin, Leonid, *1938–*
The story of a strange time.
1. Fiction in Russian, 1945–   Translations
I. Title   II. Povest strannogo vremeni. *English*
891.73′44 [F]

ISBN 0-00-271768-9

First published by Possev Verlag in 1978
under the title *Povest strannogo vremeni*
First published in Great Britain
by Collins Harvill 1990

© Possev Verlag, V. Gorachek K. G., 1978
Translation and Foreword © William Collins Sons & Co. Ltd 1990

Photoset in Linotron Imprint by
Rowland Phototypesetting Ltd
Bury St Edmunds, Suffolk
Printed and bound in Great Britain by
William Collins Sons & Co. Ltd, Glasgow

CONTENTS

FOREWORD

by Frank Williams

Gorbachev's abandonment in February 1990 of Article 6 of the Soviet Constitution, the article that guaranteed the Communist Party its leading role in society and its monopoly of power, like so many of Gorbachev's reforms was conceded grudgingly and too late. It did not, in the USSR at least, feel like the triumph it should have done. It was just another marker on the long, weary trudge towards the dismantling of a totalitarian regime that had stifled and trampled on everything that posed the least challenge to its authority.

In its own quiet way, Leonid Borodin's *Story of a Strange Time* is a literary milestone on that road.

"I have had an easy life," Borodin told a Soviet magazine recently. "I never faced the problem of having to make a choice." Born in the Siberian city of Irkutsk, Borodin started studying history at Irkutsk University in 1956, the year of Khrushchev's secret speech. A year later he was expelled for organising a group called "Free Word". His subsequent career path was very similar to others who refused to bend their views and trade their principles – labouring jobs in mines, building sites and factories, working as a stoker or janitor. Later, though, he received a diploma from a teachers' training college in Ulan-Ude. In his early thirties, when working at a school near Leningrad, Borodin joined the All-Russian Union for the Liberation of the People, VSKhSON, a group of Russian nationalist militants dedicated to the overthrow of communism and its replacement with an Orthodox Christian state. In 1967 the group's leaders were arrested and put on trial. Borodin was

given six years in a labour camp. It was there he began to
formulate the moral dimension of the struggle against the regime
in fiction, writing poetry and stories, including the ones published here, which he sent out of the camp in the form of letters
to his mother.

Borodin was arrested a second time in May 1982 on charges
of anti-Soviet agitation and propaganda. Among the items
on the charge-sheet were publishing a samizdat magazine,
Moskovsky sbornik, circulating Solzhenitsyn's *Gulag Archipelago* and sending a telegram to the author congratulating him
on his sixtieth birthday, plus the writing and publication
abroad of *The Story of a Strange Time*. Once again a Soviet
writer was identified by a court with his literary heroes and
Borodin received a sentence of ten years in a special-regime
camp to be followed by five years' exile. This is the harshest
regime, reserved for those considered a special threat to the
state, and he was not expected to emerge from Perm 36/1 alive.
Then in the summer of 1987, on the day his novel *Partings*
was published in London, news came of his release, part
of the wave of amnesties of political prisoners ordered by
Gorbachev.

Since then, Borodin has been slowly recovering his health
and also steadily entering Russian literary life. He has been
written about, made television appearances and his writing has
begun to be published in the literary monthlies. Soviet critics
have begun assigning him a place on the nationalist wing
of the literary spectrum alongside Valentin Rasputin, now
a member of Gorbachev's Presidential Council, as a writer
concerned for the spiritual regeneration of the Russian people.

Nationalism has become associated with an extreme con-
servative stance that is nakedly imperialist, demanding the
preservation of the Soviet Union in its existing boundaries,
and violently xenophobic, not to say racist. Anti-semitism is
the hallmark of the "patriotic forces" whether literary (Vassily
Belov and Viktor Astafyev), or in the Party (Nina Andreyeva).
Literary meetings in Moscow have degenerated into brawls,

while assaults on liberal writers by Pamyat street-fighters have been dismissed by "patriotic" writers as exaggerations.

Borodin, never an active participant in literary life, official or unofficial, has remained aloof. Whatever he may think of liberals, he has done nothing that might associate him with the squalid hysteria of the "patriots".

A recent article in a Soviet magazine recommending Borodin to Soviet readers and calling for the publication of his novel *The Third Truth*, drew attention to his commitment to a neglected truth, the truth that springs from the harsh daily experience of the Russian people, a commitment to a spiritual authenticity the official world tried to destroy and the liberal intelligentsia has done much, in this view, to pervert. The search, as these early stories show, has been a consistent one.

FRANK WILLIAMS
May, 1990

THE MEETING

KOZLOV HAD DONE some boxing in his time. He'd been knocked out more than once, so he well knew the feeling of coming back from oblivion, the sensation when you can't feel your own body to begin with and it's as though you're discovering your own existence for the first time. Your consciousness seems to leave your body and find the outside world. Your mind is splintered into a thousand pieces. The splinters are slowly drawn towards the centre, and then, in a last sudden rush, recreate the whole. You recognise yourself, recognise the world and you become aware of your body.

The first thing Kozlov felt was pain in his leg. He raised himself on one elbow and looked up at the sky, hoping to tell by the sun how long he'd been out cold. But as if to spite him, the sky had been a mass of dirty wadding since morning, with not a hint of a break. His sub-machine gun lay near his feet. Kozlov looked around. He called out, not too loud, but the answering silence told him he was completely on his own. His chin was throbbing. He touched it and saw blood on his hand. It felt like his cheekbone had been smashed, as well as a right tooth, several teeth perhaps. He'd been knocked out good and proper. Only why was his leg hurting as well? He felt down his boot. He hadn't been kicked as well? Couldn't make head or tail of it. The man who hit him had taken off. He'd left

Kozlov his gun, though, so that was something to be thankful
for.

But there was no time to sit and think. He had to get away.
He wasn't in the clear yet. These open birch woods were no
place to be. He had to find proper forest. And he didn't
know these parts. Kozlov looked about him, trying to find his
bearings, touched his injured cheek, shook his head, slipped
the strap of the sub-machine gun around his neck and walked
east.

* * *

He had been unlucky to start with, he fetched up in a
group of prisoners from other units. Most of them were in low
spirits, hungry or wounded . . . He decided to make a break
for it at the first opportunity and began looking for a likely
comrade. After careful observation, he fell in step with a
surly, grim-faced sergeant with a labourer's massive hands.
He made his approach. The sergeant didn't even look at him,
he just swore long and hard, then spat: "Another bloody
hero!"

Kozlov barely restrained himself from thumping him across
the ear. Then he noticed a lanky private. The man wasn't
wearing glasses, but you could tell he did normally by the way
he was squinting and the red mark across the bridge of his
nose. Kozlov summed him up instantly – Specs wasn't worth
bothering with. And put him out of his mind immediately.
But the private kept bobbing up in front of him. It made
Kozlov uneasy. Every time he looked around he caught
Specs looking away. "What's the bugger up to?" Kozlov
thought, and decided this called for a recce. He went up to the
man and asked point blank: "Got a smoke, mate?" Specs
didn't know what to say. He blinked his long fair eyelashes,
croaked a hoarse "No", and dodged away behind another
man's back.

They were marched to repair a stretch of railway. Thirty of

4

them. With a guard of six soldiers and two dogs. Not many for thirty men. More than enough for one, though. All the same, Kozlov had a feeling today would be the day.

He set to work like the others. Men dragged up sleepers, laid rails, drove in spikes, levelled ballast with wooden shovels. The work was hard. The war had been going a month. People had had it up to here.

Kozlov had fought in the Finnish campaign. He reckoned himself a professional and couldn't forgive himself for being captured. It was a short but nasty episode. Kozlov decided to blot it out of his memory and his life. There was something he had to do. He had to get away, and he would . . . By midday Kozlov felt that the situation had changed in his favour. What did he have going for him? First, the men were now strung out for a hundred metres or so along the track. Second, while the guards had begun by taking position some distance away and so been able to keep all the work-party within their field of fire, now they'd come up so close they were almost in amongst the men, yelling at them to keep going. Finally, and this was the key element, the dog-handlers had gone down to the far end of the work-party. The near end was gradually working its way to a patch of forest which came right up to the track. It wasn't of any great size, Kozlov could see fields on the far side, but it was enough for him to try and run for it.

His nerves were at breaking point. His hands were damp; sweat beaded his forehead. Then who should he see but Specs. It was more than Kozlov could take. "What are you sniffing around for, you bastard? It can't be that bloody obvious, surely?" thought Kozlov, clenching his jaw so hard it hurt. "Just you try getting in my way!"

There was a bark of German close behind. Kozlov dutifully swung his sledgehammer down on the burred head of the spike. Sharp-toed boots appeared on his left. They stopped a moment, then moved away. The shouting came again, further up the line this time.

In the very heart of Russia, amidst waving cornfields and quiet, shady forests, at the very heart of the Russian silence that felt strange to people stunned by misfortune, these men felt unreal, like they were actors in some bizarre play. It seemed that in a moment or two the author of all this would step forward, wave a magic wand and tell them to wake up. And they would straighten up, throw down their picks and shovels, laugh and slap each other on the back, tear off those absurd rags and they would all go their own separate ways. How could it be otherwise? This was Russia, it was their land! Amidst the soft, melodious polyphony of Russian was there not something unnatural about those harsh, crude, meaningless sounds? "Arbeiten!" What connection could that have with the blackbird singing overhead? Or the sky? The sky . . . Well, yes . . . the sky . . . The sky probably does have a connection with everything that happens on Russian soil. It's not clean and wholesome, it's sick. There's more to it than being simply gloomy or overcast. Yes, it is only the sky that affirms that yes, disaster has struck, it's not a dream, the disaster is real and very few people know how to withstand it. How else to explain thirty Russian men bending their backs to orders from eight foreigners, or more precisely, six foreigners and two dogs? Though it amounts to the same. The six happen to have sub-machine guns. The thirty don't. A sub-machine gun! A cunningly engineered lump of metal, no more. But the difference it makes to a man! Muscles turn to steel when the hands mould to its cold metal grips, when the finger rests on the trigger, so responsive, so obedient. With a sub-machine gun in your hands, your life is worth thirty enemy lives. Not a bad price that! Armed with only a pick, weak from hunger and wounds, what is your life worth then? The Germans are a methodical nation. They had made the calculation. Six divided by thirty makes one fifth. So he, Kozlov, was valued at one fifth of that thug with a sub-machine gun who was coming back his way.

Kozlov could see him without lifting his head. He could see

something else; the fifteen to twenty metres distance to the trees, the lone German, the dogs at the far end of the work-party. He could also see the German's finger on the trigger, the safety-catch off, and that the man knew his stuff – he was like a coiled spring. Kozlov had a sledgehammer. Three blows and the spike was in the sleeper. H-up – smash, h-up – smash . . . "H-one fifth, h-one fifth . . . " The German was just a few steps away. Five steps from the man who was worth only a fifth as much. "Whole of bloody history worked out, the buggers," Kozlov growled through his teeth. "Barbarossa, my arse! Won't work out this time!" Three steps. H-up – smash. The German alongside now. H-up . . . The German was behind. Kozlov wheeled and brought the sledgehammer down on the cropped ginger nape.

The soldier fell without a sound onto his stomach. Kozlov jerked him over, grabbed the gun, tugged. The strap snagged on the man's neck. Kozlov tugged again, and saw a second guard in front of him. For a second they both froze, looking at each other. The soldier's hands were resting on top of his gun. They both moved: Kozlov snatched the sub-machine gun off the neck of the stunned or dead German, his opponent made ready to fire. Every fraction of a second counted. Kozlov was bound to lose – the German only had to pull the trigger. But in that split second, a sledgehammer came down on the German's head. He crumpled. Behind him was the infuriating lanky private, holding a sledgehammer. He stood there looking helpless.

"The gun," Kozlov yelled.

Specs dropped the sledgehammer, fussed over the German's body. Kozlov swore, bounded over, wrenched the sub-machine gun free, thrust it into Specs' hands. "Let's go!" he yelled and ran for it.

About fifty metres into the trees, Kozlov allowed himself to look back. Specs was about ten paces behind, eyes staring, arms and sub-machine gun waving. With his mouth wide open, he looked like a fish out of water.

"Breathe through your nose," shouted Kozlov, without slackening his pace.

They were almost out of the trees when there was a crackle of shots and the first hornets buzzed viciously near his head. Kozlov knew from experience they weren't that close: you never heard the one with your number on it.

A strip of field about two hundred metres wide opened up ahead, beyond it more trees and then what appeared to be a drop into a ravine. Specs was lagging thirty or so paces behind, but he was running for all he was worth, still with his mouth open. Kozlov stopped and heard barking. The dogs were already in the forest. Specs stopped next to him, panting hard. He went pale when he heard them.

"We'll face them. Give me cover," Kozlov shouted. He could see Specs didn't have a clue what to do, so he shouted again, harder, sharper. "Stand over here. If I miss, get them with the butt!"

This was something Specs did understand. He grabbed hold of the barrel and took up position next to Kozlov.

These were the right tactics. Better to take on the dogs here than out in the open. Their handlers wouldn't risk following them. There were four of them left now. Kozlov felt peeved nobody else had got away. "They ran for it," he kept reassuring himself for some reason. "Scattered all over the place." He still felt peeved. If it hadn't been for Specs, that German would have got him. Irritating . . .

An Alsatian came bounding out of the bushes, barking. Kozlov fired a short burst. The dog cartwheeled into a tree-stump and lay still. He used a similar short burst, to conserve ammunition, on the second – to equally good effect. This dog, though, somersaulted in mid air. It got up, sort of skipped, fell, got up again. Its yelps echoed through the trees, sounding almost human. Then it began crawling along the ground, sometimes rising on its hind legs, its front paws clasped around its head as if trying to dislodge, scratch out the bullet. Certain the dog was mortally wounded, Kozlov turned to his companion. Still posturing aggressively, clutching the barrel of his gun in both hands, Specs was staring wide-eyed at the dog as it thrashed in agony.

Then they walked, without stopping and without talking, across fields, through trees, along ravines, for three hours, not less. Only when they had put about fifteen kilometres between them and the railway did Kozlov call a halt in a thick belt of trees.

"Drop," he said to his companion and flopped down into the grass. He lay face down, motionless, for five minutes or so. Then he got up, walked over to Specs, who was sitting with his back against a tree, and held out his hand: "Time we introduced ourselves, right?"

Something suddenly changed in the other man's face, a kind of spasm passed, or rather flashed from his chin to his lips and up his cheeks. His eyelids jerked, his eyelashes quivered, his ginger eyebrows twitched, and then his face froze into a mask. Kozlov could see the man was angry, furious even. When he got up and stood next to Kozlov, he turned out to be half a head taller and Kozlov found he had to tilt his head back in order to meet his companion's penetrating stare, the points of the pupils boring into him. Finally the man's bloodless lips moved and he shouted right in Kozlov's face: "We don't need any introductions! Understand? Do you understand?"

His gangly, skinny body towered over Kozlov. Kozlov stepped back in utter bewilderment. The other bore down on him shouting, mouth open wide, Adam's apple bobbing, blinking myopically. It was funny, and Kozlov probably would have laughed if at that moment he hadn't taken an uppercut on the jaw which knocked him unconscious for quite some time.

*　　*　　*

The trees petered out. A village showed ahead. Kozlov wearily lowered himself into the grass after discovering a huge patch of wild strawberries. He crawled in the grass for half an hour, never letting go his gun. The scented strawberries melted in the mouth and accentuated his pangs of hunger. He was also thirsty. All the ravines and gullies he had come across were either dry or had damp stinking mud at the bottom.

A fat, metre-long snake slid with a revolting hiss from beneath his hand. Kozlov cleared out of there like greased lightning. "That'd be one for the books," Kozlov thought with a shudder. "Escape from Fritz and be done in by one of our vipers! What a lark!" He had to press on. He decided to skirt the village from the right; there was a dip on that side and there might be water. He followed the edge of the trees, crossed a wide country road and soon came to the edge of a deep gully. At the bottom a feeble trickle meandered across sticky clay. Choosing a reasonably dry spot, Kozlov shoved his gun onto his back and dropped onto a dry slab of sandstone. Spreading his hands onto the damp mud for support, he bent over the pathetic apology for a stream and cautiously sucked up the water. He tried not to disturb the sludge at the bottom, which he could almost touch with his nose. At least it was water. It was warm, stinking and had a metallic after-taste, but water nonetheless. He rested a moment and then drank again, but when he made to get up he saw next to his own hand, by now almost completely submerged in mud, another handprint. It couldn't be his – he hadn't changed position. Next to his other hand was another print. Someone else had been drinking at this spot recently. Kozlov took hold of his gun and crept to the edge of the gully. He looked and listened. He could hear cocks crowing, people talking and the putter of motorbikes in the village. It was quiet here. Not a rustle. He went back to his drinking place. There were two sets of hand prints. The other person's fingers were longer and he had placed his hands wider apart when he stooped to drink. He couldn't be following in Specs' tracks, surely? Kozlov wouldn't have minded meeting him again, even if only to find out why he'd thumped him. He touched his chin automatically. The pain had almost gone. The blood had caked hard where the skin was split.

Carefully examining every bush, he ducked and wove his way out of the gully, thinking out each move. He wasn't worried about being hungry. Nobody starves in August: not in the midst of fields, gardens and orchards. But there was a village right here, his own, native, Russian village. Somebody from one of the houses at the end of the village would feed him for sure. Wait for night. There was a field of rye close by, cutting into the village on the right and on the left reaching to the trees where he'd found the strawberries. Bending double, Kozlov made a dash across a small clearing and dived into the golden sea. He pushed his way in a hundred metres or so to where the rye was growing thickest, went down on his knees and, bending low, pulled off his dirty, patched army singlet and spread it out on the flattened straw. First he rubbed the ears that had been trampled, then plucked more. He continued this painstaking work until he had gathered a good scoopful of fresh clean rye on his singlet. He stuffed his mouth with grain, rolled onto his back, closed his eyes, chewed and savoured it, winked to himself, rolled onto his stomach, filled his mouth again and stretched out on his back once more. And the warmth which flowed into his body and gave every muscle zest and an insatiable thirst for life came not just from a feeling of hunger satisfied. Earth was restoring to him the strength that had flowed into her from soldiers' broken bodies . . . He pressed himself, joyously, trustingly, to the earth, to his earth. And he listened, and heard its steady breathing, and his breathing was perfectly in time. So that he felt the freedom he had won with a special keenness. He might be surrounded by the enemy, he might be on his own, wandering his own land like a hunted wolf, unable to lift his head, but he was a soldier once more, with a weapon in his hands. What did that make him worth now, work that one out! What he needed was a couple of magazines of ammunition, plus a couple of grenades. In the next day or so he was bound to run into people who still meant business. If he couldn't get back through the front line (where would it be now?), he'd become a partisan. He was a veteran and knew his worth . . . Those were the thoughts that occupied his mind as he lay there, and his morale was excellent.

Meanwhile evening closed in and there was a chill in the air. Kozlov pulled on his singlet, rose to a half-crouching position, looked around, passed the strap of the sub-machine gun around his neck and made for the village. Slipping through a rail fence, he found himself in the kitchen garden of the end house. At every step he waited for the dogs to start up. Somewhere, two or three houses away, there were a few hoarse, decrepit-sounding barks. But not a peep out of this place. No light showed in the one window that overlooked the garden and the house didn't appear lived in. But no sooner had Kozlov turned the corner of the house than he came face to face with a man, who raised an axe to him and shouted: "What are you creeping round other people's houses for?"

"Quiet," Kozlov tried to hush him. "Quiet. I'm one of yours."

The old man (Kozlov could see him now) lowered his voice slightly, but his tone remained hostile.

"Don't try that on me! I know who's one of us. What d'you want? Speak up!"

"Are there Germans in the village?" asked Kozlov, dismayed by his reception.

"What do you think? Germans, Russians, all sorts. Now you get going, if you know what's good for you."

"What sort of Russians?" Kozlov didn't understand.

"The wrong sort. Polizei, that's what sort!"

The old man had lowered his axe, but he wasn't about to invite Kozlov in.

"You're sending me away, right?" Kozlov grunted.

"And why should I let you into my house when I don't know what you are!"

Kozlov wanted to say "Russian", but he remembered the polizei, and just stood there . . .

The old man went onto the offensive.

"Gets himself a gun and he wants us to kill the fatted calf. Huh!"

"I've escaped, grandad."

The old man cut him short.

"I'm no grandad to you. Over in Orekhovo the Germans have been sharing the womenfolk of big brave lads like you. Grandad he calls me."

"Yeh, you're right. You're just a son of a bitch!" Kozlov spat angrily, and grabbed his sub-machine gun as a shadow flitted behind the old man's back.

"Come into the house," a woman's voice said quietly.

The old man threw his axe down into the darkness and stamped back into the porch.

The woman touched Kozlov's sleeve.

"Come. Come inside," she repeated when she saw Kozlov hesitate. "Don't mind Dad. Come on in, else somebody'll hear. The Germans are in the schoolhouse, the polizei have taken over the village soviet, they're always snooping about."

A few minutes later Kozlov was eating an excellent borshch.

"Go and keep a look out, just in case . . . " said the woman, and the old man went obediently outside. Silently, sadly, the woman examined her guest's face in the dim light of the lamp.

"Was it you hiding in the oaks?"

"When?" asked Kozlov, his spoon halfway to his mouth.

"This evening."

"No."

"Yes, he did look taller," she agreed. She noticed his thoughtful expression and asked. "Do you know him?"

"If he shows up, feed him. He's a good lad, only he's not himself. Shell-shock. Didn't want us to stick together."

He was lying about the shell-shock. But it seemed a likely enough explanation for Specs' odd behaviour.

The old man returned and sat silently on a stool. The woman looked at him reproachfully, but said nothing.

"You'd best go."

That was what she said when he finished his soup: not leave, go. He nodded. He didn't want to, but go he must. The woman went into the other room and came back with a brand new pair of boots. The kind men wear on their wedding day. Kozlov hesitated, but put them on. The woman took his worn-out pair away into the lumber room. She and the old man exchanged looks. Again she went out into the other room and brought out a new black leather jacket. One like that cost a fortune before the war. Kozlov wouldn't have it.

"Take it," she said simply. He took it.

"You're husband's in the army?"

From the way the old man winced and the woman hung her head, he knew he shouldn't have asked. They wouldn't have given the things away if he'd been alive, they'd have kept them as a kind of token that he still was.

He said good-bye. The old man said nothing. The woman came out with him into the yard. In the darkness he was unable to see her face.

"Good luck," she said gently.

He also wanted to say something kind to her, when suddenly she took him by surprise: "My husband's in the polizei. He's living in town with some young tart."

Kozlov was shaken. He started pulling off the jacket in disgust. She seized his arm.

"No! No! It's not his. It's my brother's. He was in the border troops! Please," she pleaded in a whisper.

"You're lying!"

"Honest. My brother's dead. That's why Dad's like he is. Please," she repeated, barely audible.

Kozlov strode through the night. That confident mood which came on him in the field had gone. He thought of the woman whose husband was a traitor, thought of the old man who had lost a son, of his strange companion. Kozlov was almost certain Specs was out of his mind . . . In a month of combat he'd already encountered something similar. One day during an air attack, the commander of one of the companies in his platoon had jumped out of his trench and begun blazing away with a pistol at the dive-bombers. Death was coming down at the rate of a ton per square metre, the earth never had time to fall back to earth, men were blown to tatters, mown down in groups, and this lieutenant went mad. He scrambled onto the ridge of the trench laughing, you could only see it, not hear it, and jumped about, banging away. When he ran out of bullets, he threw his gun at the planes. Fewer than a third of the platoon survived, and the lieutenant, who hadn't a scratch, was tied up and sent to the rear.

People who are "touched" have always been treated decently in Russia. It isn't just a question of feeling sorry for them, but of something else not fully conscious, something undefined. Actually, it isn't only in Russia. It's probably because the intellect is predisposed to duplicity and deceit, common defects. And only someone not over-endowed with intellect is completely devoid of this flaw. Since ancient times people in Russia have appealed to emotion rather than reason, not that this has saved them from disaster.

During the night Kozlov passed two more villages. At dawn he burrowed into a haystack he came across in a small clearing in a birch-wood.

What woke him were voices close by, very close, German voices. A whole lot of them, not less than ten. Instinct told him, as loudly as when he'd made his escape, that he was in a real hole. Despair sucked nauseatingly at the pit of his stomach. His first thought was to lie still and wait. But how! The hay rustled right next to his head, he even felt the tang of human sweat. They were dismantling the stack. They had a bonfire nearby. One more armful and that'd be it . . .

Kozlov snapped back the breech, pushed apart the haystack with his foot and his gun and sprang out into the clearing. Right in front of him, face to face, a scruffy, weedy German holding a mess-tin stood paralysed with shock. Behind him the remaining ten or dozen stood stunned in a variety of postures. Unarmed. Their weapons stacked in a tidy pyramid to one side. Kozlov squatted down. He whistled cheerily as he put a burst into the man with the mess-tin. He swept right, swept left, dropping some of the others onto the bonfire. He kept waiting for the weedy German to fall and open up his field of fire. The German dropped his mess-tin, his jaw went slack, his eyes rolled, and he stood there with his arms spread apart. He looked as if he was saying: "What is all this? What the hell's going on?" Kozlov stitched him with another burst and watched the bullets tear holes in the battledress. But he stayed on his feet, shielding the others. Three Germans made for the weapons. Kozlov knocked them down into a heap and stopped two more making for the trees. It all took less than three minutes. There were only two of them left now in the clearing: Kozlov and the dead German who simply would not fall. The rest were lying on top of each other or scattered where he had cut them down. There was a smell of burnt rags. Kozlov ran over to the stack of weapons, whipped out a couple of magazines, stuck them in his pockets. He decided not to exchange his tried and tested weapon. He took one last look at the miracle of war – a standing corpse – and ran into the trees.

He hadn't gone more than a couple of hundred metres, when he heard automatic fire to the rear. One of them must have been able to take cover. A raspberry-coloured flare whooshed overhead. He could hear motorbikes. Kozlov turned left, soon came to a branching ravine, dropped down into it, ran along it, turned into a deep ditch overgrown with bushes and took cover. The motorbikes were closer now. Another flare went up, over to one side this time. Kozlov crawled along the ditch, then up out of it into a field of rye, kept crawling, through the field now, not in any particular direction, just to get away. He crawled for a long time. When he finally stood up, he saw a wide line of soldiers in front of him. They saw him, too. It was as though the field burst apart, death whistling and whining over his head and all around. Firing a long burst the length of the line, he forced the Germans down to take cover and he ran, not back, of course, that was impossible, but to the right, along the line. He ran, stopped, fired another burst, and ran again. The whole field to the side and behind suddenly looked as though it had sprouted black toadstools. But Kozlov would have got away, he would have, if a familiar figure hadn't suddenly sprung up beside him. The sight of Specs was so unexpected, it stopped Kozlov in his tracks. He groaned with the realisation that he had unwittingly brought the Germans down on his former companion. Specs apparently didn't recognise Kozlov straight away in his new outfit. When he did, he was no less surprised. Surprise quickly changed to his old fury: "Not you again!"

"Run," Kozlov yelled, shooting at the black torsos advancing from three sides. Specs had no intention of running. Standing full height, frowning, he held his sub-machine gun out in front of him and started firing as well. The gun leapt and jerked in his inexpert hands, and his shooting had little effect.

"Let's go," shouted Kozlov, realising that out of sheer stubbornness his companion would never leave him. Once again a patch of forest promised cover. They managed to break out of the dangerous semi-circle and were one last dash away from the trees, when Specs gasped and fell. Both his legs were shot up above the knee. Kozlov grabbed him by the arms, wanted to drag him at least as far as the forest, but Specs shook himself free, pushed Kozlov away, and screamed almost hysterically: "Don't come near me. I hate you. Listen, lay a finger on me and I'll blow you apart!"

"You out of your mind?"

"I hate you! You're worse than they are!" Specs jerked his head in the direction of the Germans. "Worse, because you're one of us. Get away from me!"

Kozlov was now genuinely angry.

"What are you on about, you idiot? Are you daft?"

There was no time for explanations. The Germans were catching up.

Kozlov leaped on Specs, gripped his arms so he couldn't resist and made for the trees. He was heavy. But in one dash, in one great gasping breath, Kozlov dragged him into the forest and laid him on the grass behind the first rows of trees. Released from Kozlov's grip, Specs pointed the sub-machine gun at him.

"Go away. I don't want your help. Leave me. I'd rather be killed by them than saved by you. You should understand that. Go away. I'll hold them off."

"Listen, you lunatic. Maybe you think I need you to save my own skin? Well you can go to hell. You're mad anyway!"

He pulled off his jacket and, stripped to his army singlet, picked up his gun again.

"Hell! We're finished anyway," he shouted wildly and began spattering bursts of fire into the rye in which German uniforms were bobbing up and down quite close to them now. Propped against a stump, Specs also began firing, still poking his arms forward clumsily. His face was bathed in sweat, large drops of sweat. Like tears. Each muscle in his creased, flushed face reacted to every jerk of his gun. Then it made a stupid kind of snort and was silent. For a while Specs blindly carried on pulling the trigger, until he realised his ammunition was spent.

Kozlov was also on his last magazine. The feeling of the end was so strong and overwhelming that he lost his usual cool and kept firing, firing, firing . . . and he took it as read when his gun turned into a useless hunk of metal. There was silence. The last few minutes he had been the only one shooting. There wasn't a sound from the field. "Are they trying to surround us?" wondered Kozlov wearily. He looked around, listening hard. All quiet. He took his gun by the barrel – it was almost unbearably hot – came out from behind the trees and walked several paces forward. All quiet. He looked back at Specs. He was lying against his stump, his head thrown back, Adam's apple jutting. Kozlov came back and sat down close to him. He tried being conciliatory: "What did you do before the war?"

Specs' whole body shook and he whispered: "Don't talk to me!"

Kozlov banged the ground with his fist and kicked a dead piece of branch.

"Oooh! If you were in one piece, I'd smash your face in, you idiot! Knock that mulishness out of you for good and all!"

Specs wanted to say something, but from the field out in front they heard barking.

Now they understood the reason for the silence. The barking was coming rapidly closer. Everything was being repeated like in one of those recurring nightmares, when you simply can't wake up . . .

When the Alsatian came flying at him, Kozlov met it with a blow from his gun that would probably have stopped a tank. The huge, well-nourished dog dropped to the ground, its skull crushed. But Kozlov wasn't given the chance to swing his weapon a second time. He had to use his hands, grabbing the second dog by the fur on its cheeks. Its snarling, slavering jaws spattered his face with saliva. Foam dripped from its bared gums and its fangs were like cartridges jammed into smaller-calibre clips. The dog's paws pounded against his chest, scrabbled to get a purchase on his wrists. He was holding almost all its weight, only its hind paws were touching the ground. He was holding it, it was holding him. It couldn't bite, he couldn't let go. The Germans were almost on him. They weren't shooting, the situation was under control. The dog, this trained beast, was taking him prisoner. Kozlov let it down on the ground and then kicked as hard as he could, aiming for its guts. The dog yelped, doubled up. He kicked it again and again. Bloody foam gushed out of its mouth, poured over his hands . . . then the sky caved in on Kozlov and pinned him with all its weight to the ground.

*   *   *

There was a wide gash in the roof of the barn, and when Kozlov regained consciousness, he was looking up into the gash, and it grew wider and wider as he looked until it seemed there was no roof above his head, he was back in the field and above him was the sky and silence.

Then the pain exploded inside his head, springs compressed and released, hundreds of sharp probes pierced his brain, there was a hammering in his temples. He dissolved completely in the pain, lost the sensation of life, turned into one shattered nerve ending that wriggled and twisted in agony, like a half-crushed earthworm. He had sudden hallucinations. Once that he was walking across an enormous field. He had on a blindingly white shirt, and in his left hand he was trailing a sub-machine gun along the ground. As he walked the German from the clearing who wouldn't fall down dead loomed in front of him. Only this German was huge, ten times his size. But he was standing in exactly the same position. The German's dead eyes weren't looking at Kozlov, they were staring over his head into the dizzying depths of Russia. And the half-spread arms and the fallen mess-tin still seemed to be saying: "What is all this! What the hell's going on!" Kozlov laughed loudly and for some reason shouted at the giant: "So where are your four fifths now, eh?"

There were times when the pain vanished for a moment as if it had never been. Then Kozlov would raise himself on one elbow and ask into the darkness: "Comrade, you hear me? You all right?"

But there was no reply . . .

*　　　*　　　*

Aleksey Vladimirovich Samarin taught at a Moscow music school, until he was arrested in connection with the case of his father-in-law, a Deputy People's Commissar. "When you cut timber, chips fly," Stalin had said. Samarin had met the captain, who was now lying a few metres away from him in the barn, out there in one of the God-forsaken places to which Russia, drunk on optimism and initiative, had shipped tons

of chips, whole echelons of waste product from the great
timber-felling operation.

They cut timber in the place he was sent to as well. In a
minor way. Chips flew. Of the usual kind. Wood. The north's
one month of autumn was coming to an end. The rains had
already died away and the snow had not yet begun. And nature
compensated for this inadequate and indeterminate state of
affairs by whipping up a biting north wind. It didn't tear the
roofs off houses or trees up by the roots, didn't skittle over
telegraph poles, but it penetrated every living thing with icy,
razor-sharp spindles, and all living things shrank and hunched
shivering, tormented by the pangs of constant, exhausting
cold. There were roughly five hundred living things in this
place. In the morning they went out from their shelter in
groups into the forest, in the evening they came back in
groups to the draughty barracks, to rest up until the following
morning.

At that time disaster struck. The tobacco ran out. In every-
day life such unexpected misfortunes are often pure coinci-
dence. Out there misfortune bore a signature. The signature
wore a captain's uniform and had a title – camp commander.
The criminals called him "The Boss". He really was undisputed
master of all those people. He could do anything with or for
them, except one thing – free them. But he hardly found this
limitation of his rights irksome, because he never felt the
slightest inclination to release them. Everything else that happened in the lives of any of these five hundred men was in one
way or another connected with him. It was the result of either
his action or inaction . . . The latter, probably, was the cause
of the fact that for a week there had been nothing to smoke in
the camp. All pockets had been turned inside out long ago for
their licit and illicit contents, so had all the likely places where
a cigarette-end might lodge, everything had been bartered that
could be bartered with the guards. Two days ago Samarin had
watched a man from the bunk opposite crawling about on the
floor with tears in his eyes using a needle to spike flecks of

tobacco which had fallen out of the lining of his padded jacket. Samarin was a non-smoker and could not appreciate what suffering these men were going through, but he believed them and, being a sensitive and gentle person, suffered with them. Not all of them, of course, behaved the same. Many put a brave face on it and didn't descend to begging from the guards or searching through the rubbish bins. But they were not the ones who set the mood and the tone. On day four a number of fights started spontaneously . . . On top of this there was the wind, that foul, revolting wind, from which there was no shelter, not even in the barracks. And, of course, the work . . .

Samarin was a hauler. The team hooked a loop of rope round the butt of a cleaned trunk, then dragged it to the road where it was loaded onto a transporter. They had to drag it a long way, over tussocks and rocks, avoid snagging it on treestumps. Three men to a tree. It was one of the heaviest jobs. The results of this operation determined the brigade's plan figures. Thirty-two men had been working at half strength five days already. They hadn't met the plan. Or at least, they were on the point of not meeting it.

"The Boss" turned up at the camp, accompanied by a guard nicknamed "Rat". When the buzz of voices had died away, the captain spoke: "There's no tobacco in the store. What do you want me to do, pull it out of a hat?"

There was dead silence. An ugly, dangerous silence. "The Boss" knew his trade though.

"You clear the whole area up to marker fifty-six tomorrow, and I'll go back to base in person and screw five cases or so out of them. You hear me? Everything cleared as far as marker fifty-six. There isn't any tobacco. You do your bit, I'll do mine."

Then he left.

The target was impossible. The odd brigade might cut through to the marker. But the whole area? In some brigades a third of the men were sick. They weren't delivering their plan, the others were covering for them. To cut as far as the marker would mean producing more than double the norm . . .

The crowd split up into groups. The silence was broken by a babble of voices that gradually intensified. Knots of men shifted, interspersed, like cards in a pack. The camp buzzed and scurried like a disturbed ant-heap. Someone calculated the number of sick, the number of non-smokers. Much depended on the latter. Why should they bust a gut? Arguments started up, shouting, speeches. Here and there fights broke out. By nightfall it was decided. Do it! There was still a week to the end of the month. So there'd be no tobacco for a week at the minimum. Do it!

What were they banking on? What untapped reserves of strength did they hope to find? Yet hope they did. Samarin didn't believe it. Though he didn't object, neither did the majority of non-smokers.

He would never forget that day. By lunchtime two men had been crushed. There was one man injured with a gashed leg. What those men did that day was not work, it would have been heroic, were it not for its purpose . . . If you ignored the purpose, it was more than heroic. By four o'clock several brigades had made it to the marker, and the men turned straight back to help the laggards without stopping for a breather. A few more injured were sent back to the camp.

Samarin was completely numb long before his brigade moved into a new place. He didn't feel tired, he just knew that if he stopped, he would fall and not get up again. He might even die. He was afraid to stop working. He was surrounded by people toiling, hurrying – he saw nobody, heard nothing, felt nothing. His consciousness and the consciousness of what was happening were detached from him, suspended somewhere between him and the outside world, they had formed something akin to his spiritual *doppelgänger*. From time to time he or it jabbered something garbled and incoherent, and the jabbering elicited a response from the shadows that flitted around him, a response that was equally garbled and incoherent.

By six it was hopelessly obvious they would not "do it" . . . , that all their efforts here had been in vain, the miracle hadn't happened. Men began dropping where they stood, at the spot where the realisation of failure dawned on them.

It took the guards much time and cursing to drive the half-dead men into the obligatory columns for the trek back. It took a long, an exhaustingly long time for the columns to crawl back to their barbed-wire beach-head. Once again there was dead silence in the camp, a silence which in that sort of situation can only be interpreted as a concentrated expression of potential violence, unrestrained violence as desperate as that silence. "The Boss" appeared once more, "Rat" by his side. Nobody stirred when he came into the barrack, every man stayed in his bunk. But this was not yet mutiny – only fatigue and apathy . . . "The Boss" stopped in the middle of the hut, young, fit, confident in himself and the might of the backing behind him, buttons and boots gleaming, everything about him – his strength, the gold crown on his tooth – gleamed like a nugget of precious metal in a heap of scrap.

"Well now lads," he said. His voice was calm, not too loud. He even managed to inject a note of sympathy. "I can't say I've got good news for you. You know that. A deal's a deal."

These last words made Samarin sit up. He slid down from his bunk, took off his glasses, placed them under his pillow, walked over to the captain and said clearly and distinctly: "You're a swine!"

A shiver ran round the barrack. "Rat" froze expectantly to attention. The captain sneered and surveyed the rows of bunks, his eyes narrowed.

"Am I to understand this man is expressing the general opinion?"

There was gloating menace in the question. Samarin stood there, face to face with the captain, demonstrating his readiness to bear the responsibility for what he had said.

The captain looked him up and down with contempt.

"What are you standing here for? You've said your piece,

now go. Or do you want me to hit you? I won't, you know.
Back to your place!"

Nonplussed, Samarin went back to his bunk. No less nonplussed, "Rat" studied his master's face. "The Boss" strode
down the barrack, stopped.

"Now, listen here. There are five cases of tobacco plug
outside. I was going to break them open, even though you
failed to keep your side of the bargain. Well, now you can rub
your spokesman and smoke him till next month. That'll be
all."

Samarin collapsed onto his bunk.

Half an hour later one of the brigade foremen came
over: "Listen, Samarin, the captain's in the work allocators'
office. Try to talk him round. Otherwise, anything might
happen. The criminals are hopping mad. Of course we'd
see you came to no harm, but we can't be everywhere . . .
Anyway . . . "

Anyway the brigade foreman wanted a smoke as well, and
the tobacco was there . . .

When Samarin walked into the office, the captain was lounging in a chair, calm, smirking. The allocators went out. The
two of them were left on their own.

"Have you got something else to say?"

Samarin took a deep breath. "I lost my temper . . . I was
tired . . . Please, give them the tobacco."

"What about yourself? You a non-smoker?" the captain asked
with feigned surprise.

"Yes."

"Then why poke your nose into other people's business?"

The captain stood up and walked over to Samarin.

"I could shoot you like a dog, but I've no intention of turning
you into a martyr. I'm going to teach you a lesson. You see
yourself as some brave intellectual fighting for the rights of the
people. But I'm going to make you understand, right now,
that the fact you're in this place means you're trash, understood? You may be down officially as an enemy of the people,

but you're not even that, you're just trash. You wanted to suffer for the people, well go ahead, suffer."

The captain sat down and held out the toe of his boot.

"See, my boots are filthy because of you. You've got a long tongue. So put it to good use!"

Samarin clattered out of the office, but out on the porch, on the top step, he stopped dead. It was dark out there. He couldn't see, but he could feel the crowd gathered in silence in front of the office. People were waiting.

Samarin sat on the step, buried his head in his hands.

"The Boss" was playing a dangerous game. He couldn't know how these humiliated, exhausted people might react if Samarin told them what had happened. And what was the result?

Samarin stood up and went inside. It was as if the captain knew Samarin would be back. He was sitting exactly as before, still grinning, his gold tooth gleaming.

Samarin went down on his knees, but the boot was held low and he had to go down on all fours. The captain chose that moment to speak.

"What was your job outside?"

Samarin didn't want to reply, but the boot was withdrawn.

"I taught music," he replied tonelessly.

"Really? Well, come on now, earn those people their tobacco, music man," the captain said airily and held out his boot.

Samarin resolved to kill him and would have done so, only shortly afterwards the captain was transferred from this island of the Gulag archipelago back to the mainland.

And then three years later Samarin ran into him in a column of prisoners the Germans had mustered to repair the railway. Samarin didn't know what to do. He had imagined this unlikely encounter so often, he so believed that revenge would relieve the burden of insuperable pain, the filthy blackness gnawing at his heart that would not let him live nor yet let him die, because for him personally the war had wiped nothing from the slate.

The fact that the captain didn't recognise him made it even more hurtful and humiliating. "What shall I do?" Samarin thought feverishly as they were marched to the railway. "Beat him up? Kill him? Expose him?" He imagined each alternative in turn and realised that whatever decision he took, he wouldn't be satisfied. He realised that everything that had happened in the camp was irrevocable: he would never be able to forget the humiliation, the pain would never go away. The wound was mortal. No compensation would ever be sufficient. But worst of all was the captain not recognising him. "Perhaps it's because of my glasses?" Samarin thought and made sure the captain saw him close to several times. It ended with the captain coming over and asking him for a smoke. That was the final straw. It was hard to say what he would have done if the captain hadn't made his escape bid. Still Samarin hit him and even though it was the first time he'd ever hit a man, he hit him so hard it made his hand go numb. He kicked him as well. He really wanted to put the boot into his enemy, but to his despair he discovered he had no enemy. There was no enemy. There was only the pain. And nobody to shift it onto. And life with it was impossible . . .

*　　*　　*

They were placed up against a wall right here, by the barn. They couldn't go any further. Both Samarin's legs had swollen up and he couldn't stand. Kozlov, who was so dizzy he was himself barely able to keep on his feet, dragged him out of the barn. Now they were standing side by side, or more accurately, propping each other up.

It was evening. The sky was clear. Except that over in the west it was as if somebody had shot a falcon at point blank range and the feathers were blasted in a fan shape across the sky, and at the very rim of the sunset there were scraps of cloud like bloody fragments . . .

Supporting Samarin's weight, Kozlov turned to him with a

LEONID BORODIN

sad smile: "Better say good-bye. Maybe before we go you'll tell me why you hit me?"

Samarin looked him full in the face, wanted to say the things he'd been so long in preparing. Those words ought to be words of forgiveness. He brought his face close to Kozlov's and saw that Kozlov did not have a gold crown.

"My God!" Samarin exclaimed.

There was a blast from the side and it caught them both with the shrill voice of death. They shuddered, staggered and fell.

ON TRIAL

WHAT COLOUR is premonition? Various colours, probably. A puffy, patchy dirty grey, with sullen black streaks, sort of arachnid – that's a premontion of disaster. While a good premonition is, of course, a slim, dazzling chink of sky blue in an old attic, suddenly stumbled on and as suddenly lost. Then again, maybe there's no such thing as premonition, only a deeply buried foreknowledge of cause and effect. Because if you think about it, if there is such a thing as a premonition of something random, something completely chance which has absolutely no connection with the past or the present, where does that leave our precise formula for explaining the world about us? And how does it affect our view of ourselves or of our empirical experience? And what is it going to do for our self-respect?

No, we don't need secrets, don't need mysteries, they all make life too complicated. So much is asked of us in life as it is, and we ask so much of it. We're all so firmly convinced everything we need and everything we do is important, or even vital. We dump the blame for everything else on our human fallibility, which, frankly speaking, is no fault of ours. And speaking even more frankly, there's no such thing as culpability, only bad luck. The difference is obvious. Culpability calls for condemnation, bad luck for sympathy. Sympathy is not complicity. It is superior, because it is has a less tangible association. It is raspberry-coloured, it is as soft and warm as

31

an Irish sweater, as a woman you love only a little, as a friend towards whom you have no obligations.

Bad luck and sympathy, such an easy combination to understand. Bad luck and complicity and we're deeply into mysticism. This is the founthead of premonition, and premonition is true slavery! It only has to be proved right once and that's it, no more pleasure in life.

Take a deep breath and make your mind up once and for all that it doesn't exist, this exhausting, paralysing burning sensation that comes straight out of Dostoyevsky. Take a deep breath . . . But it can't be done. Without the unconscious and subconscious man would be no more than a mechanical device.

Can't be done.

I

The jeep turned onto the highway. After a kilometre or so Snitsarenko handed over to Volodya. He climbed into the back seat and tried to sleep, but his stomach churned again with that nauseating sense of impending doom poised over his head. He first felt it yesterday when he was summoned to the meeting. An ordinary summons to an ordinary meeting. But the wound in his leg had ached all night and he had woken that morning with the anticipation that something unpleasant was about to happen. There was a moment when it seemed that if only he thought hard, tried to remember something terribly important which he'd clean forgotten, he would know what to prepare himself for.

But what about thought – calm, sober, dispassionate thought? All you need is to surrender to it completely, shut out emotion, discard what is secondary. Just analyse everything calmly, very calmly, and all will become clear, and what doesn't will cease to exist. It's the only way. Lean back in the seat, relax, either close your eyes or look at something colourless and boring, the driver's grey jacket, for example, or at least avoid looking out of the window, so your attention isn't diverted by the objects flashing past. The even, monotonous rumble of the engine is ideal. Its throbbing flattens and swallows all noises which might interfere or distract.

That's how it is. And yes, now you can ask: what is this all about?

Eighteen years earlier

"This is what it's all about . . . "

Shitov carefully placed the crystal liqueur glass over the neck of the bottle, moved it to one side, as if deliberately clearing a space between him and Dmitry, put his elbows on the table, cracked his knuckles, leant his chin on his hands.

"Two months ago, to be precise, on the night of May 16, fifty-two telegraph poles were sawn down by persons unknown between the villages of S-e and P-a. As these things go, the damage could have been worse. But when I got to the scene I came to the conclusion that it wasn't sabotage. What I mean is, damage had obviously been done, of course, but the intention was very different. Think for yourself, Lieutenant. Your mission is to put the telegraph line out of action. How would you cut down the poles? Bear in mind you've got the night to do it in and you've also got to cover your tracks. So, how would you do it?"

Dmitry shrugged.

"Don't know. Cut them down and get out of there. Quick as you can . . . "

Shitov frowned.

"What you've got to do is cut them down so they can't be re-used. So cut as high up the pole as possible. These poles, though, had been sawn through at ground-level. The cross-members had been knocked off, but the wires were severed in

33

only a few places. And there's nothing easier than cutting telegraph wires. All in all, the picture was clear as far as I was concerned! . . . "

. . . That was a fib. The picture only became clear the following day when he received a report that the poles had vanished during the night. There was a long and violent scene with the local government plenipotentiary. He spent the next three days rushing with his unit from one village to the next, asking questions, interrogating, threatening. The trail had gone cold. If only he'd guessed right away and sealed off the area. But he hadn't guessed, he'd only made sarcastic comments about the saboteurs' incompetence. It would only take a day at most to repair the line. It would. If the poles hadn't gone. Fifty-two five-metre poles. That meant a new bunker in his district, with good solid fortifications.

A bunker meant village soviets reduced to ashes, meant dead government plenipotentiaries and party workers, meant anti-Soviet literature, meant transparent hints from regional command. It meant the constant, wearying knowledge of the danger to his own life.

Not that Shitov had spent the past two months sitting on his backside. In that time he'd managed to achieve something, but now he was ready to play his trump card. That was going to be Lieutenant Dmitry Snitsarenko, an intelligence officer, a 24-year-old Ukrainian from Kharkov. Shitov had selected him from the list put forward by the operations department at State Security Regional Headquarters. The decisive factor was the lieutenant's typical Ukrainian face. All the other entries in his file were fine, that went without saying. Now, if the lad had the effect Shitov intended, he could finish off the underground in his patch quickly and cleanly, without all those time-consuming raids, blockades, manhunts, without too much effort. That was it!

"That's it then! You're familiar with the general situation. It's shifting in our favour. The nationalists are on the way out.

Three years ago the bulk of their forces broke through into Czechoslovakia and then on into the West. Some made it, some didn't. Anyway, they've gone. They left behind their party functionaries and diversionary groups. They've got years of experience in the underground. And they've got support. They're on the way out, all the same. Their strength is in the villages, and the villagers are tired of it. Neither war nor peace, caught in the crossfire for years. Our task is to do the job as quickly as possible, as effectively as possible, with the minimum casualties. Effectiveness is our main propaganda weapon!"

Shitov refilled their glasses.

"To our success!"

Dmitry went to raise his, but Shitov stopped him with a conspiratorial wink.

"Hey, hey, hey! Not like that. These are crystal. German crystal. Take the stem between your two fingers, gently, like so . . . don't squeeze, just keep it balanced. Good lad! Now bring the glass up from below so its rim just touches the rim of mine, just touches, like a seagull on a wave . . . and . . . up. Good!"

A thin, delicate, melodious note rang the length of the table, floated to the ceiling, drifted the length of the room and out of the window.

"Like a tuning fork," Shitov whispered hoarsely, grinning. He examined his glass minutely, as if trying to fathom the secret of German crystal, then suddenly hurled it at the wall behind Dmitry, who looked inquiringly at his superior officer.

"Your turn!"

The second glass followed in the path of the first.

When he had seen Dmitry out, Shitov swept the shards onto a piece of newspaper and took them out into the kitchen. He went to the sideboard and took out a liqueur glass – from the same set as the two just broken. He filled it and went into the sitting room, taking little sips as he went. He stretched out on the divan, then dropped the empty glass onto the rug.

There were only a few more details to sort out, crucial ones though. He had to anticipate the possibility of interference from Kalinichenko, head of the local Department for the Campaign Against Banditry. The previous head, who'd been promoted out of the Department, had been a cautious man and Shitov had had an excellent working relationship with him, in the sense that he needn't worry about him launching his own initiatives. But Kalinichenko was desperate to see action. Shitov's sources at regional HQ told him his colleague had been dumped in his patch because of some dirty business which had got him on the wrong side of the top brass.

But Shitov had been around long enough. Shitov knew, Kalinichenko might be in big trouble, but he'd still have his finger in the pie back in Lvov. When the flak flies, someone has to take the blame, there always has to be a scapegoat. Captain Kalinichenko was the perfect candidate. Give him time, though, and the old goat would stop bleating and turn out to be a wolf in disguise!

So Shitov had a tricky job ahead of him. On the one hand, he had to maintain good relations, which wouldn't be so easy, since Kalinichenko was officially his subordinate; on the other, he had to retain the initiative, which was going to be even harder, because the head of the district DCAB could in practice act independently and to all intents and purposes was subordinate to the regional DCAB rather than Shitov as the local State Security officer. It was to Shitov's advantage that there was hardly any demarcation between his and Kalinichenko's functions, and on top of that, field operations were his department, no question about it. Against Shitov was the position regarding the search and destroy platoons, which were no less unambiguously part of the DCAB's functions. Not to worry, the effectiveness of these units had been falling off recently, as had that of the DCAB as a whole. Shitov was best placed to judge that. He'd been in the district since it was liberated from the Nazis. He'd buried two lots of his staff. The first time in 'forty-five, when elements of the Ukrainian Insurgent Army made a forced march from the Carpathians and launched a surprise attack on the district centre. That day Shitov was out on an operation. The nationalists were driven out with heavy losses the next day and retreated into the forests. They left behind, though, the bodies of six of Shitov's men in the lobby of the State Security building. Their replacements carried the coffins to the cemetery. Six months later four of them were killed in a night attack on the district prison. Shitov got away with a scratch on the neck that time.

It was then they set up the DCAB to back up the security organs and also recruited the search and destroy platoons from among the local population, youngsters mostly. But they were no real match for the enemy, hardened by years of guerrilla warfare. Shitov remembered the furore in a neighbouring district when an entire unit of twenty-five men was disarmed by two bandits. The local newspapers used to run stories on the glowing exploits of the "little hawks" from the DCAB platoons. But Shitov knew what didn't make the papers. Bandits are bandits. As far as the authorities were concerned, anyone who opposed them was a bandit. Shitov, though, had seen a good deal of these people. Dead more often than not. The odd individual shot, groups of them blown up in bunkers and dug-outs, frozen in snowstorms trying to evade pursuit, breaking out of encirclement. They shot cowards and dealt viciously with people who refused to help them or co-operated with the Soviets. Shitov didn't understand them and didn't want to. But he had a healthy respect for them and to a great extent this shaped the way he operated.

"Nationalist bands" was how he described them in his reports and situationers, "victims of bourgeois propaganda" when he was speaking to the villagers. According to the tried and tested scientific social theory, those same villagers were supposed to be utterly loyal to him, Shitov, and utterly hostile to the "victims of bourgeois propaganda". If only it was just a question of "supposed". But that loyalty and that hostility were what Shitov had to deliver, and *en masse* to boot!

Any crudely formulated, blanket instruction has its plusses. Not least that nobody is terribly pernickety about the purity of the methods used to achieve it. Shitov knew the system like the back of his hand. He didn't sit up all night over his reports. He wrote them off the cuff, impromptu, using his own successful formula. He didn't blame everything on difficult circumstances, which does nothing to impress one's superiors, didn't overload with statistics, which make tiring reading, didn't make extravagant promises, which have a nasty habit of . . . He began with the overall trend, noted a "progressive tendency", then briefly, but convincingly, outlined the way in which his activities meshed in with the aforesaid "progressive tendency". No superior officer is ever going to dismiss "progress" out of hand. And so Captain Shitov was in good odour.

There was one other factor which made his position almost impregnable. Shitov was in no hurry for promotion since he had no illusions about his abilities. By his own sober assessment, he would never progress further than a district, and never higher than a major. So he preferred to keep his head down and extract all possible advantage from his situation.

How was he going to retain the initiative in the coming operation? That was the question uppermost in his mind after Dmitry left. He couldn't do it without Kalinichenko, but in that case he would have to give away information. There'd be disagreements, counter-arguments, compromises. Kalinichenko would be bound to talk his way into an appropriate piece of the action.

Shitov could see Kalinichenko's face – sharp nose, sharp chin, ever wary eyes. No, his rival was obviously a nasty piece of work. Married to that crazy girl, dragging her out with him on operations, probably to make himself feel big and brave. She was a fool, never took her eyes off him. 'Course not. He's her hero. Up on his horse, with his revolver and polished boots. A real he-man. When they first came they invited Shitov round. Complete waste of time. Kalinichenko sat there like he'd swallowed a shovel. Shitov tried to get him to unwind, but it was no use. He'd gone home and left the last glass.

Footsteps out in the kitchen. Irina was back. Shitov closed his eyes, pretended to be asleep. Irina glanced into the room, saw Shitov sprawled on the sofa still in his boots. She came over without making a sound, picked up the glass, put it on the table, then gently touched her husband's shoulder. He didn't move. Still very gently, watching him intently, she began pulling his boots off when all of a sudden Shitov sat up, roared, bared his teeth and grabbed her arm. Irina squealed, broke free and rushed back to the door, where she stopped and turned her head to look at him reproachfully. He was rolling around on the divan, roaring with laughter, his burly frame pounding the springs, his boots thudding against the plump chintz-covered arm. When he calmed down, gasping for breath and wiping away the tears, she was still standing in exactly the same position and said quietly, quite without offence, really without any expression at all in her voice: "You might have taken your boots off."

She spoke in Ukrainian. Shitov swung his feet off the divan and patted the seat.

"Sit down!"

She sat down beside him, obedient, though not timid, adjusted her dress, dropped her headscarf onto her neck, and when he put his arm round her shoulders and pulled her towards him, she didn't either bridle or cling to him, she just yielded a little to express loyalty and tenderness.

"I wanted to buy flour, waited in a queue for two hours, then there wasn't any . . . It's a miserable kind of life . . . "

She spoke, and looked at him calmly, straight in the eyes. It was the kind of look that of itself can make a man completely happy. Especially if that man's the wrong side of forty and knows for certain he'll never set the world on fire. Not surprisingly. Because that look contains nothing except the person beheld. It is completely taken up with his thoughts and wishes, as if everything and everybody else were in a different dimension.

Shitov reckoned he was lucky. Though he'd certainly given luck a helping hand.

During a raid on one of the villages in his district, he and his men had burst into a house, guns at the ready. A first examination failed to find the man they were looking for. The house was deserted, except for a woman, who throughout the search stood rooted to the spot against a partition wall between the stove and the dresser, just stood there, her hands cupping her chin. She seemed not even to see the men storming about her house. Furious, Shitov yelled at her: "What have you done with that bastard of yours?"

It was as if she was roused from sleep. She looked him straight in the eye. And though there was neither hostility nor fear in her expression, Shitov paid no attention to her at the time. She was only one of many. He shouted something else as well. She lowered her eyes, Shitov followed her look and saw blobs of mud from his men's boots, from his own boots on the pristine, scrubbed floor and on the home-made rag rugs.

"I'm alone."

She looked him in the eye again.

"My son is dead. I am alone."

That night Shitov dragged a whole crowd of mothers, old men and brides back with him to town. A day or so later, the same crowd crept back to their homes. But Shitov kept her, Irina, in the detention cells, held her in contravention of his official duties, held her in contravention of the law (though what did the law matter!), held her in contravention of everything that can be contravened in such a situation. At first he liked her the way he liked many of them. She was thirty-five or thirty-six, she didn't look younger than her age, possibly slightly older. Grief had printed lines of mourning near her eyes and mouth, had planted the stamp of fatigue on her face. But it also revealed a quite startling beauty.

To start with he liked her the way he liked many of them. But probably he just wanted to think he did, because from the very beginning she wasn't at all like any of the others.

Only the first interrogation was an interrogation proper. As always, Shitov used threats and tricks, cajoled, pumped, tried sympathy. He had no qualms about promising her that if she told him where her son was, he'd let him go; or about openly and cynically threatening to bring her his corpse in a couple of days. She knew less than he did. She wanted news of her son more than he did. What she revealed to him was something very different: Irina was the woman he, Shitov, had been needing for a very long time.

For the first few days he kept her there without admitting his interest. Later on, though, he was cynically open about doing so, perfectly conscious of what he wanted. And when in the later stages he promised to save her son if he found him, he knew he really would save him, he would break all the regulations, he was even prepared to take the consequences for his actions, which were patently not disinterested and criminal from the point of view of both the law and his conscience.

He searched for her son as he would have searched for his own. He even began to feel almost paternal, something he found surprising and disquieting.

He released her and waited four whole days, which felt more like eight, because he hardly slept.

She came to him and brought him joy. Then there was the unaccustomed, hateful trembling in his hands as he examined the casualty list from other districts. One day he found what he hoped he wouldn't – the name of her son. Then followed that terrible evening when he left the list with the name underlined on the table, went out and sat in the town's one and only restaurant until closing time. It was the worst evening in his life. Everything hinged on it, everything was being put to the test; whether he had atoned, whether his luck would hold . . . At midnight he stood on the street corner. Two more steps and he would be able to see the windows of his quarters. They might have a light in them. Or they might be dark. To find out would take just two steps. And he funked it. He was scared he might have to spend that night on his own. He wasn't afraid of the other nights. Only this first one . . . He made his way by the backstreets to one of the men from his unit, a bachelor, sat talking about nothing until morning. By six he was at his desk. The day was slow torture, and only at five did he summon the courage to ask the telephonist to connect him with his home number.

It answered.

He put down the receiver without saying a word . . . he had to fight himself from breaking down. But he won. He was, after all, a man who had seen a good deal in his time . . .

Later on he grew blasé about his luck and let himself be a little off-hand and even rude. All the same, though, luck was still luck: Shitov was the wrong side of forty, he wasn't going to set the world on fire, he wasn't going to take life by storm, just keep himself well dug in. Anybody who is on the defensive needs to have a fall-back position. Shitov's rear was secure.

He was in a good mood today. And when Shitov was in a good mood he would do as he did now, sit Irina next to him, stroke her shoulders, wink at her and ask with a giggle: "Ah, I bet you were pretty when you were courting, Irka!"

She didn't simper or feign modesty. She answered simply: "People used to say I was pretty."

He would squeeze her shoulders harder and say, with deliberate seriousness: "Now if one of your lot goes and puts a bullet in my arm or leg tomorrow, you'd be off. I know, you'd be off!"

He'd be frowning as he said it, and melt inwardly as she replied: "I'll never go as long as you don't throw me out."

"D'you love me?" he'd ask idiotically.

"And why should I not? You're a good man."

"A good man!" He'd frown. "I kill people!"

"The whole world's drowning in blood," she'd say quietly.

That was the situation regarding the personal life of Captain Ilya Zakharovich Shitov, district department head in the Ministry of State Security (MGB). He had his professional duties, which he carried out conscientiously, he had his enemies, whom he treated no more savagely than anybody else at the time, he had his woman, who thought he was kind.

And there was DCAB district head Kalinichenko, a smart-arse and an upstart, whom Shitov had to outflank or he'd be left looking very foolish.

And it was precisely at the moment when he was holding Irina, when he was swimming in the blackcurrant sea of her eyes, when he had only to gulp and disappear, it was then a wonderful idea came into his head. It was so good Shitov wasn't even sorry it came at the wrong moment, quite the wrong moment. But it came and was so marvellous Shitov let go of Irina, leapt from the divan and pounced on the telephone.

II

All around, as far as the eye could see, spread a sated, undulating, variegated body of fields. Along the seams of the hills ravines ran like insignificant, trivial blemishes on a strong young face, narrow and twisting, sweaty from the stubborn struggle for existence. Thickets of scrubby bird-cherry fringed the gullies, crawling up onto the slopes, in some places scrub no longer, but welcoming woodland, islands of it strung like lookout-posts along the world of tilled fecundity. The rustle of leaves echoed back and forth above the hills, above the sleepy fields, rolled down into the valley to the brain, the nerve centre of this huge, sentient body.

A one-street village stretches out over a kilometre and a half. Houses with windows like domino-pips. Along the lines of houses and fences, gardens make a ribbon of whipped green foam, at the back the squares and rectangles of vegetable plots.

The village is hushed. A village needs quiet to listen to the voice of the fields and the ringing of bells beyond the hills. All voices and noises here are merely the ground to one great green silence, the silence which fills everything with its scent, outwards and upwards to the very heavens where it settles, a great, blue crystal.

At night, when silence recedes into darkness, this crystal squints down with a myriad eyes into the emptiness that absorbs all form, colour, sound, then falls to earth as the pale dawn recreates anew everything that was before that night, disintegrates into the rainbow colours of this earth. The daily miracle of rebirth begins on a hill that stands athwart the village, towards which it straggles, throwing out a dusty tentacle of road in its direction.

One day, at the spot where the tentacle winds over the far side of the hill, at the moment when the first layer of morning mist slid soundlessly over the eastern horizon and came gently rolling down . . . one day the horseman appeared and reined in his mount.

He paused and then dived down into the valley, which still lay in darkness, dreaming its last dreams before morning. He flew at a gallop into the dark corridor of houses and fences, setting off the farm dogs. Somewhere near the middle of the village he turned his horse, made to gallop back the other way, but stopped, as though trying to make up his mind. He turned his horse again and went on, at a walk now, approaching first one then another house or fence, until he almost collided with a silent couple pressed up against a board gate.

"Where does Pyotr Gnatyuk live?" he asked quietly.

They didn't answer. People here didn't like strangers asking questions.

"You deaf or something?" the horseman hissed angrily.

"Fourth house from the far end."

It was the girl who spoke.

A minute later he was tapping with a revolver against the frame of a darkened window, behind which the inhabitants within appeared to wake suspiciously fast, the muffled sound of their stirring audible through the frame. An outside door screeched, shadows flickered, wavered, collided, wove and unwove. Someone came out into the yard carrying a lantern of the kind you use to see to the livestock or go down to the cellar for a well matured bottle.

The person who came out was an old man, at least he looked old in the flashes of yellow lamplight. He came over to the stranger, raised the lamp to light the stranger's face, but strong fingers gripped his hand above the wrist, and the lantern was forced back almost to the old man's nose, so that he had to look away. However, the old man was quick to recover his wits and though he spoke quietly, his voice carried a certain menace.

"Let go my hand!"

"You'll have guests for lunch, Gnatyuk. Your relatives'd do well to clear off . . . "

Though the stranger only needed a second to leap into the saddle and be away into the darkness, the old man caught a glimpse of him in the light of the lamp. He was astonished to see officer's boots and breeches underneath the horseman's leather coat. He hadn't even really tried to conceal his clothing from the old man. He could have changed beforehand. What could have been simpler. He had tried to conceal his face, but had underestimated the keenness of old Gnatyuk's eyes.

A minute or two later and the early-morning visitor was no more than a speck on the crest of the hill to the east and immediately dropped over the far side.

The old man hurried about the yard, ran back up onto the porch. Shadows of buildings and fences swung wildly for the last time before the door swallowed the old man and his lamp. A little while later six men came out of the door into the yard. They were overdressed for the time of year. Four of them were holding sub-machine guns, resembling dead firebrands in the darkness, the two others had their guns slung over their shoulders, their arms weighted down by pot-bellied baskets. They walked silently, in single file, across the yard and out through a low gate into the garden. They passed through the garden, too, without a sound. It almost seemed as though a narrow strip of carpet had been laid specially. They looked as if they were about to crash into the fence, but they passed through it like shadows and vanished into the jungle of maize that came right up to the garden and reached as far as the gentle hill. The reddening dawn had already flopped prone on the hillside, casually throwing the flaps of its dew-drenched cape over the slopes and neighbouring hills.

III

Shitov was tense. He knew Kalinichenko had come back a few minutes ago. It should have gone like clockwork. The possibility of a hitch could be almost ruled out, yet Shitov was tense. The game he'd started was too big, the stakes were horrendous, and he was out of his depth. It was frightening, but at the same time the realisation that he had set the game in motion made him deliriously happy. He had thought up this undertaking, taken the entire risk on himself. All of it! It was actually a rather pleasant sensation, taking all the risk, it made him feel younger, perkier. The thought even occurred to him that, had he been bolder in his time, he might have gone further. But common sense dictated something else: that he had only one head to lose, that he could do with it a bit longer, and that miscalculating, these days especially, was as easy as pie! Of course he felt he was something special at the moment, but this was the first and last time. He was middle-aged, level-headed and realistic about himself. One thing he didn't need was trouble. Let the Kalinichenkos of this world make the sparks fly. Which of them would come out of it in one piece nobody knew.

The thought of Kalinichenko made his stomach churn, and at that precise moment he heard brisk footsteps in the corridor. The door opened and Kalinichenko strode into his office, without knocking or greeting him.

He was quite a sight! His jaw was working, his pointed nose was even sharper, its tip all pale, as if freezing cold. Shotgun eyes fired both barrels at Shitov and then aimed at the bust of Felix Dzerzhinsky, founder of Lenin's secret police, the *Cheka*, patron saint of later generations of *Chekists*, on a stand behind Shitov's desk. He was gripping a map-case and the whiteness of his knuckles betrayed the degree of his fury and of something else besides that made Shitov suddenly feel his office was chillier than usual.

"What's happened, Vasily Grigorievich?" Shitov asked. It came out very naturally, though it was that first question that scared him most.

The thin, pale lips trembled and then spat: "Empty!"

"Gone?" Shitov gasped, again very naturally.

The eyes opposite Shitov sprayed him with machine-gun fire.

"They won't get away from me! At three this morning somebody rode into the village from this direction and warned Gnatyuk."

"The bastard, he even found out what time," Shitov thought with loathing, while looking at the DCAB chief with professional sympathy.

"My information was absolutely reliable," snapped Kalinichenko. Shitov sniggered maliciously to himself: "Could hardly be otherwise since I supplied it! You're a fool, my lad, a fool, for all your airs and graces. Smart-arse!"

It felt colder and colder in the office. Shitov shivered, at the same time putting on a show of serious thought.

"What do you suggest?" His question was simple and to the point. Once again he was extremely pleased with himself.

Kalinichenko stood up, put his map-case on the table, walked behind Shitov and stopped in front of Iron Felix as if consulting an oracle.

It's not a very pleasant feeling to have someone like that behind your back. But Shitov stayed as he was, didn't look round, just shrank with a shiver and didn't even really seem to notice when Kalinichenko reappeared in the armchair. The pupils under the thin blonde lashes were firing full blast now and little spurts of dust from the bullets danced a devilish jig right under Shitov's nose.

"Who knew about the operation, Ilya Zakharovich?"

Shitov flushed scarlet. At this moment he even half forgot he was the author of this comedy and felt genuinely angry. "Pipsqueak! Suspects me and doesn't even bother to hide the fact!" It would have given Shitov a deal of pleasure to smash the heavy marble paperweight in the DCAB chief's foxy face or give him a good old-fashioned thrashing or put several rounds into that smooth white forehead.

But he didn't do any of those things. Quite the contrary. He adopted the tone of Kalinichenko's senior officer and mentor: "Let's be calm, Vasily Grigorievich. If you do have any suspicions, let's discuss them. What do you know about this horseman?"

A hard case, this one! The spurts were throwing dust right into Shitov's eyes and he took the first opportunity to look down at the sheet of paper in front of him, gathering strength for the next dash. But what was there to be afraid of? Kalinichenko had no proof whatsoever, though there had been a cock-up: somebody'd seen Dmitry. Still, if the worst came to the worst, Shitov would wriggle his way out of it. He'd been forced to do it, and he wasn't obliged to give details of all his actions and plans to the DCAB chief.

Logical thought boosted Shitov's confidence. He looked up, and the awareness of his own rightness delivered a mighty salvo that immediately silenced the opposition. Drawing himself up to his full height . . . he rose from behind the table.

"I think the best thing for you is to get some rest, Vasily Grigorievich. We can discuss it with a clear head in the morning."

"Who was the lieutenant you assigned me for the raid?"

That damn machine-gun was in action again, but this time he was aiming too high.

"Lieutenant Snitsarenko has been sent from regional HQ to

familiarise himself with conditions in the field. It looks like they want to give him a district and he's been sent here to learn the ropes. Your bad luck today will be a useful lesson to him, of course. Anyway, you can always complain to HQ if you've got something against him. But you know as well as I do, that can cut both ways . . . "

Direct hit. Kalinichenko sagged, the fire went out of his eyes, his shoulders drooped. Now he looked like a hawk that mistook a wolf for a rabbit. He stood up, drily took his leave and left Shitov's office.

Only when the footsteps died away at the end of the corridor did Shitov slump with relief into the armchair, ready to savour his victory. All he could feel, though, was fatigue. An apathy he had never known before spread through his body and soul. He felt not a drop of satisfaction, not an iota of pleasure, just indifference and fatigue . . .

Ilya Zakharovich had taken on something that was too big for him. Much too big. He was used to living straightforwardly, to plain dealing, to playing dirty only when instructed, to cheating only when orders required it, and if he acted outside them he did so openly, brazenly. His job presumed a modicum of rule-bending and licence. This modicum was enough for him. The entire nature of his work, its methods and principles, blurred the distinction between what was the law and a violation of the law, because his job was to combat something, and in combat it is the outcome that is important. Shitov's job called for initiative, and he showed just as much as was necessary to preserve his head. Most important of all: his department always felt like home, his men were allies. At home he was the master, with his men he was the boss. Now it was all turned inside out, everything had changed places, a new kind of danger called for more than the usual spunk and cheek. And Shitov was nearly fifty, he'd never get beyond major, whatever happened . . .

He walked slowly down the stairs from his now empty department. He didn't answer when the duty officer coming on shift greeted him, didn't nod to his driver as he usually did, didn't bid him good-night or shut the car door.

Irina met him in silence. She immediately began laying the table. One long perceptive look at her husband and she went to the sideboard, fetched a bottle of brandy and a glass, placed them next to his plate, then stood back silently, waiting for her husband to wash and change.

He noticed the bottle immediately and immediately felt better. It wasn't so much the brandy as Irina, his wonderful Irina who understood him at a glance. His wife was his one true ally. He went up to her, took her gently by the shoulders, then took her face in his hands, kissed her arched brows, her wrinkles, pressed her to him hard.

"You're so warm, Irka, so warm. I'd freeze without you. They aren't people out there, they're splinters of ice. We'll be out of here soon; go back to Mother Russia. I've had a bellyful of your Ukrainians. I want to hear Russian. And you can learn Russian, too, right?"

She nodded.

"It's good you don't say much. Most people never stop and the devil knows what they're on about. We'll buy a house in Russia, with a little garden! We'll work. I'm still strong. What are you smiling for? Don't believe me, eh?"

Shitov stooped, picked her off the floor and swept her around the room. And she threw her arms around his neck, her cheek rasped against his. He felt her tears somewhere near his chin and understood. He never did show her much affection . . . At last he put her back down again, and she pressed her ear to his chest, where his ageing heart was fluttering shamefully, and she laughed, licking the tears off her lips. She laughed about as often as her husband showed tenderness . . .

"It's fine, it's fine. A heart can be fixed. Get a spade in my hands, I'll be right. I know the soil. That's where I came from. You know the calluses I had? The sort you slice off with a razor blade! Human blood washes them off so fast. The amount of blood I've spilt, Irka! The times we live in . . . Before I get old, I'll cover all the blood up with calluses . . . One nail drives out another."

Shitov also wanted to say: "We ought to have a son." But he didn't, remembering how Irina's face turned to stone whenever he said it. He spared her that. He went over to the sideboard, fetched two more glasses and put them on the table. Then he brought two more chairs to the table.

"The lieutenant's coming."

Irina blushed; he never sat her at table when one of his men came. Today was going to be special . . .

Dmitry was preoccupied when he came. Shitov noticed and unceremoniously sent Irina out after a few minutes.

Dmitry answered his questions in detail, described what happened, but he kept something back, or had doubts about something . . .

Kalinichenko had organised the operation brilliantly. They didn't go straight to the village, they detoured into two other villages further east first and picked up a dozen or so of the best men from the local search and destroy platoons as reinforcements. They came down on Gnatyuk's house like a whirlwind, instantly sealed the house off from the other gardens, from the maize field and neighbouring houses. A mouse couldn't have slipped through. One man went into the yard and fired a burst at the stove pipe. Dmitry guessed right. It wasn't just for the hell of it. Gnatyuk, his wife and their teenage lad came tumbling in fright out of the house. Kalinichenko grabbed the old man by the collar, shook him so hard his legs gave way, threw him to the ground and shouted: "Where are they?"

That was the start of a comedy which only Dmitry was able to appreciate. And though he could not but be impressed by Gnatyuk's skill as an actor, Dmitry felt a bit uneasy about Kalinichenko, a brave and resourceful officer, being taken for a ride, especially as he wasn't entirely clear as to the purpose of Shitov's plan. The situation the DCAB chief found himself in was utterly ridiculous. He set two companies of armed men to turning over the whole house and yard, frightened the life not only out of the Gnatyuk family but the whole village, and found not a trace of the bandits. He personally went over every inch of the outbuildings – kitchen, cellar, hayloft, tapped every square metre of floor, probed the entire garden and vegetable patch, all for nothing.

Kalinichenko went grey with fury and embarrassment. When it was finally obvious the operation was a dud, he charged about the yard, yelling first at the old man, then at the old woman, then at the boy (who didn't bother to conceal his glee), then in the end did something extremely stupid. He shot the family dog, a beautiful, silky haired animal with brown patches under its eyes. Gnatyuk lost his temper. You wouldn't have thought he'd ever been frightened. He stormed up to Kalinichenko, waving his fists and shouting. He was going to lay a complaint, it was against the law and the captain would answer for it, the Soviet authorities wouldn't allow honest people to be treated this way . . . Kalinichenko let the old man have his say, never taking his eyes off him, and when Gnatyuk eventually broke down in a fit of coughing, ordered him to be arrested. Then he went off to the village soviet, where he spent two hours questioning the other villagers using a system that was a mystery to everyone but himself. As a result they took another lad with them when the unit moved back to town.

Shitov pricked up his ears. Kalinichenko hadn't said anything about arresting Gnatyuk. The lad was, of course, the one who had told Dmitry the way to the house. Shitov couldn't forgive himself for not giving Dmitry precise directions, because it turned out that when Dmitry came to the village he didn't know which end to count the fourth house from. An elementary mistake.

"Gnatyuk recognise you, you reckon?"

"Probably," Dmitry replied, after a moment's thought. "He did get one look."

"Bad."

Shitov tossed his cigarette-end at the ashtray, but missed.

"It's a bloody mess!"

"Why?" asked Dmitry.

"Kalinichenko may break the old man."

Dmitry finally screwed up the courage to ask: "Ilya Zakharovich, why do you want to keep him out of the operation? He knows what he's doing. I know he's a bit unsubtle, but you should have seen the Gnatyuks playing the innocent! I don't know if there's any other way to deal with them, perhaps it's none of my business, but . . . "

Shitov cut him short: "They can and must be dealt with differently . . . I can't say anything about Kalinichenko. I wasn't the only one who planned the operation."

Had Dmitry been a little more experienced he would certainly have detected that Shitov was being less than honest. The crucial adjustment in the plan for the raid was last-minute and obviously Shitov's idea. But Dmitry still had the mentality of a frontline officer. He was used to carrying out orders, not discussing them.

Shitov was already giving orders.

"As soon as Gnatyuk gets back, you'll start infiltrating his band. It may even be tomorrow. I'll try to stop Kalinichenko breaking the old man. At any rate, I won't give him more than three days. Another possibility is for you to organise his escape. Anyway, we'll see. Be prepared for action – any time from tomorrow morning. Meanwhile I'll fix up somewhere cosy for that old fox Gnatyuk in Siberia!"

They drank. Shitov forced Dmitry to tell him about the exploits in intelligence for which he'd been decorated. They were both well oiled when the telephone rang shortly after one in the morning.

Kalinichenko made no apology for the lateness of the hour and snapped only one sentence, one that sounded very like an ultimatum: "I'll be with you in ten minutes; it won't wait."

The phone went dead on Shitov.

"Never a dull moment with him around," Shitov muttered grumpily. "He's cracked Gnatyuk. I can imagine what he did to him!"

"You don't think he used violence?" Dmitry sounded alarmed and at the same time puzzled.

Shitov looked at him the way you look at a child that asks questions about babies and gooseberry bushes and waved dismissively.

"Get next door and sit quiet. I underestimated old smarty-pants. Irina!"

Irina appeared instantly, as if she'd been waiting all that time just for that summons.

"Everything off the table. Quick. Get a move on!"

To Dmitry he said: "In there. Go on. And not a squeak!"

Meanwhile he grabbed the ashtray, emptied it, pulled the chairs back, examined the room carefully, the mat in the doorway. He sniffed the air, frowned, went over to the sideboard, opened a bottle of cologne and passed it several times round the room, covering the top with his palm. Finally he drew up a chair by the radio-set and began twiddling the dial. Suddenly he was up again. He dashed over to the sideboard and from somewhere deep inside the bottom shelf pulled out a small Browning which he dropped into his trouser pocket.

Irina opened the door. Kalinichenko strode into the room and came straight to the point, dry as always, but sounding rather boastful and self-satisfied: "Lieutenant Snitsarenko is a UIA agent. An important one, too, I believe. Gnatyuk identified him. Another half hour and I'll have the horse he rode to the village."

"So, Gnatyuk confessed he recognised one of our men as his visitor last night?"

"Yes."

"Did he confess of his own accord or did you have to persuade him?"

It was a meaningless question and Shitov knew it. But he needed time to think.

Kalinichenko's entire face was aglow with gloating smugness.

"I didn't persuade him, Ilya Zakharovich. That's the investigator's job, not mine. I just made him come clean. I don't need his confession, that's the investigator's affair. I needed a name. I got it. Tomorrow morning Gnatyuk can take back everything he said, but I'll have hard evidence. What I insist on is Snitsarenko's arrest, now. I don't want to get involved in discussions on this, so I'm telling you. If you refuse, I'll phone regional HQ immediately."

It was good Kalinichenko kept talking. Shitov had made up his mind.

"If there's any phoning to HQ, I'll do it. My orders to you are – detain, I repeat, detain Lieutenant Snitsarenko, but nobody is to lay a finger on him! You can see to that?"

"I can."

There was something human about the pipsqueak, after all. Because when Shitov gave the order he could see the DCAB chief's face light up with the joy of a man who has at last been understood. He saw it and for the first time he thought perhaps there'd been no need for all this business, perhaps they could have rubbed along together . . . The thought even flashed through his mind that if they had got along, in time Kalinichenko might possibly have put in a good word for him at HQ, where he clearly had somebody looking after him. Shitov was certain of that. Only the strong of this world are brazen, that he knew. Of course he knew you also found the so-called "idealists", but they don't survive when they stumble. Kalinichenko had. So he must still hold some trump cards.

It was a bit late to start thinking about that now. He'd started this game and he had to carry on playing it. Winner takes all.

Kalinichenko left. Dmitry emerged from the next room, shaken.

"What are we going to do, Ilya Zakharovich? I don't get this at all!"

Shitov puffed nervously at a cigarette.

"There's nothing to get!"

He went over to the table, searched for something in the drawer, pulled out a map and spread it on the table, then looked in the drawer for a compass, checked it, put it on the table.

"Now, you'll leave my house and go down this street here. Keep to the fence. The street ends at the park. Beyond the park is a forest, beyond that a cemetery. Walk six kilometres due south from there using the compass. You'll come out at the end of the village where the Gnatyuk house is. By morning you've got to be in the bunker."

"But Ilya Zakharovich, Gnatyuk isn't there!"

"No. But his son is, his wife is. Or do you think they know less than he does? Put pressure on both of them. Play on their fear for the old man. Use any means, just make sure you're in that bunker. Kalinichenko might raid the village in the morning. If the worst happens, only if, don't surrender immediately . . . Fire a couple of shots in the air . . . "

Apparently Shitov regretted the last sentence, because he added: "Not that it's likely you'll have to do that. Be in the bunker. Throw the compass away before you get there."

Shitov went to put his hand in his pocket, but suppressed the gesture. Instead, for appearance's sake, he went out into the next room, stood there a minute or so, then came back out with the Browning in his hand.

"Take it."

"Why? I've got my own."

"Take it. It'll bring you luck. Never fails."

Snitsarenko left Shitov the way he had come, by the back door.

IV

Arriving in a strange city always makes you feel happy, even
if it is misfortune that has brought you there. A strange city is
as alluring as a maze. Every city is something of a puzzle,
because it's more than a collection of houses and people, it's a
slice of history as well. It always has some famous names
associated with it. Besides, every city has a character, a meaning
of its own, and this meaning unfolds gradually as you walk
from the station, which is slightly away from the centre as a
rule. You walk blindly, by feel, and you sense the quickening
pulse of the city and, guided by this sensation alone, without
help either from passers-by or street signs, you come at last to
the main arteries. One turn, then another, and you've reached
the heart of this huge, sprawling being called a city. At this
point, to solve the puzzle, to fathom its meaning, you have to
walk very slowly, look carefully, read every sign and poster,
study the faces of the locals as often as possible, and not just
their faces, the season's fashions are significant, too.

It can happen you only need a day to fall on your feet in a
strange city, while sometimes you still feel out of place after
years and years.

Every city has plenty of new things, so that getting to know
it is always a joy even though nothing good awaits you there.

But if your life is going to begin in a new city, if you're
certain things are going to start happening for you right here,
and on top of that your heart has never been wounded, never
had to bear a single parting, a single disappointment, and
you're incredibly open to the whole world, to everything in it,
how can you hide your happiness and excitement as you step
out into the unfamiliar city streets down by the station!

Tanya didn't hide anything. She looked at the people in the
street with undisguised curiosity, stopped innocently to read
the signs and memorial plaques and smiled at anyone who
looked her way. There was no explaining the strange, but

happy feeling of warmth that filled her heart and which
came from this completely unfamiliar, completely strange
city.

Tanya stopped in a small square in front of a building with
a clock tower. Statues of Roman deities closed off the square
at the wings of the building. The first person she stopped told
her it was the old Town Hall. And though the traffic was
sparser than in other streets and the pedestrians fewer, Tanya
felt rightly that she had found the heart of the city.

Here, in these streets, among these buildings, was where
she was to live, heal the people who passed her by, race in an
ambulance up to these entrances, arches and yards. She was
certain the city would take to her, because she had fallen in
love with it, this unusual city built on hills and overshadowed
by hills. She knew everything would be fine, in fact everything
was fine already. The one bad thing was that she was alone
and had nobody to share her joy with, nobody she could just
embrace and kiss and see her own joy reflected in the smile
and eyes of the other.

Up the road from the Town Hall she crossed a tram-line
and went into a little public garden to rest and have something
to eat. There weren't many benches, and all of them were full.
Eventually she squeezed onto the end of a bench, opened her
bag, and tucked into her breakfast, which comprised two
homemade pasties. She thought a moment, then put one of
them back.

Over on a corner of another bench opposite, a tall young
man sat slumped. He wore a yellow leather jacket with slanting
pockets and officer's boots. His elbows were on his knees and
his face was buried in his hands, as if he was not just on the
verge of tears but about to begin howling like a woman. That
was ridiculous. He wasn't going to do anything of the sort. He
sat stock still in that position, while his chestnut forelock
gradually slipped over his hands and covered his long slender
fingers. Sitting in that position could mean one thing only –
deep distress. His neighbours on the bench sensed it. They

looked at him sideways and shifted away, perhaps out of a feeling that distress might be contagious, perhaps for some other reason. At any rate, they were clearly unsympathetic and Tanya felt a little ashamed for them. Several minutes later the man was still in exactly the same position. Tanya tried to imagine what could have happened to this man to make him ignore the presence of other people and bury his face in his hands.

What use was that? Tanya stood up to leave the gardens. She was right at the gates when she stopped and did something quite unexpected, something that made her astonished at her own boldness. She turned and went back to the man on the bench.

"Excuse me, please."

She said it louder, probably, than was called for. The women looked at her, hostile and suspicious. She glared back and said again: "Excuse me, please."

The man lifted his head and looked at her blankly at first. He turned out to be young and very handsome. Tanya was embarrassed and didn't know what to say.

The blankness in his eyes that so surprised Tanya vanished. It was followed first by an expression of surprise, then of polite attention.

"Could you tell me how to get to that hill over there?"

Tanya was pointing at a wooded hill which rose steeply at the far end of the city and was framed in the arched gateway to the garden.

"High Castle?"

"Pardon?"

"The hill, High Castle Hill."

He felt uncomfortable sitting while she was standing. He stood up, he towered a whole head taller than she.

"You take a tram as far as the railway crossing . . . " he began rather uncertainly. He stopped and looked penetratingly at Tanya. She wanted the ground to open up under her feet.

"Thanks," she murmured quietly. She almost ran off, the

stares of the people on the benches hot on her back. She left the gardens, turned into the first lane she came to and stopped. She leant back against a wall. "Little idiot. Made yourself look a right fool," she kept saying, covering her burning cheeks with her hands. "That's enough romance. Go to the station and fetch your bag. Find yourself a room. You've had all the adventures you need for one day."

But her adventures were only just beginning.

"Come on we'll go together. I have to go to High Castle as well."

He was standing in front of her. The words were said in a tone that did not admit the possibility of a refusal, a tone of voice that was the preserve of strong, straightforward men, a tone that precluded the very thought of any ulterior motive.

By the time they'd walked through the city to the railway crossing where the path began to climb High Castle Hill, she'd already told him about her parents, about being evacuated to Siberia, about nursing college and Lord knows what else besides, while he had told her nothing about himself except his name. He was called Vasily. As they climbed the hill she was silent. And was scared by his silence. She sneaked a look at his face and it was enough. She calmed down and cursed herself for being such a chatterbox.

The view from the top took her breath away. Though she'd told herself to keep quiet until he said something, she couldn't help herself. "Fantastic," she sighed, or something like that. She glanced at Vasily and the words died in her mouth. The expression on his face was tense, alert and hostile as he looked down on the sea of green in which church roofs and towers of different shapes and sizes lay like ships at anchor.

"Don't you think it's beautiful?" Tanya wanted an explanation for this look of his that was as cold as steel.

His expression, when he replied, didn't change, as though he was continuing his train of thought, only aloud now.

"Beautiful? I suppose it might be for some people. As far as I'm concerned, it's an enemy city. The enemy's out there

under every roof . . . If I had my way, I'd plough all that
beauty into the ground. I'd breathe easier not having to look
out for a sniper behind every apple tree, behind every fence.
Kiev's in ruins, Stalingrad's in ruins, and this place is like
some fat bourgeois who sat it out in a cellar!"

He was silent. Tanya couldn't understand what he was
talking about, but she decided not to ask. When she'd been
posted here, they'd said something about a difficult situation,
nationalist bandits and so on. But the joy of victory was still
fresh in the mind, and after beating an enemy like the Germans,
dealing with a few bandits didn't seem serious. Now she
couldn't imagine, didn't want to believe that there were people
to whom her joy meant nothing.

She didn't ask. He told her. He told her about Fascist
henchmen and Kulak leftovers, about hired killers and bought
agents, about brave *Chekists* and cowardly locals who only
helped a just cause under duress. He told her about the lack
of foresight at the top which hindered people like him who
were trying to extirpate the enemy root and branch. He spoke
of the need for red terror and a party purge.

He spoke with such painful honesty and conviction that
Tanya, without as yet understanding the heart of the matter,
already sympathised with him, already shared his pain and
frustration.

The qualities of a person that most often dispose us favourably
towards him are integrity, single-mindedness and honesty,
qualities that have individual worth in their own right. That
worth we perceive as something aesthetically beyond dispute.
We yield to the sheer force of those qualities.

The sacred idealism of the mind! Has it not been the source
of both the most divine good and the most monstrous evil?
But who has not surrendered to it, who has not trembled before
it or been inspired by it? Only the lazy and the luckless.

It is only the wisdom born of making mistakes and taking a
tumble, of losing and paying the price, this wisdom alone is

capable of discerning in idealism the germ of the ideal that brought it into being. This wisdom alone has the right and the inner resources to sanction or condemn the single-mindedness that blazes in a man's eyes, his ruthless vehemence, the irreversible finality of action! Wisdom alone.

All the others either recoil in timidity and fright, or are dazzled by its appeal, rush to submit, to become a part or receive a part of another man's integrity and obsession.

On encountering such a will and surrendering to it, a man wants to die in defence of it, a woman to live serving it.

That was what happened. Two weeks later Tanya emerged from the city registry office nestling against Vasily Kalinichenko's shoulder, the way a young pine tree clings to a cliff on the edge of an abyss, lending all the strength and tenacity of its roots to the ledges that give it nourishment. They walked through the streets of the city which was never to be hers.

For insubordination and violations of the law, State Security Captain Vasily Kalinichenko was transferred to one of the remoter districts of the region to be in charge of the local Department for the Campaign Against Banditry. He was to atone for a crime he did not feel he had committed, which did not coincide with his concept of crime. And as they walked for the last time round the city, he told her they'd be back, he'd settle his scores with the city and the people who, by being soft on bandits, were doing real harm to the principles of revolutionary struggle. He was certain that sooner or later his view would be recognised as correct. This would happen when the demagogues and opportunists realised, after their own methods had failed, that you couldn't make a revolution in white gloves, that Iron Felix's sword, far from being a museum piece, was a weapon tempered in the forge of class struggle.

He also described to her the great spirit of internationalism which would soon sweep away the national differences that only produced enmity and hatred.

Tanya listened to him carefully, not so much to what he said as to how he said it. He spoke the language of the heroes from the novels she had grown up on, but which until now had been purely fictional. In real life everything was so much more banal and boring. She was so lucky! She'd met a man who was the living embodiment of those literary heroes, fearless and unshakeable in their convictions . . . Then there was his chestnut hair, his blue eyes. He was tall and slim, he was tough and intelligent and he loved her. She knew he had fallen in love with her only for her looks. Of course he thought she was better than she really was. But she was no fool. She wouldn't let him see what she was, she'd quietly become the way he wanted to see her. And when she became that, he might as well think she'd always been that way, that he hadn't been wrong.

Now, though, she was just a silly girl. No matter what he said, she could not but like this city which had brought her happiness. Later on she could reconsider it all seriously and understand what a ninny she'd been. But this evening, before she got on the train, she was going to say quietly to herself: "Thank you, green city!" He didn't have to know . . .

They stopped in a little square in front of a church. They had to split up until evening – she to the hotel to fetch her suitcase, he to complete formalities at the office. But at the precise moment when she had resolved to tear herself away from him, the church doors flew open, there was a surge of human voices and a newly wed couple emerged. The bride was in a long white dress with a large white bow on her breast, the ribbon hanging almost to her waist. On her head she wore a little filigree crown, a white veil trailing behind it to the ground. The groom was elegant in a black suit with an embroidered Ukrainian shirt showing beneath it. He, too, had a white bow pinned on his chest, only the ribbon was longer than his bride's. The bride was as dark-eyed as Tanya and the groom as fair and as blue-eyed as Vasily, only slightly shorter.

They came down the steps of the church. A whole crowd of people, friends probably, followed. Then two older couples appeared on the steps. The parents. Everybody, the newly weds and all the rest, was happy and cheerful. They chattered, joked, embraced. They headed straight for Tanya and Vasily, and there was such a lump in Tanya's throat, tears came to her eyes. She and Vasily were so lonely, so superfluous in this city. Nobody had any time for them, they didn't know a soul, and nobody knew that an hour ago they had become man and wife. Vasily was handsome and elegant in his dress uniform, but now she desperately wanted to see him in a black suit with a white bow. And a Ukrainian shirt would have set off his masculine neck. And what a sight she'd have made in a white veil and high heels.

The procession came nearer. It was two or three metres away. They were standing in the couple's way, they ought to step aside. Vasily had already begun to do so, but Tanya suddenly felt that if they stood aside now, if these people passed by without noticing them, it would hurt so much she'd break down in tears there and then. She abandoned Vasily, ran to the bride, embraced her and kissed her on both cheeks. She and Vasily were both immediately engulfed by the wedding party, someone embraced her, one man even kissed her. Out of the corner of her eye she saw the groom embrace Vasily. They were nearly swept round the corner with the wedding party to the horse-drawn cabs that were waiting there, but they managed to slip away down the nearest side street and return to the square. Tanya again nestled against her husband. But when she looked at him, the smile died on her face. His expression was stony, impenetrable, almost like when he was talking about the enemy. She already knew this mask, the unseeing eyes and clenched jaw. She already knew it and during their brief courtship had been scared more than once by the thought that one day he would wear that mask because of her. And it was all her fault, of course. Her lips were trembling.

"That was a stupid thing to do!"

It was the voice of a station loudspeaker announcing arrivals and departures. It was the voice, probably, of a judge pronouncing sentence.

She must have looked utterly pathetic, because his look softened a little and she felt his hands on her shoulders. Then the ghost of a smile flickered at the corner of his mouth. Flickered and vanished.

"We'll talk about it in the train."

He kissed her, and though it wasn't quite as she'd have liked, it wasn't as coldly as it might have been.

The little district town they were sent to was green, comfortable and quiet. They were allocated a proper flat, which even had a back door.

Vasily didn't require comfort, but he did like order. Tanya found life easy because she was madly in love with her husband. Of course she wished he was home more of the time, was more affectionate and talkative, wished they could see more people, wished he would pay more attention to her meals, dresses and hairdos. But all that was secondary. The main thing was, she wished she didn't have to be afraid of losing him, or at least that the nights weren't so long when he was away.

By the tenth or twelfth day she was holding back the tears as she bandaged his wounded leg.

The time came when she rebelled. To her surprise and joy, Vasily gave way and a month later she was sitting confidently in a saddle and quite handy with a revolver.

The night before the first operation Vasily had agreed to take her on, they invited round the local State Security chief, Shitov. Even at this stage Tanya could feel Vasily wasn't getting on too well with his new boss. Shitov turned out to be middle-aged and pudgy, with bags under his eyes and all the signs of an alcoholic. He shook her hand for an unnaturally long time and his palms were sweaty . . . When he drank he coughed and smacked his lips. He was vulgar and tried to play the bluff, good-natured boss. Vasily, though, kept his dignity. Tanya watched her husband with pride, he was obviously superior to Shitov. No *Chekist* should act like that. Vasily was worth two of him. Shitov probably looked like a sack of potatoes in the saddle. But Tanya was courteous and her husband was pleased with her.

In the morning she galloped side by side with the dashing captain, her husband, at the head of the unit. A pistol hung at her belt. It was like a dream or a scene from a film, and she was both heroine and actress and the happiest person in the world.

But the day ended badly.

Everything happened quickly without her having any part in it, and she couldn't make any sense of it . . . Shots were fired, somebody shouted, somebody swore, and two big strong lads were lying tied up on the ground. They didn't beg for mercy, didn't cry and promise never to do it again, they just spat contemptuously at the soldiers and at her as well. One of them was broad shouldered, hook nosed, with straight black brows and a scar on his chin. The other was shaved bald, broad faced, thick lipped, with tattoos on his arms.

The men were all very pleased, they talked loudly and laughed too loudly, slapped each other on the back, slapped the horses' necks, rattled their rifle bolts for no good reason . . . Tanya felt wretched. As though she'd been cheated, as though somebody had said something foul to her. She couldn't for the life of her understand why she was there and what she was supposed to do. At last she heard her husband's voice as he came out of a house. She was terribly afraid he would be pleased as well, and she was scared to look at him. When she did, though, she was relieved. Vasily was serious, calm, not an iota of self-satisfaction.

They rode back slowly, because they were escorting prisoners on a cart surrounded by horses.

It happened in a gully where the unit stopped to water the horses. Everybody was in a hurry, except Tanya and three soldiers. The unit broke ranks, men and horses all bunched up together at the water. Suddenly the shaven-headed lad jumped from the cart and ran dodging down the gully. His hands were free. Despite a momentary advantage of surprise, the attempt was doomed. The lad had covered less than fifty metres when several shots rang out, followed by a burst of sub-machine gun fire. He dived headlong into the mud, bowled over several times and lay still. Tanya was the first to reach him. She slid from the saddle, abandoned her horse and literally went down on her knees in front of the lad. Numb with horror, she carefully turned him on his back and put her ear to his chest. There was no breathing, she felt something wet on her cheek, touched it, and saw blood. The lad's forehead and chin were smeared with mud, but his half open, glassy eyes and his slightly twisted boyish lips gave his face an expression of drunken bliss. Her eyes were held by his dulled, milky pupils. Then she began to howl, to cry as she had never cried before. It was more than tears, it was nearer hysterics, and she might even have passed out had she not heard her husband's voice overhead, like metal grating on metal: "Stop it at once! Back in the saddle!"

She rose to her feet with difficulty and saw the sub-machine gun slung across her husband's chest. She even thought she saw smoke wisping from the barrel . . . but it was only the tears misting her vision . . .

"Back in the saddle!"

The words were like a whiplash. Somehow she clambered into the saddle and when she rode up to the unit she could look nobody in the eye except the boy sitting bound on the cart. But the look he gave her was beyond her comprehension.

Back home she cried herself out. Then she calmed down and asked to be forgiven. He forgave her. And only when they were in bed did she whisper quietly: "Why are you so cold, Vasily?"

V

Eighteen years later

In spite of all his forebodings, the expedition turned out highly successful. Through the *Agrotech* office he managed to wangle spare parts for the combines and tyres for his drivers. Given these were in extremely short supply, this was an unheard-of success which in time would cost him no more than a bottle of cognac. As for the meeting, it was exactly like all the others past, present and future – no use to anybody except the regional bosses, and then only because it was the done thing. There was some kind of dreary nonsense about plan-deficit farm units, there was the usual lecture on the international situation, somebody went up and told a long-winded story about his operational methods, there was the obligatory ritual slaughter of a backsliding *sovkhoz* director *pour encourager les autres*. Anyway, Dmitry Petrovich Snitsarenko used those six hours to devour a collection of Maigret stories bought specially for the occasion. He even managed to leave the gathering not only not tired, but positively clear-headed and refreshed.

Volodya was supposed to have the car at the conference hall at six. Dmitry Petrovich had a good five hours in hand. This time he had no errands to run in town for his wife, so those five hours were his own. He bought a paper, looked through the cinema listings, found a film he wanted to see and went to the trolleybus stop. There weren't many people waiting and a trolleybus soon pulled up. He got on and stayed at the entrance door at the back, surviving the jolts and turns by clinging to the metal bars across the back window. He was going to be naughty and jump out by the entrance when they came to his stop.

At the third stop a middle-aged woman climbed into the bus. She was about to step past Dmitry Petrovich when she stopped and wheeled towards him. Her eyes were wide with surprise and with what was probably fear, because her face contorted and she clutched at her heart. Snitsarenko looked at her in astonishment. He was on the point of asking what the matter was, but she grabbed the sleeve of a man standing next to him, pointed at Dmitry Petrovich and hissed: "Murderer!"

The man looked blankly at Snitsarenko, then at her, then back at Snitsarenko. "She mad or what?" thought Dmitry Petrovich. He stepped towards her. She gripped her victim's sleeve in both hands and, ducking behind his back, cried hoarsely: "He's a murderer! Don't let him get away! He's a murderer! He murdered my husband! Call the militia! Stop him . . . Murderer!"

The man wasn't the heroic type. He just stood there, gawping. But some of the other passengers, their curiosity roused, moved towards the back of the bus. They stared at Snitsarenko and the woman. She sidled further to the front, begging and pleading with the entire bus, never taking her eyes off Dmitry Petrovich.

"Do something! Grab him! He killed my husband! He's a murderer! I know him! Don't let him go! Please!"

Snitsarenko couldn't take any more of this.

"Listen, if you're in your right mind, you've made a mistake. I've never seen you before and you've never seen me, either. Stop shouting and look at me carefully!"

The woman shut up. She was staring wildly, but it was obvious she was convinced of the truth of what she was saying.

"Calm down," Snitsarenko spoke again. "Where and when was your husband murdered?"

But the woman didn't hear him. She carried on looking pleadingly at the other passengers. It was as if she didn't want to hear him because she knew he would only lie and try to worm his way out of it.

"Would you like to see my papers?" Dmitry Petrovich asked.

No she didn't. All she wanted was a militiaman. Her certainty was beginning to infect the other passengers and the atmosphere was becoming tense. There was an ugly silence which hung like a cloud over Dmitry Petrovich. His head was throbbing and his leg ached.

"Well, this is a fine mess you're in," he thought. "Good thing there's nobody here you know. You'd be a complete laughing stock!"

"All right," he said, smiling as reassuringly as he could. "All right, we'll get out at the next stop and go straight to the nearest militia post. I'd like to ask you all to come with us. Just in case she starts shouting or calling for help in the middle of the street. That's something I can do without. Will you do that?"

He was speaking to all the dozen or so passengers facing him, all of them men.

"It won't take more than ten to fifteen minutes."

The tension was relaxed by what he said and the way he said it, but it was not eliminated entirely.

They left the trolleybus in a crowd and had to walk some distance before they found a militia post. He couldn't see the woman while they were walking. She hung back, as if she was frightened he might attack her. Who knew what was going on in that sick mind of hers? But as soon as they reached the militia post, she was back in front again and in a moment or two disappeared into an office. Not long afterwards Snitsarenko and the accompanying retinue were called in. An elderly major inspected his documents calmly and unhurriedly, asked him a couple of questions. All the same, despite his reserve, he did not return Dmitry Petrovich's papers, but kept them in front of him on his desk. Clearly he was preparing himself for a long and thorough questioning of the aggrieved party. By now Dmitry Petrovich was utterly bored by the whole business. He interrupted the major, took out his notebook, found the right page and placed it on the table.

"Please phone regional State Security on this number and then pass me the receiver."

The major looked at Snitsarenko, examined the page with the number, looked back at him again and dialled. As soon as the other party was on the line, he handed over the receiver. Snitsarenko tried to speak calmly. The people in the room hung on to every word, trying to work out what was being said at the other end.

"Sasha? Dmitry here. Hello . . . Fine . . . No, I couldn't . . . I'm telling you, I couldn't . . . Listen, are you very busy? Right. I need you urgently."

Snitsarenko turned to the major.

"What's the number of this post?"

"Number three."

"Militia post three . . . No, it's urgent . . . See you."

Snitsarenko put down the receiver. The major produced a packet of cigarettes.

"Like a cigarette? They're filter."

"Thanks, I don't smoke."

Dmitry Petrovich put the notebook back in his pocket. There was an awkward silence. Finally the major decided to try and clarify the situation.

"Citizen Kalinichenko could, of course, be making a mistake. It's quite a few years ago . . . "

It suddenly hit Dmitry Petrovich with a blinding flash.

"What's your name?" he asked her anxiously.

"Kalinichenko!" She flung the name in his face, not concealing her triumph. "My husband was Vasily Grigoriyevich Kalinichenko."

Then she added quietly, wearily, without looking at him: "I recognised you immediately."

"When was your husband murdered?" asked the major, on his guard now.

She told him.

"What is all this? Am I dreaming or what? This can't be true! It's crazy!" All his reason, all his faith shrieked desperately: "It's a lie. A lie!"

Snitsarenko turned on the woman. She shrank back trembling into her chair, the major hastily slid open the desk drawer where he kept his service pistol.

71

"Why are you lying? I don't know what happened to your husband later, but nobody killed him then. What are you lying for? Answer me!"

The men crowding the office were nonplussed. Something weird was going on. Either there was a dreadful, tragic mistake, or . . . there was no limit to the depths people would sink to! There could hardly be a third category. A man was either guilty or not guilty. Was life capable of producing something that was not subject to judgement? What a person did might be *predetermined* by a mass of circumstances, what a person did had to be *judged* quite unequivocally, otherwise how could you tell the difference between good and evil?

She described what had happened. Not to Dmitry, though. She spoke softly. And it was clear there would be no tears, they had dried up long ago.

"He was dead when they brought him back to the house . . . Three bullets in his chest . . . "

"Bullets . . . " muttered Snitsarenko. "Bullets . . . "

So, that was what had happened! Oh Lord! He'd felt at the time it was a dirty business. But he hadn't wanted to know, because he was clean. That was certain. He'd wanted to find out what happened to Kalinichenko, and Shitov, but hadn't. Why? What had stopped him? Fear? What? Anyway, what did it matter? He was a murderer! A murderer, because he'd killed a man. A murderer because he'd believed being conscientious was enough in life, it was enough to believe! This would spare you having to think and bearing the responsibility. Even now he was certain his was the true faith. But why didn't the promptings of his conscience come into the system of his faith? Had not this supreme measure of everything in this world been given to him? But it had been driven deep inside and become atrophied from moral cowardice, from the total subordination of all his motivation and actions. Living and dying were easier that way. Never speak ill of the dead. Still, Kalinichenko was a bastard. But Kalinichenko was dead. He, Dmitry, had survived, and now he had to answer for it all to himself and to this woman here whom he'd also in a real sense killed that dreadful night, the night which marked the sum total of his faith in carrying out orders.

He was guilty. Guilty! Instinct had told him he was mixed up in something dirty, but he hadn't wanted to complicate life. And now he was a murderer. A murderer by his own and by society's laws. And nothing could atone for it, nothing could wipe it away . . . He had been a dedicated, yet blind servant to an idea, an idea which promised everything in the future. But he had not understood then that there was no such thing as past or future, there was simply the man, at each and every second one and indivisible with his own past and his own future. There is always just this one man. This man is on trial before a judge who is out considering his verdict and may reappear at any moment. And the man steels himself to hear that verdict. A verdict which cannot go to appeal . . .

A KGB colonel walked into the room. With Dmitry Petrovich he was friendly, with the major businesslike, with the rest affable. Snitsarenko caught the colonel's eye and nodded at the entourage.

"Please would everybody not directly involved in the case leave the room." The colonel reacted instantly, without knowing who was or was not directly involved.

When the four of them were left alone, Snitsarenko again caught the colonel's eye and nodded at the major. The major, too, was politely ejected from his own office, displaying no feelings of any sort, other than a willingness to obey his superior officer.

"Sasha, eighteen years ago this woman's husband was killed." Dmitry Petrovich turned to her: "Please tell the colonel who you believe killed your husband."

She hesitated a fraction, but looked Snitsarenko full in the face and said with conviction: "You did."

The colonel's eyebrows arched. He stared questioningly, uncomprehendingly at Dmitry Petrovich.

"That, basically, is why I phoned you," said Snitsarenko, walking away from the desk to the back of the room.

The colonel drew his own conclusions from Dmitry Petrovich's remark and sat down next to the woman.

"What's your name? . . . Well now, Tatyana Alekseyevna, I don't know the details as yet, of course, but in this particular case that isn't important. I don't want to think you're slandering comrade Snitsarenko here. So I'm telling you, absolutely and unequivocally, you've made a mistake."

She wanted to say something, but he wouldn't let her.

"I'll listen to what you have to say, but I want to tell you this. I went through the war with Dmitry Snitsarenko and watched him rise from sergeant to platoon commander. I personally recommended him for the security organs, where he proved himself a true *Chekist* and Communist. He was given a medal for eliminating a large UIA group. What's more, he was seriously wounded during that operation. For six years now he's been director of a state farm here and I've never heard a word said against him in that time. Your allegation is unfounded also by virtue of the fact that men like Dmitry Petrovich could never, well, by their nature, let's say, be involved in any murky business. Our system rests on people like him, Tatyana Alekseyevna, they put it in place, they held it together and strengthened it . . . "

Meanwhile Snitsarenko stood there, listening to this paean of praise and thinking: "My dear colonel, if only you knew what you were saying. In fact, do you know where the dividing line falls between what is clean and what is murky business? And was your progression from intelligence captain to KGB colonel so very clean? Is some piece of ancient history waiting for you at a tram stop somewhere? You probably think it was all justified and the slate's been wiped clean. But the time has come for one of us to answer for it. And that one of us is me. Maybe you're next? We felt the ideal justified what we did. How are we to be justified? The dead are the lucky ones!"

The colonel finished his speech. Snitsarenko came over.

"Tatyana Alekseyevna, in the very near future you'll get a letter from me explaining exactly what happened to you and your husband. Leave me your address and I'll give you mine. Believe me, I won't try to hide. Just be patient a few days and everything will be explained."

When she had left the room, exhausted and downcast, Snitsarenko said: "Sasha, I need your help to find a man . . . Ilya Zakharovich Shitov. If he's still alive, that is . . . It'll be bad if he's dead . . . Then I'll . . . "

VI

Eighteen years earlier

Shitov hit the bottle the day he returned from regional HQ. Kalinichenko had denounced him, accusing him of giving aid to the nationalists, of sabotaging an operation, of conspiring with the traitor Snitsarenko. Shitov had been given a frosty reception at HQ, even though they were aware of his intention not to keep the head of the DCAB in the picture.

"Why all this elaborate farce?" they asked.

"To make it look convincing," Shitov answered.

He wriggled out of it, of course. But he was given to understand that if he failed, he'd pay for it. If that bunker wasn't found, and found fast, the six people he'd sprung from under Kalinichenko's nose would cost him his job. At best it'd mean early retirement, with all the consequences that implied. And he'd better make sure nothing happened to Dmitry.

Shitov drank steadily. There'd been no word from Dmitry for six days now. Shitov kept drinking. Irina watched over him fearfully from the far corner of the room. Her only weapon, tenderness, was powerless against the panic and despair that had gripped Shitov. He wouldn't let her near him. He wouldn't talk to her, he didn't notice her, and if he did, her presence irritated him so much he could have beaten her.

75

He neglected his duties and Kalinichenko gradually began to take over the reins. The investigators and operations men began muttering to each other and going to the DCAB chief for advice, by-passing Shitov. Shitov didn't care. He knew he was as good as dead if the operation went wrong. He was also certain that if it worked he could have everything back in place in a day. He couldn't go into the DCAB office. At HQ he'd at last found out why Kalinichenko had been transferred. He was no angel himself, but the thought of what Kalinichenko had done filled him with disgust.

Maybe it wasn't quite like that. It can happen that discovering somebody's worse than you are makes you very happy, because you can pour all the self-disgust that's built up inside onto him. One way or the other, he hardly saw Kalinichenko.

The latter sensed his senior officer's agony. He started pushing his own methods, openly ignored Shitov, made disparaging remarks about him in the presence of other officers.

But Kalinichenko, methodical and sober-minded as he was, underestimated Shitov. He failed to take account of the phenomenal tenacity and cunning that surface in the Russian character in desperate situations. At such times there are no limits, no boundaries. No barrier is insurmountable, no distance too great, and woe betide anyone who stands in the way. Many great strategic minds have been defeated simply because they thought they were watching their enemy's death throes, when suddenly that agony was transmuted into an incredible, inexplicable force which nothing could stop or blunt. And whether it was good or evil that force unleashed depended simply on the circumstances that brought it into being.

The worst did come to the worst. Dmitry found the bunker, but failed to get a fix on its location. At first everything went smoothly. Dmitry did as Shitov told him, made his way to the Gnatyuk house and used threats and blackmail to pressure the wife and son. Finally the boy whispered in his mother's ear and disappeared. He was gone an hour and a half. He came back alone, but showed Dmitry the direction he should take from the village and where he would be met. Dmitry made his way down a path where sowings of maize and potatoes met. He had gone about half a kilometre when several hands seized him from behind, disarmed him and bound an evil-smelling rag around his eyes. He tried in vain to calculate the direction they went in. These people knew what they were doing, so that when they were finally challenged by a sentry and stopped, Dmitry couldn't be certain they hadn't come full circle back to the village. He was taken down steps, then they sat him on a chair in a lighted room. He could just detect the light through the blindfold. They kept it on throughout the questioning. The voice was calm, but commanded authority. Dmitry repeated the cover story he had worked out with Shitov, deflected the trick questions and on the whole put on a faultless performance.

Still blindfolded, he was led into what appeared to be a separate chamber. It was pitch dark in there. His blindfold was removed and he was pushed onto a mattress. There were other people in the chamber, but there was hardly any talking and nobody took any notice of him. Besides, he was asleep almost as soon as he hit the mattress.

He couldn't tell how long he slept, a good while, probably, because he felt hungry and his head ached from too much sleep. They brought him food in the darkness, then bound his eyes for another interrogation. From the questions Dmitry realised that the men in the bunker knew he was wanted, but it wasn't clear whether Kalinichenko had been to the village. It was the same man asking the questions. He was making it harder this time, probing the depth and sincerity of Snitsarenko's nationalist persuasions. He'd seen enough of their propaganda to answer convincingly, but this time he didn't have that inner certainty that his answers were the right ones. And the way the questions were put meant he couldn't get away with stock answers. He had to prevaricate, work his way into the subject, and at the same time maintain the right tone and style. Then it was back into the darkness, followed by yet another interrogation, followed by an interminable wait that seemed like a month to him, but which was in fact a week. On the tenth day they blindfolded him again and brought him out into the usual room. This time the voice that spoke to him was harsher, more clipped.

He was told he had been accepted into the Organisation of Ukrainian Nationalists and could be assigned his first operation, to test him out, naturally. The voice read out a document stating that for such and such crimes a tribunal of the organisation had sentenced Vasily Kalinichenko, a traitor to the Ukrainian people, to death, this sentence to be carried out by Dmitry Snitsarenko. Dmitry was not asked if he wished to volunteer. Then he was taken back up the steep steps, led for what seemed hours over ploughed fields, through maize, potatoes, along a road. When the blindfold was finally removed, it was night, the lights of the village winked in front of him, and a voice from behind told him to keep walking and not look back. Both his pistols were returned to him.

Dmitry was shocked when he saw Shitov. Puffy eyed, unshaven, stinking of booze, Shitov looked unkempt, derelict and dirty, with a feverish glint in his eyes. He was overjoyed to see Dmitry and perked up no end. But when he heard that Dmitry had come back empty-handed, he was crestfallen. He slumped, his elbows on the table, and just sat there, oblivious to Dmitry's presence, rocking gently from side to side, from time to time swearing under his breath.

After a while he raised his head and looked pleadingly at Dmitry.

"Come on, Dima! Surely we can come up with something between us, eh?"

Dmitry shrugged.

"Perhaps we could stage an attempt on his life?"

"Stage? This isn't a theatre! This is war!"

He hunched as he spoke, and it made him look like a mole emerging into the fresh air.

He made up a bed on the divan and asked as Dmitry began to undress: "Still got the pistol? Give it here."

He put it in his pocket, grunted good night and turned out the light. As he lay there, Dmitry could hear him prowling in the next room, and just as he was about to drop off he made a mental note that the footsteps sounded firmer.

When Dmitry awoke, Shitov wasn't there. Irina fed him without saying a word and produced, on Shitov's instructions most likely, a set of fresh linen, too broad and too short for him. Dmitry tried to draw Irina into conversation, but a few brief words from her were enough for him to realise that conversation was not part of her duties.

He looked through the papers, listened to the radio, cleaned his revolver. The Shitov who walked through the door that evening was not the Shitov he had seen last night, nor was it the Shitov he'd known before. There was a sharp decisiveness to his movements, to the expression on his face, to his tone of voice. There was something barbed that put you on your guard. Dmitry could feel it, but didn't want to probe too deeply.

A plan had been drawn up to stage the assassination of the DCAB chief. Kalinichenko knew about it and had agreed. After the mock assassination Kalinichenko would be hidden out of sight until the operation was over . . .

Dmitry asked at some point: "Is it true Kalinichenko shot . . . "

Shitov didn't let him finish.

"That's none of our business. The people who need to know, know."

Dmitry went off to complete the operation. He was not able to see how for the next two hours Shitov put away one vodka after another, pacing the room, straining his ears in the darkness, swallowing pills and powders, before the glasses trembled from the echo of distant shots and he collapsed onto

the divan like a rotten tree as the window-panes tinkled a thin
"finito".

The three blanks Dmitry watched Shitov load into the Browning sounded satisfyingly authentic. The way Kalinichenko
doubled up and crashed headlong to the ground was masterly.

Dmitry caught a glimpse of this performance before vanishing and felt genuinely sorry for Kalinichenko. He'd have one
hell of a bruise on his forehead next morning. He even saw the
look of horror on the face of Kalinichenko's pretty young wife.
He thought they might well not have told her, just in case.
Might well not have done. They were both of them – Shitov
and Kalinichenko – quite capable of that . . .

A day or so later they stormed the bunker. Dmitry was badly
wounded and taken to hospital. He underwent two operations
and it was as he was recovering he heard about the medal and
refused point blank to serve in the security organs any longer.
Shortly afterwards he was transferred to the Urals and never
met Kalinichenko again. As for Shitov . . .

VII

Eighteen years later

Eighteen years later Dmitry Petrovich Snitsarenko was walking
down the streets of a *dacha* settlement in the prosperous
black-earth belt of Russia. Painted houses nestled like beehives
in the green depths of the gardens amongst vivid flower-beds.
Raspberries hung over wattle fences into the road, while apples
and black drops of wild cherry hung overhead. These cosy
fairy-tale nests reeked of jam-making, television sets and en-
hanced personal pensions.

Snitsarenko stopped at the gate leading to one of them, put
his hand into the special opening and slid back the bolt. He
walked into the garden. At the far end a brightly painted porch

marked the dwelling of the proud owner of this corner of paradise. At the porch he was met by a boy of about twelve with delicate features and girlish brows.

"That's my dad," the boy said in answer to Dmitry Petrovich's enquiry. "He's with mum in the kitchen garden at the back."

He set off, showing the way through flower-beds and past gooseberry bushes.

So, Ilya Zakharovich Shitov was a father. Snitsarenko hadn't expected that. Not that it changed anything, but Snitsarenko was in no hurry now, he wanted a chance to think before meeting Shitov, as though something new had come up that demanded careful thought. But the boy walked fast and there was no time for reflection.

Shitov and his wife were squatting beside the vegetable patch examining the plants and didn't notice Snitsarenko come round the corner.

"Dad," the boy shouted, pointing at the visitor, and immediately ran off.

Dmitry Petrovich walked up to Shitov slowly, very slowly. Shitov, grey and old, straightened up just as slowly as he approached. The old woman, whose feminine instinct sensed impending disaster, just as slowly clasped her hands to her throat.

"Stand please. The court is in session," Snitsarenko said.

But he didn't say that. He said: "Hello, Shitov."

"Guilty," Shitov replied.

No. The words were: "Hello, Dima."

"Stop!" screamed Shitov's wife.

No, she didn't. She, too, said hello, though Dmitry had said nothing to her, probably because he couldn't take his eyes off the man who had made him a murderer and was himself a murderer.

Shitov didn't offer his hand, even though he wiped them extra thoroughly on his gardening apron, playing for time to collect his thoughts. You could see from his face he was finding it hard going. Shitov, grey, ageing Shitov was stumped. There was something about him, though, that Snitsarenko couldn't remember from before. Old age weighed heavily on Shitov, but his eyes were younger than ever . . .

"Well, now, come on into the house. Be our guest . . . " Shitov said eventually. He sounded hesitant and most unenthusiastic. As he walked past Snitsarenko, he attempted a friendly smile. The attempt was a failure.

As they turned the corner, Dmitry Petrovich looked back automatically. Irina was still standing there, hands clasped to her throat, her face a mask of melancholy longing . . .

They sat opposite each other at a low table in a little attic room. Everything down to the last tiny detail had a Ukrainian flavour. Even Shitov was wearing a Ukrainian shirt with an embroidered collar. Snitsarenko was taken aback by all this. He remembered how Shitov couldn't stand anything Ukrainian.

Their conversation was strictly to the point.

"Tell me why you've come, Dima. It's not a social call, I can tell that. Let's not beat around the bush . . . We're both soldiers. Out with it . . . "

Shitov gestured listlessly and stared past Snitsarenko. He looked tired.

"It's time to settle accounts, Ilya Zakharovich. Everything has to be paid for sometime. Now it's our turn."

Dmitry Petrovich spoke quietly. He was surprised to feel no bitterness towards Shitov, let alone hatred. Their conversation had started on the wrong foot but there was nothing he could do to alter that, because something had altered in him, and only the hopelessness of his own situation had driven him into it.

"So, you've come to see justice done, and it's crucify old Shitov!"

Whatever he might have thought, Snitsarenko had never expected to hear such hostility in Shitov's voice, and so he replied in surprise: "It seems to me, Ilya Zakharovich, you

can't have any claims on me. After all, as I told you,
I . . . "

Shitov interrupted him rudely and angrily. "I don't give a
damn about you, dear boy! Not a damn! Got that! You can
feel as guilty as you like! All right, put on sackcloth and ashes!
I'll spit on you for it, you fool. Got that! Come to see justice
done! Perhaps it was done a long time ago! Here!"

He jabbed himself in the chest.

"Perhaps I've taken all the suffering in the world on myself
and been granted forgiveness! What do you know about justice,
anyway? Expected me to go down on my knees and start
snivelling? Not likely! You can't touch me, you can't touch
anything of mine. I don't know anything and I don't want to
know! Did you see that pistol being loaded? Did you or didn't
you?"

"I did . . . " Snitsarenko murmured at last.

"Right then, so wriggle out of that one yourself. Perhaps
you loaded live ammunition later. Because I loaded blanks,
my friend. And whose idea was it in the first place. Yours!
You wanted promotion! I never heard anything. I don't know
who shot the bastard, you or the nationalists. That's my version
and I'm sticking to it, Dima!"

Shitov coughed, clutched at his chest, went pale.

"So you want to dump it all on me, Ilya Zakharovich?"

"Did I come looking for you, Dima? No. Did I try to make
you talk? No I didn't. I won't surrender. I'll bite and scratch
to the end. I won't give in! Don't you have any hopes on that
score, Dima!"

"That's your privilege, Ilya Zakharovich. But during the
last few days I've come to understand a lot . . . "

"Understand? A lot?" Shitov cut him short sarcastically.
"Dima, you don't understand one hundredth of what you'll
understand before you're finished . . . Perhaps not even
then . . . Forever the puppy dog, all innocent. And who knows
. . . maybe that's what's best for you. You mightn't have the
strength to take it all in . . . Now you can scamper round

grabbing pussycats by the tail and feel ever so proud of yourself."

Shitov was becoming emotional.

"Ilya Zakharovich, a woman recognised me in the street, Kalinichenko's widow. She wants justice . . . We did kill . . ."

Shitov pulled a face.

"Killed, you say! Who? Her husband? How many others did we kill? Does anybody demand justice for them? The old Gnatyuk woman died of heart failure under interrogation, her boy rotted in the camps, old man Gnatyuk died from loss of blood, and does anybody demand justice for them? Eh?"

"It's not the same, Ilya Zakharovich!" Snitsarenko could barely restrain himself. "You're mixing two different things! There was a war on and they were the enemy. You put a pistol into my hands to kill one of our own people!"

"You accuse me of mixing things up!" Shitov exploded again. "I've spent the last eighteen years unravelling the things I'd got tangled up. Eighteen years I've been trying to wipe my hands clean of human blood with the soil and they still reek of it. I look at my son in the morning, hoping he hasn't inherited it from me! Who has the right to judge me? Name me one single person who has the right. The younger generation? Too young to have any rights. The older generation? Too deep in it themselves. Killed one of my own people, you say! When he *was* one of my own, that was the time to put me on trial! Now they can put me on trial for the whole lot, everything, so everybody'd have to be up there, themselves included . . . Either everybody and for the whole lot, or I'm not guilty! And tell that stupid bitch how many innocent people that husband of hers did in, and how many more he'd have bumped off if I hadn't eliminated him to save my own face. Put old man Shitov on trial just because he wiped out some piece of vermin? That wouldn't be justice. That's pie in the sky! Enough of this, Dima. You do as you see fit, but leave me be."

Suddenly Shitov leant across the table, his face close to

Snitsarenko's. "No. I don't believe you. I don't believe you want justice. You want to dump it all on me and get yourself off the hook on the grounds of extenuating circumstances!"

Dmitry Petrovich got up from the table. He walked across to the window and opened the shutter. Shitov's son was squatting under an apple tree, patiently whittling a stick with a pocket knife. There was a submissiveness about his pale face which made him look exactly like his mother. He had to have something of his father, but Snitsarenko couldn't see it. And for some reason he felt an urge to find the answer to some question he couldn't pinpoint.

When he turned around again, Shitov was changed beyond recognition. It was an old man he saw at the table, old and weak and tired. Snitsarenko suddenly realised that Shitov wouldn't fight back, he'd lay his grizzled head on the block and close his eyes.

So, everything would now fall into place. The guilty would be punished. Justice would be done. Shitov's old wife would fall to the ground weeping in despair and the pale face of the boy under the apple tree would be clouded with grief forever. And if not, what then? Dmitry Petrovich imagined a flat in a far-off Siberian town, a flat where a lonely woman who had lost her husband and remained true to him lived. This woman thirsted for justice and rightly so, because this thirst had drained the life out of her. Shitov had his concept of justice, weird and incomprehensible though it was. And he, Dmitry Snitsarenko, had his. After all, he had not, essentially, committed a crime. He had killed nobody. His guilt lay elsewhere and that elsewhere was under the jurisdiction of a different court, where both judge and defence counsel were all rolled into one and the same person – himself! There was more to the question of justice than met the eye. It was now up to him whether the thirst of a lonely woman in a distant town would be quenched, whether Shitov's wife and son would be made wretched. There was also the simple justice of punishment for a crime! But how come justice is unable to break the chain of evil, how come it merely prolongs it? And what about him? What ought he to do? Take the responsibility himself? But why him? He had a wife, children. So what to do? . . .

Shitov interrupted his thoughts. His voice was flat, without malice.

"Did you track me down yourself or through the organs?"

"Through the organs."

"Right."

Shitov stood up, tugged his shirt straight as he would have done his military tunic, stood at attention, looked unflinchingly at Dmitry Petrovich. He appeared resigned.

"Well, let's not beat about the bush. If you've not come on your own, call them in, no point them skulking behind fences."

"I came on my own, Ilya Zakharovich."

"Right."

Shitov's expression didn't change. He stood ramrod straight, as if in the dock. He stood without speaking, looking past Snitsarenko.

"Good-bye, Ilya Zakharovich," Dmitry Petrovich said quietly and stepped quickly past Shitov to the door.

Shitov caught up with him with a clatter of boots on the porch.

"Who d'you think you are . . . ! Don't want to sink to my level, eh? You despise me! Go right ahead, despise me! I wanted to spit on you! So do me a favour. What am I supposed to do? Get my things together right now?"

Shitov was gasping for breath.

"I won't let you past until you tell me!"

He blocked Dmitry Petrovich's path, legs spread apart, hands behind his back.

Snitsarenko was confused, still finally undecided. He was surprised to hear himself say crisply, quite involuntarily: "Let's just say this conversation never happened."

He walked quickly, ran almost, to the gate. Shitov overtook him all the same and blocked the path. There were tears in his eyes. The tears were choking him, too, because he was unable to speak at first.

"Forgive me, Dima," he whispered.

Snitsarenko nodded and the killers parted forever.

THE STORY
OF A
STRANGE TIME

"I WANT to be honest! I want to be honest! I want to be honest!"

I could write those words a thousand times. Recite them every morning when I wake, remind myself of them dozens of times a day, fall asleep saying them, weigh them and measure them against my every action, no matter how trivial. But I know now that this is a delusion. Being honest doesn't depend on an individual wanting to be so. At least it doesn't depend on a desire on my part to be so, because it is not given to me to know what is honest and what is dishonest. I understand this now. Still, I want to be honest, honest above everything else. And so I have decided to end my life.

This idea first came into my head a few days ago, when I found out everything. Then it was just an idea that flashed through my mind, past my mind even. But it happened to be stronger than anything that was left in me, and I yielded to it. On the other hand, no. I didn't give in. I armed myself with it. But not wanting to seem to be just full of hot air, even to myself, I did not rush to make a final decision. I mulled over the pros and cons for several days. Quietly and systematically. I analysed all imaginable variants with a thoroughness that is only ever possible in a business such as this, and they all proved unviable.

So I decided to end my life. And I want to be honest in this decision, if only because this is the one honest decision.

Though I still don't know if it's honest, me writing all this, because I don't really know *why* it is I'm writing. But I still have five days ahead of me, time enough to think through all the secondary detail. I have done so much thinking these last few days that I have had to start scrutinising my thoughts from the outside, reading them as if they were someone else's. Though, once again, I don't know why I need to since I've made up my mind.

For the first time ever I'm travelling in a first-class single cabin on a steamer. Sort of uncomfortable. Though that's just what I need. The steamer's going right into the wilds and we'll be arriving five days from now. Today's day one. It's almost over. Four more ahead. Once I'd fixed on this solution, it was interesting to see how I would react to the time left me. I thought I'd probably want it to pass as quickly as possible and let things just happen. It might possibly have been like that if my decision hadn't been so firm. But as it happens, once you've made your mind up it's a matter of supreme indifference how many days are left.

The steamer hardly rocks at all. I stroll round the cabin. There's a big mirror over the basin, the kind you find in public toilets. That's why it's so uncomfortable in here. I examine my reflection in the mirror carefully. There was a time, a long time back, when I was about thirteen, when my looks caused me no end of bother. To be blunt, they didn't suit me on principle, though the primary cause was just one defect – my nose. It was snub, dreadfully vulgar. And my dream was to be an actor. Playing *The Gadfly*. An illustration from it used to hang over my bed. The hero, black hair, dark eyes and straight nose (yes, straight nose), would look down and scoff at my puny efforts to find one iota of similarity between him and me. This might, I felt, have been possible, were it not for my nose. And so I tried to correct this genetic defect. I'd spend days out in the forest with an elastic band stretched over my nose. It was extremely painful, but I stood it. And then in the evening I'd be in a complete state, staring at my profile in the mirror for ages. One day she caught me red-handed . . .

Went up on deck. Looked at the water, at the far bank, into the sky. Nothing's right. But what do we mean by right? When has it been, when was it ever right? Something has gone dead in the world, or changed beyond recognition, or had its true inner meaning turned inside out . . .

That time she caught me at it, she said I shouldn't be preening myself in front of the mirror like a girl. I don't know which I felt more, ashamed or insulted. Ashamed, most likely, because at that time I felt she had the right to make me feel ashamed of myself. She didn't actually have that right. In fact, she had no rights at all. But I didn't discover that until recently.

There are tourists on the deck below. They're happy, not a care in the world. Sing, dance on the deck to a guitar, play cards. They're my age. I tried studying their faces, but they're completely faceless. They're all so self-absorbed, playing some sort of game of their own invention and pretending not to notice that all the others are up to exactly the same game. I didn't notice that either until recently! But then it was hard for me to notice, because I was playing a game with a much more complicated set of rules. And it wasn't me who thought them up. The people who did were much more cunning and inventive than I. I was playing an honest game as a young man of promise. Which is what I was, as far as the rules of the game allowed. I had good marks at school, though I didn't try to be top. I wasn't bad at sport. I was politically aware and patriotic. I was polite, hardworking, brave and strong when need be, alert and quick off the mark. Those were the rules of my game and until I was fourteen I made a first-class job of it. The role model I adopted for myself was that of the "honest individual".

But honesty proved impossible in a world rooted in absurdity. And I paid for the excessive ambition of my model. I did something which threw me down from the pinnacle of my apparent decency into a pit I will never be able to climb out of. At first I protested my innocence, because my idea of what constituted guilt was too narrow and formal. From my point of view, none of those events was the result of a conscious act on my part. I hadn't known what I was doing. And there was no law that could find me guilty. The tragedy was, though, that I had played my game over-scrupulously so as not to be able to accuse myself of lacking scruples. Had I been a little less rigid in my choice, had my model been a little less ambitious, I might possibly not have done what cannot now be undone or forgotten. However, none of the other alternatives depended on me, and I don't know who they did depend on. They were excluded a *priori* by my environment and by all those people who had played a part in my life. And my model collapsed, everything collapsed round my ears, everything turned out back to front, head over heels. Good was shown to be evil, honesty perfidy and sense senselessness.

When I was about nine she gave me a slide-projector. In those days it was called a magic lantern. It really did seem magic to me. I liked it even better than the movies. I could put in a slide, sit right close to the screen, absorbed by the amazingly vivid colours of Africa or Australia, picture myself in that strange world and tell myself wonderful tall stories in which I was inevitably the hero. Sometimes when my imagination had run wild, at the climax of some adventure when the hero, i.e. me, had to show real initiative, I'd get so carried away I'd leap to my feet. Which meant, of course, my head came in front of the beam and everything went black, the fairy tale on the screen obliterated by an enormous shadow with two grotesque ears.

The same happened in real life, in this great perfidious fairy tale, when I did actually use my initiative one day. The results of that cannot truly be described as base, but they were at the same time horribly worse than base.

At first I had the sensation that I had been propelled by an effort of muscle and will high above the earth, and the earth had gone whizzing off lord knows where. Meanwhile I was hanging in the void, freed from the laws of gravity, without the strength to grasp the stupidity of the situation. This feeling was pretty close to the reality. I genuinely was hanging in mid-air, completely on my own. Without a past, since I had had to disown it, and without a future, because there is no future without the past. And I was no longer me, just a vague shadow of what had once been my self. I didn't even have a name any more. It took no more than an instant, and there was not a single person left in the whole world who I felt I needed. All the people around me had either stopped being themselves or proved complete strangers, because the ties binding us turned out to be an illusion. They had no inkling of all this, but I still wanted to be honest (I could not abandon the last of what I had left in me) and broke with them all on my own initiative.

Getting dark now. The steamer slides up to some anonymous landing stage. The strings and knots of lights on shore unravel and swell in my cabin porthole. Down below it's bedlam – noise, shouting, pushing and shoving. Nobody comes near first class, though. It's all quiet here. We long-distance travellers sit in our own reserved dining saloon or shiver out on our own deck, far from the scrum of tourist class, the stench and racket of the lower orders. It's peaceful up here, as if the inhabitants of all the cabins were suicides.

I went through some nasty moments when I was selling my belongings at the flea market to procure this peace and quiet. I wanted to be on my own for the last five days. Hear nothing, see nobody . . .

I grew up in a town, but never really felt at home there. Not that I felt out of place or lonely, as migrants sometimes do. I just felt more at ease with myself in the country. If I can just blow my own trumpet, (I know my own worth), I always felt bigger and better in the country. I liked going back to town and every time having to readjust to its unpredictability, to the fickleness of its criteria and affections. But I liked going out into the country even more.

From the vantage point of a nearby hill, the little settlement at the foot of a mountain range looked like a cluster of beehives hidden in a luxuriant, if somewhat overgrown, garden. Paths fanned out from it up into the mountains. I had my favourite places up there that I'd visit the first few days after arriving.

Night now, and the steamer crushes the darkness in the very middle of the current. So, go up on deck and stay there till frozen. Then to bed and one day will be over . . .

After all, time is purely our own invention. In relation to matters eternal, time does not exist. There is darkness and we call it night, there is light and we call it day. We invent it. We give it a name. But there are other nights and days. A man's life is his day. Everything that comes before or after is night. Night is longer than day, but if time is an invention, they are always equal. All people's days are equal, their nights are equal, nights and days equal *vis à vis* each other. A day more, a day less, a year more, a year less . . . More and less are relative, artificial. So, tomorrow morning I will be left with as much as ever I had – an instant . . .

II

It was his first day at his new posting, and the first time he had had to receive the public. He ought to have seen her first, because she had come several hours before he began seeing people. He had noticed her the moment he walked into the office, had registered her presence. But he called other people in first. They all had pressing and difficult problems. He became involved, began to run late, burdened himself with promises to help or investigate or phone the right people, scribbled notes on his calendar and in his diary. And when time was up he emerged into the waiting room, tired, exasperated with himself, looking completely washed-out, at which point he completely gave away his lack of experience by announcing almost apologetically that he couldn't see anybody else. And then he saw her and remembered. She was sitting in exactly the same spot and when he glanced at her in surprise, she started fumbling with her bag and in a moment would have been gone. But he walked over to her.

"You were here before the rest. Why didn't you come in?"

She was silent. She hung her head, avoided his eyes, opened and shut her bag mechanically. From the way her ashen lips were trembling, he knew she was on the verge of tears. He asked the question again, but she only hung her head lower. He had no option but to ask her to step into his office.

She had big blue eyes and a snub nose. She was thin, little more than a girl, either convalescent or in great distress, maybe both. Her dress was extremely modest, though her hairstyle was the latest fashion . . . But seeing modesty was in fashion at the time, her hair did not conflict with the overall impression she made on him during those first minutes of their acquaintance.

To defend against tears, he spoke to her with deliberate courtesy. This was also to dispose her towards being frank with him. But at the same time his manner was sufficiently distant to keep at bay the hysteria she was close to, judging by the state she was in.

"What's your name and what's the trouble?"

She bit her lip repeatedly as she struggled to retain her composure, then replied very softly: "They're evicting me from my room."

"What's your name? Where do you live and where do you work?"

She answered as quietly as before. He wrote down the details, put his pen aside and leaned towards her.

"Now, calm down and tell me who is evicting you and why."

She lifted her head and now he saw her huge eyes, so full of tears they made him feel horribly awkward. He picked up a pencil, hesitated, put it back down again. He saw nothing now except those eyes which, should they overflow, would flood the world with molten pearls – at least, that was the tawdry metaphor that sprang to his mind later on when thinking about her. But that was afterwards. At that moment, though, he merely felt awkward, the way you do when confronted suddenly by a person who has suffered a great misfortune of a kind you only know from second hand.

"They've taken my husband."

*   *   *

"Taken". In those days everybody knew what that word signified, instantly. Nobody ever said "arrested", the word was "taken". What seems especially surprising today is the way this peculiar (there's no other way to describe it) word, so vague, so wide in its implications and at the same time so unambiguous, caught the special spirit of its time with extraordinary precision; a time about which so much – both truth and nonsense – has been and, God knows, will be said. Perhaps people's courage will fail them and they'll carry on looking for a scapegoat and will, no doubt, find one. What could be easier! It'll make this chapter in our history seem like a cruel and pointless farce, but it'll make them feel better. But then again, maybe people will find the necessary courage and, instead of looking for a scapegoat, try to find the source of the evil. Finding it and understanding it, if they ever do or can, will be painfully difficult, because a whole epoch will have to be described as a tragedy, one that spans several generations.

A strange time of strange words and strange happenings! Perhaps you should say no more if you want to avoid being simplistic? The important thing is, that time happened and there are people who remember it.

Even more important; one day they took a nineteen-year-old's husband away.

Every one of us selects his or her own personal scale to measure up against the outside world, a scale which on the whole matches his or her spiritual needs and capacities. With statesmen and generals it's one to one. They measure up as equals. Some women take a man as their scale. Which of them gains more out of such an alliance is hard to tell, but if it breaks down, the woman always suffers. Even if only temporarily. She has to grope her way along, a bit as if she were short-sighted and had broken her glasses on the road.

"They've taken my husband," the nineteen-year-old told the official. Only a moment ago this personage was prepared to hear her out and then help, do everything he could for her. He had the power and the resources to do that. All she did was say one strange sentence and he grasped the entire situation in a flash. And the clarity which radiated from that sentence, that special clarity of understanding which the people of that strange time possessed, crushed the man against his official desk, stripped him of his power and his resources, rendered him helpless and useless.

Meanwhile she looked at him with blind eyes, and hoped against hope. He hadn't said no yet and she hoped he wouldn't say that word . . . if he was just the tiniest bit kind . . .

Yes, he probably was kind. After all, in every period of history being kind has only ever meant not being cruel, or not very. And cruel he was not. That was a fact and everybody who knew him would vouch for it. He often tried to help people and he didn't like it when he failed. He felt very bad, in fact. It is a human quality known as fellow-feeling. That's what they said he had when he embarked on the first steps of a career which, though hardly brilliant, had taken him by inertia through a steady progression of promotions and success.

Obviously it would be naïve to think that fellow-feeling was the key characteristic noted in the reports on him. Of course not. He was also invariably described as politically literate. And the higher he rose, the greater the weight attached to this, while fellow-feeling was no more than an added bonus. It didn't hurt to have it, but all the same it was an expensive luxury for a man burdened with responsibility. Kindness, fellow-feeling and other such sentimental fripperies were simply not to be recommended at that strange time.

99

Political literacy, on the other hand, was like a second passport, particularly for a person in an official position. The term is still in use today, perhaps will be forever, and it signifies no more than the possession of a certain amount of a certain kind of knowledge. But at that time it indicated a capacity to reconcile the irreconcilable, to see things only as they ought to be seen; a capacity to capitulate while retaining a sense of freedom or liberate oneself while capitulating. In other words, it was a phenomenon that could have been either superior or inferior, but was most certainly right outside the bounds of normal common sense.

. . . And it was because the man the woman had brought her troubles to was politically literate that he not only understood exactly what she meant but also realised that her case was hopeless and that he was helpless. But if he was unable to do any good for this woman, it was still within his power to try not to do her harm. So he did not inform her that the wife of an enemy of the people had no moral right to leniency on the part of the executive organs of people's power. He did not tell her that, though he could have done. He did what she wanted him to. He asked her to tell him what had happened.

There was nothing unusual in her story. A young lab assistant had fallen in love with an engineer ten years her senior. Why had she fallen in love? When she first saw him, she thought his eyes were strict and tired. In reality they were very kind eyes. This was something she'd picked up straight out of trashy fiction, of course. She said he was handsome. That his hair was wavy pepper-and-salt grey. Stupid way to describe it! She said his lips were rather unique; they were thin and his smile had an oddly melancholy line. And his chin was determined. Naturally. Oh, those determined chins!

And this was all completely beside the point. His eyes might have been perfectly ordinary, his lips quite run-of-the-mill. He may even have been the classic chinless wonder. The point was she loved him. Please God, if only he'd notice her! He didn't, of course. She was certain of that. (It'd be interesting to hear his side of the story!) All right, so be it. He hadn't noticed her. So, burning with embarrassment and cursing herself for a hussy, she started making sure their paths crossed as often as possible. He did notice her, eventually . . . He was cool and correct . . . Much drenching of pillows . . . Deeply significant shadows under the eyes . . . Squabbles at work. But then gradually . . . like water dripping onto a stone . . . The rest was boring. And what was he listening to all this for, anyway, encouraging this trite confession by being sympathetic? Who needed it? It was all perfectly obvious. Her husband had, at best, been mixed up in something. That is, if he wasn't a genuine wrecker or a Trotskyite. As far as she was concerned, you could see right away she was an idiot and they didn't want anything from her. The flat, though, belonged to the state and would have to be repossessed. But it seemed as though she had clean forgotten the flat and was telling him the whole story, as if lifting the receiver and ordering her husband, he of the handsome lips and determined chin, to be brought round here would be simplicity itself. If only it were. But if they hadn't let him out straight away, the Almighty Himself couldn't help now. He knew the boys down on Zelyonaya Street. He'd had dealings with them before. Not a bundle of laughs, and quite enough to keep the experience fresh in his mind. You found yourself sitting opposite somebody your own age who made you feel like a naughty schoolboy. And that was when your conscience was crystal clear! What would it be like if it wasn't?!

. . . Yes, what was she on about now? He didn't catch it first time . . . Ah, so that's it! Pregnant. Worse. Been given the sack . . . Expelled from the Komsomol . . . Damn those hotheads! You really have to be a complete halfwit not to see she's a fool, a dishy little fool with big blue eyes . . .

The Trotskyite was no fool, either . . . Or the other way about, a total idiot not to have noticed those saucers straight off.

It wouldn't be a bad idea, of course, to think of something

for her, fix her up somewhere . . . She wouldn't get maternity leave after this. He could make enquiries about the engineer. He did have one channel . . . not one hundred percent reliable, but he could do it discreetly. He'd well and truly lumbered himself! Why had she come here and not the Party District Committee? What? Because the City Executive Committee represents Soviet power? That's as maybe, but who really makes the decisions? What's she on about now? What mistake? Some mistake when their factory missed its targets two years running!

Time to wind it up. She should come back in two days. We'll think of something as far as work and housing is concerned, but she shouldn't bank on there being a mistake with her husband.

Oho! Give her just the faintest glimmer of hope and she starts regarding you as a father and benefactor! Damn it all! You feel good, though, being the benefactor of a blue-eyed madonna! You know, if only . . .

He showed her out of his office and met the blistering stare of his secretary. That shrivelled old maid will have drawn her own conclusions, no doubt about that! Get rid of her at the first opportunity . . . But now straight down to the canteen. He had a meeting with the First Secretary at four . . . He still hadn't read his mail . . . When he went to toss his mac onto the counter of the canteen cloakroom, he turned automatically towards the large mirror on the wall and paused. The line of a smile . . . What sort of a line did he have? He tried a smile but it came out a grimace. There was no line, just lips and teeth and wrinkles. No, he was no great shakes at smiling. And his face had looked a bit effeminate from the start. Not that it had stopped him getting on.

Her eyes were so blue. So blue they were unreal. As if they'd been drawn in with a colour-pencil. And so incredibly deep. Brimming with sky-blue tears. No, not tears, molten pearls . . .

She's on her way home now, thinking what a stroke of luck to have seen someone who was good, who was kind. He had been so sympathetic, asked her to tell him all about it. He couldn't *not* help, he was bound to. He'd get to the bottom of it and everything'd be fine. Those people on Zelyonaya Street would apologise to her husband and to her. They'd have to apologise to her. Because they hadn't believed her when she'd spoken up for him, when she'd proved her point. They'd apologise for shouting and swearing at her. And she'd forget about it, no harm done. She understood. They had a difficult job to do. There were so many wicked people and it's hurtful when people you've trusted for ever such a long time turn out to be wicked. It's very vexing. She understood and so she didn't hold anything against them even now, when they'd acted so unjustly and been so horrid. Because you can't keep cool and collected in that job, nobody could, when you're responsible for the entire State.

She was just a simple nobody. Why did disaster have to strike her? She'd only ever had one real stroke of luck, she'd been very lucky with her marriage. That's all. Did her one piece of happiness have to turn out a catastrophe? No, that couldn't be! That'd be so unfair! And what good things in life had come her husband's way in his thirty years? Not enough to eat, studies, work . . .

The factory manager's wife believes her husband's been taken by mistake as well. She's been doing the rounds and knocking on doors. Perhaps that was a mistake, too. But if there's been sabotage at the factory, who is responsible if not the manager? The manager isn't a shift foreman who only knows what's been happening in his shop and even then only during his particular shift. She'd done right not to start writing letters to Moscow. They'd got the manager, the Party cell organiser and the chief engineer. One of them was bound to be guilty and so her husband oughtn't to be on the same list as them. They were running the place. Let them carry the can. But she was going to try another way. Sort it all out here, on the spot, without complaining about anybody. There are good people everywhere and, anyway, things couldn't necessarily be seen better from Moscow. You just have to find a good, honest person. And she had found him, it seemed. He had asked her so many questions, even though his time for seeing people was up. She'd told him everything in a way she'd never told anybody else before. She was even embarrassed about some of the things she'd told him. But she'd had to do it like that. She had to make this man believe there'd been a mistake. And he had believed her. Otherwise he wouldn't have started making promises. Otherwise he wouldn't have told her to come back in two days. Of course he knew what he was saying and promising. He felt sorry for her. He knew she was sincere in what she said. You can't help but feel when somebody's being sincere. Because it's not just the words you use, the way you use them is special. You have to be heartless not to feel when somebody's being sincere and telling the truth.

. . . And this man wasn't heartless. You really could say, without exaggerating, he was kind. Because he paced his office for a whole hour in a state of great agitation, chain smoking. During this time he saw nobody and took no calls. He was agitated because he was scared about the impending encounter with the woman he had promised to help two days ago. It was utterly irresponsible to have made that promise in a fit of hopeless sentimentality, knowing full well he was powerless to help her. He hadn't promised anything concrete, but he had given her encouragement. And now he was going to have to pay for it.

The day before he had tried rather half-heartedly to find out what had happened to the husband and had been told in no uncertain terms to keep his nose out of it. Which led him to conclude that the business was so serious even his rank would be no protection were he to do something foolish. He was given a second rap across the knuckles when he tried to pull rank and intervene in the housing committee's decision, to get them, at the very least, to postpone the eviction of the blue-eyed wife of the enemy of the people. Some harridan tore a strip off him over the phone, telling him what she thought of the imbeciles she found in some departments and their level of political vigilance.

Now on top of that he would have to put up with, at best, floods of tears and probably even hysterics. Why had he gone and got involved?

And when she walked into his office and sat down on the chair he showed her to, it was he – not she – he, a man without any serious moral blemishes that he was aware of, except an overdose of philanthropy, it was he who averted his eyes and pretended that he was either hunting for some important document among the papers on his desk or simply trying to put them in order.

However, he took himself in hand. He told her very solemnly and in tones of deepest sympathy that she must be brave and understand correctly (he stressed the word), understand correctly everything he, to his deep regret, was going to have to tell her. He glanced at her and realised it was best not to look at her at all.

He went on to tell her that her case looked as bad as it possibly could do, that her husband had not been arrested by mistake and consequently he was not the man she had taken him for. This meant also that either she was the victim of a cruel deception or she was herself partly guilty, because by surrendering blindly to her emotions she had failed to see through an enemy of the people.

Only when he had delivered this basic message did he finally look at her. What he saw made him so disgusted with himself, with his office, with what he said, with everything in this world, that he suddenly wanted to be a long, long way away, in a different world altogether where everything would be different, himself first of all. He wanted that half-woman half-child to be sitting next to him the way she was now, only not looking at him with those dead eyes, but smiling like a normal nineteen-year-old does. Nor would they have that terrible, incomprehensible, insurmountable tragedy described so bizarrely and guardedly as "transitional difficulties" come between them. He would have liked to be the dumbest, most politically illiterate social element just to rid himself of the burden of faith. He couldn't take it – a faith which demanded knowledge and which at the same time had no room for it, which called you to action and yet condemned you to passivity, which passionately denounced lies but which did not permit you to be honest.

What was he talking about! If the impulse had been that strong he could have satisfied it. The terrible thing was that he had many other impulses besides this one that were constant and overwhelming, and which, taken together, constituted his character. Anyway, is it really possible for a person just to decide to drop out? That's something only a very strong person can do, probably. Or a very weak one. He was neither one nor the other. He was average. Which meant he was one of the pillars of his time.

Distressed as he was by her predicament on a purely human level, what could he offer to replace what she had lost? He suggested she try and salvage what still seemed salvageable. In the interests of her unborn child, in her own interests, he urged her to disown her husband, revert to her maiden name and move right away. The motherland was sufficiently vast.

She dutifully agreed to everything. He dictated the text of a statement then and there, promised to have it sent immediately. He could see she was not herself and consciously exploited her condition, knowing that later she might be stricken with doubt, might hesitate, despair. If she didn't sign it now she would be caught by conflicting emotions and that would complicate matters.

He was giving her some long and complicated piece of advice when he started to hear his own disembodied voice. And in addition to this voice, a coarse and unpleasant one, he heard another two which kept interrupting each other. One told him that he must do something very important right away, the first real action in his life, while the other, absolutely identical in tone and vocabulary, was yelling at him to do nothing of the kind because the devil knew what would come of it. But neither told him what exactly he should or should not do now, as if that was blindingly obvious. So for some time he kept on talking mechanically like an old friend or mentor, feeling more wretched with every word, most likely because he didn't know how to stop. He began every sentence as if it was going to be the last, the end, and every time launched into some explanation, piece of advice, recommendation, caution, tied himself in knots and talked drivel. Finally, though, his conscience rebelled and he terminated this interminable, shabby monologue quite unexpectedly with a sentence so loathsome it made them both wince: "Well, you must excuse me, I have an appointment . . . "

She rose to her feet. "Thank you," she said, and though her voice was deadpan, the words were like a slap across the face. As she opened the door and then pulled it shut behind her, the impression she gave was as if she'd suddenly gone blind . . . The door closed. He grabbed a fat directory and was about to hurl it. But thought is quicker than the hand and it urged that chucking heavy, useful objects around your office was no way to behave. His hand froze and a moment later the directory plummeted with all the weight of that tightly-bound useless verbiage onto the desk.

The inhabitants of the strange time should have had a few cheap glass objects to hand for occasions such as this. The therapeutic properties of the sight and sound of splintering glass are well known.

He remained standing behind his desk for a while. Then he suddenly dashed across to the window and immediately drew back. Just as he thought. She was on the far side of the little square looking up at his office window. He grabbed his mac and cap, called to his secretary on his way through the door that he was going out and wouldn't be back for some time. He shot down the stairs, crossed the square and hurried over to her. She was more scared than surprised. He took her arm, roughly, hastily, and asked where she lived.

They walked a long way across town. Very fast at times. He was almost dragging her along. She stumbled. He apologised. And dragged her on again. She did not resist, but then she didn't show any kind of reaction. She simply submitted.

The self-contained two-room flat on the first floor was neatly furnished. Better than his own. On the table he noticed a photograph of the man with the supposedly stubborn chin. The chin was actually perfectly ordinary, something that made him happy beyond words and reinforced his determination.

It took all day to pack. He made five or six phone calls. The first to his secretary to cancel all his appointments and tell her not to expect him. The second to organise the truck. The third to check the trains. Then some more to sort out some other details, make some arrangements.

There was a difficult moment when they came to the photo on the table. She sat on a chair with the picture in her hands for half an hour or more, crying so hard it was useless to console her or say anything. There was one moment, or so it seemed to him, when something might have happened, as if an electric charge was accumulating on the end of a naked wire and was on the verge of earthing with tremendous explosive force. And at this dangerous moment her eyes met his, stern, silent, with their implacable demand. Yes, he was demanding, he was dictating conditions. The demand and the conditions were logical and sensible. The charge was neutralised by the last and largest tear. The photograph was hidden amongst the jumble.

That evening the blue-eyed nineteen-year-old whose husband had been taken left the town.

That night the man who had fellow-feeling, but who was also politically literate, paced the one room of his bachelor flat, tormenting himself with the knowledge of his own stupidity.

The next morning an old woman in a remote Siberian village nestling in the foothills of a mountain range found herself taking in an unexpected guest who arrived with a letter from her son. In it he asked his mother to treat the guest as she would his sister, asked her to give her all the help she could and told her to expect him in a month.

That same evening, all through that night, the next morning, all that day and many days subsequently, a man with an ordinary chin who, in the opinion of competent and politically literate comrades, had committed such monstrous crimes as a dozen men with genuinely determined chins would scarcely be capable of, rattled along in a filthy, smokey railway wagon that reeked of all the odours of human misfortune.

III

The second day of my allotted five is coming to an end . . . I have not put pen to paper all day. Nothing to write about and didn't feel like it anyway. But now that night has come peering in through the porthole, my hands reach for the exercise book and the urge to write comes more strongly than ever. Maybe not to write, but to make a clean breast of everything to myself. Somebody once found he had toothache in the heart, while my head's aching strangely somehow, somehow peculiarly, something's hurting inside my head. Several times today I was up on deck and I caught myself wanting to lean over and put my head in the water. That's probably what they mean by brainwashing! But I really do feel as though my head's stuffed, a total mess, and all I'm doing is putting it into order and introducing some sort of logic. But a lot slips away, it seems, drops out of the chain and lodges in the nooks and crannies of the mind, and order is only maintained by an effort of the will, not sheer force of logic. I have to churn all this out onto paper, incoherently perhaps, but at least in some tangible form . . . Then I can go over it all again . . . Not that it can influence my decision, that's irrevocable, but just to be on the safe side . . . This afternoon I suddenly felt the urge to look at the bullet. I fished out the magazine and unloaded it. Bear shot . . . I held it tight and jabbed it against my chest . . . Hurt . . . Somehow it's hard to imagine this blunt piece of lead penetrating my chest like a needle and then tearing the muscles, smashing through bone, extinguishing the brain. And the thoughts in it will go flying off somewhere, vanish . . . But perhaps they'll get lodged somewhere? . . . Though not in the disgusting, naked, rotting skull! That would be dreadful! But it's even more dreadful to think a lump of inert metal can turn the world into nothingness! And where does that leave the law of the conservation of matter, then? . . . But this is nonsense!

After lunch I went below. The tourists were lounging on a pile of rucksacks. Playing cards. The boys eyeing the girls, the girls eyeing the boys, guitars strumming, steamer hooting, everybody all smiles.

To hell with all this! I felt I was going to pass out . . . What a fiendish camouflage this is! Who thought it up? Because it's all a fraud, the whole thing! *The* most important element is missing – the truth! Why do those people smile? Why the gleam and splash of water? When the most important element is missing! If everything you do has a double meaning! If honesty is impossible! Don't they all know or are they just pretending? Or do they know something I don't? Perhaps there's some sort of higher wisdom or higher meaning? And if they do exist but are unattainable what's the use in that?

Why do I get scared when I watch those kids having a good time? Not scared exactly. It makes me want to switch them off, put their grins and voices out, make them stop dead, shut up and listen to the world about them. How can you hear it when you're talking and smiling so much? A wood-grouse doesn't hear the hunter if it's too busy calling.

But then perhaps it hasn't happened to them, never will . . . After all, not everyone is fated to kill their own father. I was. What for, though? Surely not just because I badly wanted to be honest!

And people keep on smiling and talking, talking away. They talk especially loudly about nature. About how wise and lovely and full of purpose it is. They snap little bits of it in their cameras as souvenirs. And nature gives generously. So they enthuse even more.

This is also a game with a set of rules, the most important of them being to pretend you don't know that running right through nature, right down to the individual cell, there is constant enmity, a constant battle for the brief instant of existence.

Out of these instants, which resemble exposed frames of cine film, a mirage of immutability, wisdom and perpetuity is formed. And in the same way that the life on a cinema screen is really no more than technical juggling with a fixed sum of dead frames, so nature's perpetuity is an uninterrupted sequence of deaths. Which is there more of in nature – life or death? Wisdom or meaninglessness? Even today nobody has managed to synthesise the simplest living cell. Yet a lump of lead is sufficient to do away with a man, the subtlest of all living creatures . . . But people are the slaves of their instant, they have nothing else. They project the instants, their own and other people's, for each other and what emerges they call history. They speculate on the meaning of this juggling, they prophesy and excel at extracting universal meanings.

Maybe the tangle of general meaninglessness is beginning to unravel, but that's a job for other people who haven't put their hands to it, to untangling it yet . . . I have decided to end my life. In three days this steamer will reach its destination. I'll disembark and walk off into the taiga. I'll walk north for as long as my strength lasts. I don't want the body to be found. I'm not committing suicide. I'm simply walking away from people and from the world. The world couldn't give a damn and there's no reason for people to know. As far as they're concerned I've vanished, lost forever. I told everyone I needed to I was going away and never coming back. That's what'll happen. I'm never coming back.

I told her that ten minutes after it all happened. There were tears for the next few days. Even her hands were red from crying. But I didn't feel sorry for her. As far as I was concerned she wasn't my mother any more. She was an accomplice. She didn't try to justify herself. There was nobody in the entire world who could justify what she'd done. Or what I'd done. Or the man who had spent nineteen years claiming to be my father but who was, in actual fact, the biggest killer of the three of us.

I told them that to their faces. They said nothing. In the space of a few days they aged twenty years. He went wrinkled practically overnight, his eyes sank in and lost their colour, his hands began to shake, he lost weight, began to stoop. To say nothing of her . . .

"Does it have to be this way?" she groaned when I told her I was leaving. "How are we to carry on living?"

"Same as the last nineteen years, keep going!" I answered.

"If you can keep going," I felt like adding . . . But I didn't. I once read a story about a man being bitten by a cobra and hacking his own hand off with a knife. He was screaming as he hacked. I screamed, too. Not at home, of course, but later, at the side of the road when I was waiting to hitch a lift. I rolled on the ground and howled like a baby. If it was only my hand I was cutting off . . . But I couldn't go on living with them. How could we look each other in the face? Anyway, staying alive meant only one thing as far as I was concerned – absolving my guilt. And that was what was impossible! My guilt was just a part of the general meaninglessness and was I supposed to start sorting out other people's problems? Why should it be me who had to unravel tangles that had been generations in the making!

Whenever I remember the enviable and idyllic picture our family life used to present, it makes me want to laugh and cry. Our family oozed prosperity and happiness. So it seemed. But its well-being was founded on treachery and was to end in murder. They – that man and my mother – had committed a foul deed and hoped to see themselves absolved in me. But I have become their retribution. Could it really have been otherwise? Can honesty really be born of dishonesty, truth of lies, good of evil? The more they instilled honesty in me, the worse the fate they prepared for themselves.

They tried to justify themselves, said they hadn't known, hadn't understood. Who'd believe them! What kind of people were they if they could understand anything you like except the voice of conscience! Nobody'd believe them, nobody'd say they weren't to blame!

IV

The nineteen-year-old was expecting a baby. When the man who had been her eyes and her shoulder disappeared into the maelstrom of that time, she groped wildly in the air hoping to touch on some support, however minimal. Because what would become of her without a prop of some kind? The harshness and senselessness of the world stunned her and she turned away from it to hearken to the one thing which was authentic beyond a shadow of a doubt, which was her meaning, her continuity, her justification and her hope. She was expecting a child. Her blind, outstretched hands happened on a support and she put her trust in it, trusted everything she had to it. She was expecting a baby. She was expecting. If she had nothing to expect she would either have departed this world which had cheated her of her happiness or lost her head completely and thrown herself into the flames. But she was expecting. And for that reason she placed her trust, without reflection, in the man who reached out a hand. The hand seemed sure and strong. She simply didn't have time to think about the rest.

But a matter of hours later the official was cursing himself for not having thought through what he was doing. Why, he asked himself, had he gone and sent her to his mother's? What would his mother think? What was he going to say to his mother in a month's time? What was he going to do with this woman and her baby? And how would all this reflect on his c.v., on his impeccable c.v.? He'd taken in the wife of an enemy of the people!

He was in a torment of regret. He was in agonies of remorse. But when he tired of putting the wind up himself, he began to feel moments of satisfaction at what he had done. Of course he knew he had done good and had done it out of a pure sincerity which had overridden his instinct for self-preservation. Was this not a mark of the decency people had valued so highly in him before fate raised him above the most basic human relations?

It was in that contradictory combination of remorse and self-satisfaction that the official with a philanthropic streak and of some social standing drifted into sleep at the end of that day.

His awakening was bleak, as only it can be when you carry one day's problems over to the next, banking on a clear head in the morning, though in reality giving way to indecision and sloth.

He was sullen as he walked into his office, ready for unpleasantness, from his secretary first and foremost. If only he could slip past her without saying good morning. He couldn't and so prepared suitable ripostes in advance, absolute killers which he could select depending on the venom of her attack. He took it as read she'd watched from her window as he walked away with his visitor . . . He walked into reception fully primed, on the alert, bristling, and was utterly taken aback when his secretary greeted him with a warm smile, said good morning absolutely naturally, ran through the list of calls after he left the day before and asked when he would like to see his post. This display of good nature was unexpected and suspect and he could not immediately change tack. He growled something incoherent and made straight for his office. Here an even bigger surprise awaited him – a vase of flowers on the window sill.

"I'm sorry, I thought it looked more homely like this."

Embarrassed, he was on the point of rounding on her, but she spoke first: "I've been wrong about you. Forgive me. I know, I'm positive, you did help that poor unhappy child? You did? What times we live in . . . "

"We all know what sort of times these are . . . " he began awkwardly, but broke off and told her to fetch his post. He wanted to be on his own.

The day went well and passed quickly. He got through everything, difficult business was resolved easily, the switchboard was prompt and efficient, queries answered and documents to hand instantly, he felt young and full of vigour.

That was during the day. In the evening, though, he wandered about his bachelor flat like a lost soul. He couldn't concentrate on anything. He felt lonely and sick at heart. He had an urge to get drunk, but there were no spirits in the place and he couldn't be bothered to go out.

That was during the evening. But in the night he realised that all these past days and hours he wasn't being decent or generous at all, he was simply being hugely selfish. Because everything that he had done for that woman had been done, essentially, for himself. He wanted her to be his. He had fallen in love and that was the cause of his kindness and generosity. It was very hard to admit, but it did make everything fall into place. And it was only because of the times they were living in. The times were working in his favour.

He was good to his adopted son, and not out of a sense of duty but because he genuinely liked him. He could have done nothing to bind his wife more closely to him, even if he'd tried deliberately. Their marriage worked so well the other man never came between them. He had vanished to the other side of the living world, turned into a fragment of that unfathomable secret which only ever had any reality when it was displayed from time to time in cold clipped sentences in the papers or in brief announcements on the radio. From time to time you became aware that somebody from a neighbouring flat or office had disappeared. The eyes of the people who had been close to that person would glaze over with shock for a while, that was all.

It was, indeed, a most peculiar time. People knew and didn't know, guessed and couldn't guess, believed and didn't believe. All you can say is that what they believed in was immeasurably greater than what they would admit to having doubts about. The object of their faith was so huge and splendid, so omnipotent in the scheme of human relationships that any individual sensitivities, any personal criteria were almost completely supplanted. Everything was determined by it, even scarcely significant aspects of morality. An astonishing social phenomenon had come into being which encapsulated present and future, ends and means, faith and knowledge all at once. At some time in the future people may call this magnificent, if monstrous, idol a social Narcissus, and they'll be right. That's what it was. The idol not only lived and acted on its own behalf, there was also nothing it would not have sacrificed in order to preserve its own image. It was a fantastic idol. The fantastic, though, has limits beyond which the symbols that are required to comprehend it can no longer be found. At that point the human mind shifts categories and the fantastic is accepted as something perfectly probable or even as the norm.

The idol had that kind of fantastic quality. Considerations of reason and fact were powerless against it. Human nature is susceptible to miracles, longs for miracles. Which is as it should be. There was a miracle. But in all the turmoil people forgot about it, though the need remained. And then they began to create the miracle for themselves, each according to his abilities, each according to his needs. They still are. And have achieved much.

But what is to be the yardstick of human responsibility? Is it to be merely the sum total of effects? If that is so, it's very sad, because effects can always be understood without any reference to their causes. Consequently people never learn anything. You can recite them a litany of all the misfortunes which have sprung from the inexhaustible well of the utopian fantasy, force them to repent and bewail their fate and the fate of their children. No one will tell them whether they are guilty or not guilty. Who would have the audacity? An outsider? But what business has an outsider with another man's grief?

Two people came together at a time when an obscure and shadowy misfortune was stalking the world like a masked fakir, prowling from house to house to garner an abundant harvest. They pretended to know nothing of its existence and even persuaded themselves that that was so. They expunged everything that reminded them of it from their lives . . . They had no name. All that was left was a faded snapshot in an old-fashioned passepartout frame stuck away in a pile of junk.

Naïve egotists! They failed to reckon on chance. One summer day chance rolled up in a jeep at their garden gate. The man they'd sacrificed, the man they'd been so careful to forget all those years had never forgotten them. All those years the memory of them had been the only ray of warmth for his tormented body and his humiliated soul. And when he reached the limit of patience and hope, the man took a desperate decision. He told himself he must see his boy and the woman who had betrayed him. He must see them because he was beginning to doubt their existence. He must see them, and then – *que sera* . . .

The captain in the jeep asked to be informed immediately should the man appear in the locality. The captain wanted the boy to be brought in on it, too, but the father objected categorically, forbade it absolutely. He had many reasons for doing so, though he could not give a single coherent one. The captain had no reasons. For him it was the case in hand first and foremost. And he went about it his own way.

Father and son returned from the river one day to find the mother in tears. She was even, the father felt, badly frightened. When the two of them were alone together, she pressed a handkerchief to her lips and whispered: "He was here . . . I spoke to him . . . "

"What does he want?"

"To see his son."

"What did you tell him?"

"I asked him to go away."

"And?"

She collapsed into a chair, her shoulders heaving. "He said . . . what for? . . . he hadn't done anything . . . he said I'd betrayed him . . . "

"Where is he now?"

"I don't know . . . he went away . . . "

They did not speak for some time. Then he said: "They mustn't see each other. I'll phone town."

She rushed at him, grabbed his arm.

"No! No! Don't do that!"

"Why not? Do you want everything to fall apart?"

She clung to his shoulder, sobbing. All she could do was keep on saying: "No! No! I don't know! I don't know anything . . . he was like . . . "

She couldn't speak for sobbing. Not that she had anything to say.

"What shall we do? Go back tomorrow? But what if he turns up in town?"

Suddenly she was quiet. She backed away from him, looked him straight in the eye and said with a deep sigh: "Let's just let things take their course . . . "

These words filled them both with fear and for several minutes they stood in a silent embrace in the middle of the room, until they heard their son's footsteps in the corridor.

V

That summer, as always, we were staying in the country. We had come earlier than usual, when the northern slopes of the nearby hills had begun to exude the pink aroma of wild rosemary and the southern faces exploded in blinding white clouds of bird-cherry. I had seen it many times before, but it always struck me afresh, and that summer I distinctly remember having a heightened sense that something out of the ordinary was in the air.

It all began a week after we arrived. I was on my way back from the river with a decent catch. I had only just pulled the garden gate shut when a jeep pulled up. I couldn't tell which direction it had come from. A man climbed out. He was in his fifties, dressed in breeches and a simple tunic, but without a hat. He called to me as if we were old friends.

"Hi there. How's the fishing? Is your dad at home?"

"Yes, he's here," I replied, trying to remember if I'd seen this man before somewhere. No, I hadn't.

My father seemed taken aback and immediately took him off to his study. I was intrigued. Who was this person? I walked past the study a few times and what I eventually heard shook me. They were obviously winding up their conversation, because they were standing right by the door.

"Don't exaggerate," our visitor was saying. "He's a big lad. He's perfectly capable of understanding it all. At his age I . . ."

Here my father interrupted him, and in a tone of voice I'd never heard before. "Not on any account! I don't want to talk about it any more!"

I managed to dodge round the corner in time before they came out.

At lunch our visitor talked a lot. He told all sorts of hunting and fishing stories, praised my mother's cooking. But most of his time, it seemed to me, was spent watching me, and once he even gave me a wink, doing it so neither my mother nor my father noticed. I only knew his first name, I didn't know what he did and couldn't bring myself to ask, because curiosity is a vice and I did not permit myself vices.

It was during lunch that our visitor announced that he would like to spend a day with us, to go fishing. As he did so he looked questioningly, as though seeking permission, first at my father and then at my mother.

"Do stay, of course," my father answered hastily, and in that haste I distinctly heard disguised annoyance. But I was the only one to pick it up, knowing as I did all the nuances of his voice. Our visitor noticed nothing and immediately began picking my brains on the best tackle, time of day, fishing conditions, in other words launched into a purely technical conversation which my father followed, barely concealing his anxiety and thinking hard all the while. I was almost certain I was the intended catch of the fishing expedition. But how was I involved in all this? In short, a mystery – a disturbing, romantic mystery that winked – had come to stay. And the mystery was centred on me, on me alone. I had always possessed a highly developed imagination, but in this instance it had nothing to latch on to, which made the mystery even more seductive. I lost my appetite completely and that night I dozed fitfully until four, even though, to be quite honest, there was no particular need to be up quite so early. But I stood on principle and at half-past four we – i.e. my father, the visitor and I – were shivering in the dawn chill as we tramped down the narrow path which twisted and turned as it followed the mountain stream plunging into our bird-cherry- and rosemary-bedecked valley. There were grayling in the stream. Grayling are a canny, capricious fish which call for patience and skill. I was soon disappointed to learn our guest had neither. He was always fidgeting, wouldn't stop talking, got in the way and was generally a complete nuisance, especially to me. But I sensed that fishing was not the real object of the exercise. What he wanted was to talk to me. My father had obviously cottoned onto that as well, so he would never leave us on our own together, even though it's desirable to keep a distance between you when fishing.

It was the start of a game in which each player knew what the others were after and so played with a completely open hand. But the forces were unequal. We were two against father's one. We succeeded in outmanoeuvring him and slipping some fifty metres away. As soon as we were alone, our visitor underwent a sudden metamorphosis. His face became stern, his edginess vanished and a predatory look came into his eyes.

"I need to talk to you," he said, darting a quick glance to where my father was standing. I nodded my assent, giving him to understand I had guessed his real intentions long ago.

"You're in the Komsomol?"

I nodded again.

"Good," he said and edged closer. "Your father thinks you're still a kid. All fathers are the same. Nothing wrong in that, of course, but I can see you're a big, grown-up lad. So I can talk to you on the level. Right?"

He was looking at me intently. I just kept nodding, speechless in anticipation of an adventure.

"Do you know who I am?"

"No."

"Have you heard of the security organs?"

" 'Course."

He paused, and during those few moments of silence I rehearsed the plots of a dozen detective stories in my mind, trying to guess the rough outline of the good fortune which, it seemed, had come my way.

"Nobody else must know what I'm going to tell you now. Not even your mother and father. That's the most important rule in our work. Understood?"

"Understood," I replied, swallowing hard.

"A few years back we arrested a very dangerous Trotskyite wrecker. Do you know what a Trotskyite is?"

"Somebody who's for Trotsky."

"Exactly. So, two weeks ago he escaped . . . from prison, and we have information he might be heading for your village."

My surprise when I heard this was genuine.

"What would he want here?"

Strangely enough this question rather threw our visitor off balance. At any rate, he shuffled uneasily and a shadow of doubt about this business crept into my mind.

"There's something here that interests him. You don't need to know exactly what. So, if you see a stranger, I repeat – a stranger, because you know everybody hereabouts – if you do see one, don't breathe a word to anybody, run straight to the forester. Just say two words to him – 'He's here.' That's all we want you to do. No following him and absolutely no clever stuff. Just two words to the forester. Not a word to your mother or father. No sense in worrying them. Everything understood?"

"Understood," I muttered bitterly. My disappointment was complete. That was a mission for a three-year-old. Anyway, the man mightn't even show up. And if he did, he'd probably lie low.

At this moment the fish began to bite, unexpectedly as always. First my float dipped, then our visitor's. I'd soon taken more than half a dozen, but he was always slow with his strike or struck so hard the line came whistling out of the water, flew back overhead and snagged in the trees. Our visitor started to get rattled, lost his temper and in the end, as he attempted one more strike, snapped his line and threw his rod in the river, the ultimate sin in the fisherman's book.

As we moved from place to place, my father and I worked steadily downstream, first fishing the rapids and then the backwaters, while our grumpy visitor wandered after us and gave himself the job of hunting out the grayling which fell off into the grass and of disentangling our lines when they snagged in branches and bushes. The fish stopped biting and we lit a fire to cook our catch. Our visitor perked up. He turned out to be an expert cook and showed us methods we had never even heard of before. Father was unusually taciturn. He suspected something. I couldn't for the life of me figure out what was worrying him. After all, the business was so trivial, there was no reason to be that worried. But it wasn't just that he was anxious, he was irritated. And his irritation surfaced in a most unexpected manner. Our visitor suggested fetching a net and rigging it across the stream. Father reacted very sharply, almost rudely, to the effect that greed was something you found in a poacher, not a fisherman. Our visitor pretended not to notice father's tone of voice and passed it off as a joke. That was something he did rather well.

I was fourteen at the time. The world was older and slyer than I was, though I didn't believe it. I felt I was its equal. Could it have been different? When you're faced with an end result, it's hard to imagine the processes involved in arriving at it. Finding the world already fixed in a set pattern, I accepted its history as a plausible construct. And at fourteen who seriously believes there was a time he did not exist, but everything else did? And how can you talk about existence without presupposing yourself as part of it? That's how I thought, or roughly like that. Or perhaps I didn't think at all, but just knew it at heart, and the heart always does just know and never thinks. Was I really capable of supposing that by the time I came into the world those who were there before me had already tied the knots for me? So that when I did emerge into it I immediately inherited all their problems, misfortunes and mistakes. So that from my first steps, from my first words, from my first stirrings of self-awareness and emotion, I had never been free.

I knew nothing. And it was probably for that reason I didn't notice something had happened in our family either the next or on subsequent days. Since everything was as usual, I read my mother's inflamed eyes in the mornings as a sign of illness. That was what I was told. I interpreted my father's silences as concern for my mother. I was both worried and disappointed by this. But I didn't want mysteries. I wanted things clear and straightforward. I wanted too much.

Several days intervened between the day I have just described and the day when everything happened, but I remember nothing about them. Those two stand together in my memory.

Early one morning I set off for the forester's winter hut. It was six or seven kilometres upstream at a place where the current danced past rock falls which had tumbled from an overhanging cliff. In early summer the grayling had to force their way up these rapids to spawn in the headwaters in the taiga. The grayling hung back in the frothy whirlpools, gathering strength to leap up the plunging masses of water. You could catch enough here to make fish soup without any trouble, more than enough, but I wasn't greedy and I came to this spot largely because it was so beautiful. The cliff lowering over the stream, the gnarled pines with their spreading branches at the top, the massive piles of boulders at the bottom, the roar of the rapids and the cosy little log cabin built on an outcrop nearby . . . It had been built by the forester, the man our visitor mentioned. I knew him well. He had taken me out into the taiga, taught me how to read tracks, fish, stalk game, light a fire, find water. He had no family of his own and he treated me like a son. We often used to go up to the rapids together and spend several days at the hut. My parents trusted the forester implicitly.

But if anything I preferred to come here on my own. I wasn't afraid of the taiga. By the time I was thirteen I'd already been given a shotgun and I wasn't a bad shot, either.

I caught the smell of the fire too late, at the last turn of the path, and my mind hadn't properly started to function when I saw the glowing embers near the hut and the man next to them. He was sitting with his back towards me and didn't hear me as I slid from between the trees. Everything about him was peculiar; the way he was sitting cross-legged on the ground, swaying from side to side, and the way he was dressed – in a ragged padded jacket, with a pair of enormous blunt-toed boots standing nearby. His feet were bare. He had a battered winter hat on, and this was June!

My surprise was short-lived. I clearly remember not feeling any fear. There was something helpless and harmless about him. Perhaps because he sat with his face in his hands, his head hung low, and because of the way he was rocking, too. You might have thought he was praying, or crying, or he had a bad headache. It was immediately obvious this was the man. And then came a feeling of light-headedness from the sheer joy of an act of heroism, of risk, of adventure or of something else, a feeling which possessed me and dictated my decisions and actions. My model was being tested.

I cocked my gun, raised it and tried my deepest bass. "Hands up!"

The man jumped. For an instant a look of fright crossed his face, but only for an instant. When he saw that he was confronted by a boy, he didn't so much relax as simply begin to scrutinise me carefully without making any attempt to put his hands up. I repeated my order, not so loudly, but no less firmly. His lips moved. "Puppy," he snapped. He walked straight towards me. He was coming for me, but I remember distinctly not being scared. I knew I would shoot. When he was about ten paces away I put my finger on the trigger and shouted: "Stop or I'll shoot!"

At that moment I was horrified to feel my finger would not bend, as if it was suddenly paralysed. Then I knew what fear was. It flowed into me like an electric current and instantly seized my whole body. I started to tremble. I was shouting "Stop!" and could hear the fear in my voice. He was about five paces away. Suddenly a miracle happened. The man stopped. There was confusion on his face, indecision and something else besides . . . I don't remember what . . . He suddenly went pale, his forehead most of all. I saw somebody go white for the first time in my life. It was terrible! His lips were moving incoherently and he began to examine me intently. I couldn't have known then, of course, quite what he was searching for so frantically in my face. And if only I had never discovered what!

Then I heard his voice, low, staccato. "What's your name?"

I regarded the question as a trick and I fought my trembling lips to repeat my order: "Hands up!"

He wasn't angry any more. He continued his scrutiny of my face as he asked: "If I put my hands up will you tell me what your name is?"

I kept my gun on him and said nothing. I didn't know what to do next. Tell him he was under arrest?

"So, you're putting me under arrest?" he asked, as though he was trying to be helpful.

"Yes," I replied.

"Are you sure I need arresting?"

There was something about his voice that was very unpleasant, unpleasant because dangerous . . . That wasn't how he was supposed to talk and act. When he was coming for me, I felt afraid. When he started talking the fear receded a little, but uncertainty crept in and for me uncertainty was more dangerous than fear. Now I could have pulled the trigger, but wanted very much not to.

"Are you going to take me in to the militia?"

"Yes," I said as firmly and as sternly as I could manage.

"And you won't tell me your name?"

I said nothing.

"You won't regret it later?"

"No!" That was rich! Me feel sorry for a Trotskyite wrecker?!

"Then let's go!"

"Where?" I asked, slightly taken aback.

"The militia, where else?"

He was looking at me differently now, the way people do when they want to get their own back. At the time I thought he was up to something and warned him, not very confidently: "One false move and I'll shoot! I'm warning you!"

A malicious grin flitted across his lips.

"Wrong!"

"What is?" I asked in surprise.

"You got it wrong. Goes like this: 'One step either side, one step back, one jump will be regarded as an attempt to escape! The escort will shoot without warning!' "

I hadn't a clue what he meant.

He pulled his boots on and we were actually on our way. He went first and I followed eight or ten paces behind. By the end of the first half kilometre, though, I knew I had bitten off more than I could chew. Already my arms felt they were about to drop off. I had to watch my feet all the time, as well. If I tripped he would, at best, just make a run for it, though equally he might turn on me . . . He knew this perfectly well, too, of course, and submitted either in the hope of escaping at some point en route, or . . . he had decided to turn himself in . . . If that was the case, I reasoned, in the first instance he'd take off anyway and in the second what did I need to keep him covered for if he was going to turn himself in?

"Halt!" I shouted.

He stopped and turned to face me.

"You want to turn yourself in, don't you?"

I emphasised the word "yourself".

"Who told you that?"

He knew what I was going through and was making the most of it. "I'm not about to turn myself in. But since you've arrested me, go on, take me in. But you watch out; put that gun down and it'll be the worse for you. Understood?"

I realised I had got myself into a real mess.

"Let's go!" He was giving the orders.

We started walking. Half an hour later it was a ship's cannon I was carrying, not a shotgun. I was half blinded by tears and that made everything seem like some stupid bad dream. An odious back was bobbing up down somewhere in front, and every now and then it would bare its teeth in a malicious, jeering grin and screech at me. Then my arms, which had turned into sticks of lead long ago, would lift themselves mechanically . . . Finally the moment came when I felt I was either going to drop the gun or collapse. Which is what probably would have happened had my resourcefulness not come to the rescue. I guessed how I could recover the initiative. I ordered him to halt and announced a rest for a smoke.

He was sitting about five metres away from me, while I was almost lying. My gun was balanced on a bush, pointing at him. I kept it steady with my left hand, the less tired one. He had no tobacco, or he was a non-smoker, because he just sat motionless and watched me strangely from under his brows. I felt uneasy under his gaze. We still had halfway to go, or a little under. I knew I couldn't make it. I had to think of something. Then suddenly he spoke.

"So, you're fourteen, you're in the Komsomol and you already feel able to shoot a man?"

I was surprised. How did he know I was fourteen and in the Komsomol? . . . And I didn't like the last bit of the sentence.

"I couldn't shoot a man, but I can a wrecker!"

"So that's how it is!" It was his turn to be surprised. "You know I'm a wrecker, do you?"

"I do."

"And there's nothing else you know about me?" he asked in the same peculiar tone of voice which I disliked so much, and which I also found so demoralising.

"I know you're a Trotskyite."

He clapped his hands and burst out laughing. I don't know why, but I couldn't abide that laughter, it made my stomach churn, it annoyed me, infuriated me. That was no doubt the reason why I grabbed the gun and started yelling at him. "What's so funny? What's so funny? All I need do is pull the trigger and go home! You think I'm going to let a wrecker mess me around?"

He stopped laughing, shuddered and then spoke quietly: "And where are you going to shoot me? In the chest? Face? Back, maybe? You could shoot me in the legs. I'd be still alive, but couldn't get away. What ammunition are you using?"

Why did I want to cry at that moment? How do you describe what I went through then? What kind of a feeling was it? I only remember feeling bad, even worse than when I was walking with my gun at the ready. It was worse than the exhaustion! I sprang to my feet and shouted: "Move!"

Incredibly, we made it. I tripped three or four times, but I was back on my feet immediately and aiming at the man walking in front of me. After a while the barrel of my gun began to point downwards and was almost bumping along the path. He would turn on me threateningly. Sometimes it was just a gesture, but sometimes his face was distorted by such fury that my finger automatically went back to the trigger. Finally I could control my arms no longer. I uncocked my gun in despair and trusted to luck.

We made one more stop for a smoke. For some reason I wanted him to talk this time. I wanted him to very much! But he didn't say a word, just sat there, gloomy and morose.

Half a kilometre from home, I stopped again. My conscience was uneasy. To all intents and purposes he had come of his own accord. He'd had a hundred opportunities to escape if he'd wanted to. If that was the case, why should I escort him through the village at gun-point?

While I was thinking all this over, he suddenly asked: "Well, you tired then?"

"I'm tired."

He gave a sickly smile.

"You're a good lad on the whole! You'll turn out a real man . . . " He paused, then added: "If you finish up human, that is."

"Are you really a wrecker?" I asked.

"What a question!" he said in his old, unpleasant tone of voice. "He arrests somebody, nearly shoots him, and asks questions later! You don't do things like that, sonny. If you're going to bring somebody in, do the job properly!"

"What do you want me to do?" I was almost shouting now.

"What do I want you to do? Escort me in to the militia."

"Why? Why do you need me to do that?"

"I don't need it. You do. You and some other people . . . "

Once again I could see that now familiar expression of vengeful fury on his face. My uncertainty increased. Events were no longer so easily understood, so black and white. They called for some other set of criteria which required time and effort to evaluate. I was only fourteen. Was I really capable of understanding the people of that strange time?

"Are you truly a wrecker?" I asked again.

He stared at me in silence and I did not like that stare. In it I could feel almost physically the gulf between my conception of the world and the world in reality.

There was no militia post in our village. I had to take him to the forester. The houses in the village were dotted about at random. The first one we had to pass was ours. And so we were approaching our gate. Him in front, hands behind his back, me behind with the gun. Before we reached the village he had thrown his hat away for some reason and without it he looked even more of a fright. Unshaven, hair all matted, wearing a tattered padded jacket and square-toed boots with filthy foot cloths poking over the top – this was the sight that confronted my mother and father when they suddenly appeared at the gate.

Things happened very fast. For the second time that day I saw somebody go white, my father this time. Meanwhile my mother started screaming. The sound was so painful I nearly dropped my gun. My father rushed over and put his arm rather clumsily around her, either to comfort her or lead her back into the house. She was trying to push him away, staring with crazed eyes first at the stranger and then at my gun. I was paralysed with fear. My prisoner was standing with his back to me, so I could not see his face. I guessed, though, that he was looking at my mother. And no sooner had that thought occurred to me than he turned in my direction and I saw the tears streaming down his dirty, unshaven, angry face.

The events of that day were fraught with consequences. The following day we went back to town and my mother was admitted to hospital. The diagnosis – so they told me – was nervous hysteria brought on by the dangerous situation I had got myself into.

A few days later I received a summons to the four-storey building on Zelyonaya Street and was presented with an engraved pocket watch.

Five years later I smashed that watch against a corner of that building and bought a ticket for the steamer which is now, thirty-six hours later, carrying me further and further from my past . . .

VI

The wheel of reckoning turned slowly, but inexorably. When she saw father and son together she knew the worst had happened, the worst imaginable. And realising the next instant the monstrousness and irrevocability of what had happened, she almost lost her reason. A cry of pain, horror and protest burst from her, nearly tearing the shotgun out of the hands of her fourteen-year-old son.

The forester, an old friend of the family, came to see them off. He had been drinking hard, something he rarely did. While they packed the things in the car, he stood to one side, scowling, silent, clearing his throat from time to time and tugging at his eyebrows. At the last moment he came over, shook hands with them, and when he came to the boy he kept hold of his hand and turned to his father.

"Good boy you've turned out . . . he'll go a long way . . . "

The boy took these words at face value and blushed, but the person they were aimed at understood what was really meant. He looked round in alarm and, when he was sure the mother hadn't heard, snapped at the boy to get into the car. Then he took the forester aside and they talked for some time. They shook hands again and a minute later the car jolted off. The passengers spent the first few moments settling themselves comfortably for the long journey ahead, so they none of them saw the tipsy forester spit in their wake.

Years passed by.

The woman who had been nineteen was now thirty-four. But if a year ago people said she looked not a day over twenty-five, she looked past forty now.

Years passed by.

Many big events were taking place. And though these events didn't actually touch them, they did have a direct effect on their lives. They brought the day nearer when she saw a man she'd forgotten about long ago. He was the manager of the factory where she had once worked with her first husband. They'd been taken on the same day. When she saw him, she felt that now was the time for the thing to happen that she'd been waiting for these last few years, as if waiting to be sentenced. She could have walked past and deferred sentence. But no, quite the contrary. She threw herself at this man, like a moth at a candle-flame. He didn't recognise her. She reminded him.

"Ah, it's you . . . " he said limply, indifferently. "Well, there you are, you see. All over . . . My wife told me you disowned your husband . . . Is that so?"

She stood silent, awaiting sentence.

"He was shot for escaping. He attacked the escort and got away. Only somebody on the outside turned him in . . . But you, excuse me for saying so, were too hasty."

And he walked off.

But she stood for a long time in the middle of the pavement. People walked past her, looked round but did not stop. She scared them . . .

VII

Mother! Mother! What have I been doing? How could I have said the things I did? Where did that hard, cruel streak in me come from? Who was I trying to avenge? Who was I trying to settle scores with?

I woke up suddenly in the middle of the night last night. I felt I could hear you screaming again, like then, all those years ago, when I was bringing my own father in at gun-point. This time, though, your voice was coming from far away. It went on for a long time, over and over again. I jumped out of my bunk and dashed to the door for some reason. I felt you'd be there, behind the door! The illusion dissolved and I was back on my own again in the cabin of a steamer heading north into the back of beyond, where I was going to settle my score with life for real.

I will not accept that by preparing to commit suicide I was a coward. I was not. A coward is not capable of that. But even now, when the fishing boat is bringing me back south, closer and closer to home, now that I have reconsidered and decided to live, I know that this is not an act of cowardice.

I shan't read over everything I wrote in this exercise book during those three days. Time enough for that later. And not just five days, either. I'll read it all again, consider everything I wrote and did not write, everything that was said and not said. Later, though.

Now I crave one, just one, piece of luck – for nothing to have happened at home these last few days!

That's how strange it was with me! My mind was clear and sober. The arguments were irrefutable, the emotions genuine. And then suddenly in the middle of the night I saw my mother's eyes, heard her scream, and everything was turned upside down. I ran to her call, forgetting everything else. I had, you see, denied nothing, revoked no decisions. I simply submitted to her appeal.

Mother! We will go our separate ways. But not before your

eyes have forgotten your tears, before your smile returns to our house, for good! I'll smoothe your wrinkles yet, teach you how to laugh again. I won't let a single hair on your head turn grey. Just wait for me. I have a lot to tell you. I have to tell you something that will remove from our family at a single stroke the stain put on it by time and circumstance. As yet, I don't know what to say. But the moment I see you, I'm positive the words will find themselves.

Let the dead bury their dead. Oh yes, we will talk about the dead! But the living must live! And I will call him father. That is what he is to me, after all!

And then we will go our own separate ways, mother, all the same! But you'll understand that's the way it has to be . . . You'll understand, and give me your blessing.

Because I want to be honest! I want to be honest!

THE OPTION

THE HAY-LOFT was opposite the house. In theory it was the second storey of the barn, but actually it was no more than the space under the steeply pitched roof. One gable of the loft overlooked the village street, the other, on the kitchen-garden side, had a rickety staircase built on that creaked alarmingly when Andrey climbed it. There was not much hay, but the scent was headier than home-distilled vodka, and when Andrey flopped full-length into a bed he'd made of it, he felt dizzy and the wooziness tossed and turned and tumbled him from side to side. It was a delightful state. Happy and serene. The smell of hay was so unexpectedly powerful it swamped all other sensations. On top of that . . . it was the smell of his childhood.

Childhood for him meant the war and his childhood games were war games. Why had they never played soldiers but always partisans? And why had he always, but always, been the commander? Perhaps because a partisan commander was his own boss, with nobody to order him about?

This notion surprised and disappointed Andrey, because it implied that as a boy he had had distinctly anarchist tendencies! Yet the other boys always followed his lead. Not just ones his own age, older ones accepted his authority unquestioningly as well. Why? What made them do it? He was physically strong, but not exceptionally so. More imagination? Perhaps. But more likely it was his attitude to their games. He always played for real and if a game called for some particular skill, he mastered it, at any price.

Looking at it another way, he simply did not distinguish between life and play, which was maybe why his life came to resemble a game. At the same time he always believed passionately in sticking to the rules. Breaking them was unforgiveable. This attitude he carried over into life, which he wanted to be as clear-cut, meaningful and noble as children's games. He couldn't tell when he stopped playing at life and when life proper began. If so, all this made him one of the Don Quixotes of this world, likeable but misguided.

Yes, everything that was happening to him now had been mapped out in childhood and he ought to have appealed to childhood memories sooner. He should have come here years ago, to drink his grandfather's homemade vodka, climb up into the loft, plunge into the sweet-smelling hay and remember . . . Although maybe no memories would have risen to the surface then? Maybe it wasn't the hay, maybe it wasn't the crimson sunset, every tint and smudge fixed in the memory forever, like everything else here. Hadn't he dreamt a hundred times of the smell of hay and the colour of sunset and the voice of the river over the shallows and him here in the middle of it? Perhaps it had nothing to do with this? Perhaps it was the pistol weighing on his chest, crushing his chest, punishing his breathing which was already laboured after his grandfather's potent brew?

Girls didn't like him when he was a boy. He wouldn't let them join in. They called him a spoilsport and ganged up on him. It didn't work. He refused to treat them as real people. They were a useless freak of nature. When he did eventually begin to show an interest in them, he was slightly contemptuous. At school he thought Romeo was a bit crass, and later at college he thought Werther was more schizoid than anything else. His heroes were explorers and revolutionaries. He overheard one girl say he was as boring as a doublebass solo. He was rather proud of that. To be interesting to women meant being a clown in the eyes of his fellow males.

Did he love Olga? He believed he did. That is, he treated her differently to any other woman. But it was only now he began to realise that he could have really loved her, and this "could have" and the subsequent conditional train of thought suddenly clouded his tenderly sentimental mood and brought him, no not brought, plunged him back into reality, which that evening had retired graciously to the back of his mind, giving respite, a break, a sigh of relief to a man on the run.

How long did he have left? Don't try to guess. Reckon on an hour, thirty minutes, ten minutes. That'd keep him in a permanent state of readiness. There'd be no tension then.

Life goes on. Or the game. No matter. Stick to the rules to the end. That means you win.

I

The Five

The room was dingy and squalid, the windows unwashed and the parquet scruffy. Four people were waiting for a fifth. He was late. The conversation had dried and they sat in silence. One fingered a russet beard and stared abstractedly out of the window, the second flicked his way yet again through a dog-eared book, while the third sat hunched in the one and only armchair, battered and moth-eaten, and picked thoughtfully at the insides of his watch. The fourth was sprawled on an old couch. He was worse dressed than the others, to be more precise, with less regard for appearances. He was unshaven, haggard, and his hair was an indeterminate colour. He alone fitted into this room. It was his, after all. He paid twenty-five roubles a month, with no bath or telephone, no right to a residence permit, but with the right to do as he pleased with the accommodation. This right he had enjoyed for several years now, and since he was a bachelor and a sloven, the room was too far gone to bring it into decent order now. There had been remonstrations and reproaches. He had been contrite and promised, but nothing happened. A couple of girls might have saved the room, but you couldn't bring them here. This was a safe flat. The rules of conspiracy had to come first.

Five fives are twenty-five. The five each chipped in five roubles to pay for the flat. True, they didn't all of them always have it spare when required. Especially the tenant. Kolya the tenant lived on a student grant. He refused help from his friends on principle, and had to be forced to let his share be paid for him. It was Konstantin who paid, the one in the armchair. His father was a well-known Leningrad Party boss and generous with pocket money. Konstantin's clothes were almost dandyish, his manners were aristocratic and his speech refined, and so not surprisingly he seemed completely out of place in this company, to the uninformed and uninitiated eye, that is. Were it not for Konstantin, Vadim would have looked just as alien in this room, not because of his clothes or appearance, however, even though he was the only one with a beard. It was hard to say what marked him out, but if an outsider had wanted to know what was going on, it was Vadim he would have asked. Yes indeed, an outsider might well think they had come together by chance, since the fourth, Pavel, with auburn hair, also seemed out on a limb.

Pavel slammed the book shut and turned to Kolya the tenant, who was manfully fighting off sleep.

"Listen, this was the time you were told to be here?"

Konstantin and Vadim also looked at Kolya. He merely assumed a hurt expression and snorted.

The fifth was late. This was so out of the ordinary that not one of the four uttered a word of complaint. There had to be a very good reason. "All the same!" Konstantin remarked, yet it was no more than an expression of genuine surprise at the unusual behaviour of their leader, their "comandore", whose absolute punctuality at times seemed an affectation.

Had there been the four of them, the group would have fallen apart long ago. But there was the fifth, the cement and the iron. It was thanks to his undoubted talent that these four very different young men had been as one for several years.

This was happening not in the nineteenth century, nor even in the early twentieth, but bang in the middle of this. The underground action group was in crisis. Two years ago they'd scattered their first leaflets and waited for the storm to follow. Apart from the odd whisper, it hadn't. They were surprised, hurt. The people had not heard them or had not wanted to hear. They had told the truth about the regime, the truth which they had discovered was irrefutably obvious, blindingly obvious. But the people out there had not heeded their call, it was as if their ears were stuffed with cotton-wool or filled with wax or they were deliberately deaf.

And they loved the people. Or rather they wanted very much to do so, even though they suspected their love would not be reciprocated.

It was not the nineteenth century but the middle of the twentieth, and they were not aristocrats or radical *raznochintsy* but young communists, *komsomoltsy*. History, nevertheless, was repeating itself and they could sense it was so, and that like any repetition, it was banal. They could sense it, but were powerless to break the circle of banality and so were gradually overwhelmed by a feeling of pointlessness and futility.

Occasionally they heard that somebody somewhere had been arrested and sentenced for something similar, and then they banged the table with frustration because once again they'd failed to spot somebody like themselves, and they so needed reassurance that they weren't on their own.

Time passed. Making mischief was no longer enough. Youthful optimism collided with a reality which was in no hurry to see itself transformed. The people did not awaken and they had a sneaking doubt whether the people were actually asleep.

Before, when they had gathered, there had been so much to

talk about, they had argued themselves hoarse. Today they sat in silence for almost an hour. Waiting for the fifth. And the wait was irksome.

At last, at the end of the third half-hour they heard the long-awaited pre-arranged knock on the door. Kolya leapt up from the couch, suddenly wide-awake.

The fifth member of the group was called Andrey. He was tall and slender, with light-brown hair and hard features. He was no older than the others, though he seemed it. He ran a critical eye over them, like an officer inspecting his troops before battle. Nobody said a word. Not even a greeting. The fifth always spoke first.

He saw an empty chair, sat down, frowned, making himself look even older, and said nothing. Then he stood up, walked over to the table and leant on it with his fists. Then he spoke. "Nothing's happened."

His voice was flat, heavy as his fist.

"Nothing's happened. Not that you could expect anything to happen with us lot! We're yellow!"

This was quite an opening. They all looked at Andrey, uneasily, somehow sullenly.

"I've spent the last hour and a half walking up and down the Moika canal. A few days ago I decided I was going to tell you something very important. But I still needed an hour and a half more today."

All this was said in a tone of conviction that nobody would question the speaker's right to do so, or his rightness. Nobody did.

"It's a complete fiasco. We all know that. For one simple reason. Russia is not ready. The time is not ripe. It's pointless carrying on."

Now they were all looking at him in surprise.

"Nobody needs us. Us trying to tell the world what the world already knows is ridiculous. We wanted to tell about the millions who perished. We'd only just found out about it! But who were we trying to tell? The people who'd watched it all happen! As for the people who survived the camps and came back, you know as well as I do the kind of crap they talk. There's something wrong here . . . We're trying to smash down the wall instead of walking through the door . . . "

He brought his fist down on the table, as if placing the full stop he failed to achieve in his words. When he spoke again, his voice held an intonation his friends had not heard before.

"You must understand. There's some kind of a mystery here, it's as though we're trying to solve higher mathematics using multiplication tables . . . In other words, we're packing in, liquidating our business because we lack operating capital!"

The "comandore's" announcement was so strange and unexpected, they were completely taken aback, all except Konstantin. And when he decided to speak, they all turned to him in hope.

"So what's there to live for? A career?"

Konstantin was not asking Andrey, who was sitting, head bowed, frowning, his fist pressed against the table. His question was addressed to all of them, so it didn't make things any easier.

Konstantin looked at Andrey, who said nothing. But there was something left unspoken in his silence and the "comandore's" right-hand man sensed it.

"Have you told us everything, chief?"

"Not everything. I came to a decision, decided I had an option. We all of us have and each must decide for himself. Our options might even coincide."

"Come on then, tell us!" Kolya the tenant leapt to his feet.

"No," Andrey replied. "I'll speak last. So, what are your options?"

There was silence at first. Then the long-haired bearded boy at the window shifted with embarrassment. Everybody turned towards him.

"My option . . . I'm sure it won't be the same . . . I mean, I know it won't . . . I've thought about it for a long time, but I kept quiet . . . "

Andrey looked at him suspiciously, as though he didn't have much hope of them coinciding, either. The boy hesitated, blushed, and for some reason cracked his knuckles.

"Well . . . I don't know how to put it, really . . . It's like this . . . I'm devoting myself to . . . no, that's not the right word, interested is more like it . . . in Christianity . . . I'm serious . . . That's it . . . "

He spread his hands with a guilty smile. Guilt was written all over his face.

The silence that followed was proof of general astonishment. Even the "comandore's" face changed from its usual harshness of expression to one of utter bewilderment.

"I don't understand," he said. "I'm interested in yoga, seriously interested. Have been for a long time. So what?"

"It's not the same, Andrey," Vadim answered as gently as he could. "It's hard to explain . . . "

"You mean, you believe in God?" Kolya the tenant asked point-blank, grinning idiotically. Kolya didn't pretend to be intelligent and so could get away with more than the others.

Vadim's answer was scarcely audible. "Yes."

He said it the way a bashful schoolboy confesses to his friends he's in love, expecting to be teased. It was also said in a way that made them all feel uncomfortable, as if they really had forced their friend to confess something dreadfully intimate that you couldn't take seriously, but was no laughing matter, either. None of them could look Vadim in the eye. And he stared at the table, blushing. Even the "comandore" was momentarily lost for words.

"I don't understand," he said, irritated. "If we're talking about religion as a social institution with a positive moral charge . . . I've been thinking about that myself. If you've got any thoughts along those lines, tell us, we'll discuss them . . . Perhaps we can use . . . "

"No." Vadim cut him short. "It's different. I don't have any ideas." He looked as if he was going through torture.

"He doesn't have any ideas, but he does have an option," Andrey shot back.

"I did say it was my own personal option, it doesn't stop me doing anything. I've done everything you have. You asked, so I told you. If you want to suggest something new, the one doesn't exclude the other."

Vadim was calmer now. Andrey recovered his former abruptness.

"I'm afraid it does," he said harshly.

Kolya the tenant looked the length of the table at Vadim.

"Vadka, you been christened, right?"

"Leave him alone," Konstantin cut in sharply. But Vadim replied. "I was christened when I was a kid."

"I was christened, too!" For some reason there was joy in Kolya's voice.

"Cut it out, I tell you!" Konstantin's put-down was even sharper.

Kolya took no offence. He left the table and flopped back on the couch. Konstantin turned to Vadim.

"All right, Vadik. It's your business, of course. But . . . I can't believe you see there's any kind of future in your option . . . Or it's just a way of getting out of a contradiction . . . I could understand that . . . I mean, fill us in a bit more."

Vadim hesitated. "No, it's not a way out . . . To be honest, it's still more a kind of feeling . . . I haven't sorted it all out in my own mind yet, but it's not a way out, I'm certain of that . . . "

"But religion's on the way out everywhere," insisted Konstantin. "If it isn't finished already."

"That's a matter of opinion," Vadim answered cautiously. "But honestly, it's hard for me to talk about this."

He looked around helplessly. In the wall opposite, which backed onto the courtyard, were the traces of a doorway, evidence of old alterations to the building. He pointed to it.

"Look. We know there's nothing on the far side of that door. But what if we opened it and suddenly discovered a hall there and dozens of rooms . . . It's the same thing . . . Christianity's a whole world people don't even suspect exists . . . "

"Rubbish," said Pavel, who had been silent until then.

"Hardly likely," objected Konstantin.

"In any case," Andrey said curtly, signalling the discussion was over, "one thing is clear. At this point we part company with Vadim."

Vadim was alarmed. "Andrey!"

"Yes," he snapped. He turned to Konstantin. "Anybody else have any suggestions?"

Konstantin shrugged. Kolya rose from the couch and came to the table, his whole attitude showing that his options were the "comandore's". Pavel spoke for them all: "No options." The ball was back in Andrey's court.

Vadim was at the end of the table by the window. Pavel was between him and Andrey. Andrey walked behind Pavel to Vadim. He was grave. Vadim stood up in confusion.

"Vadim," the "comandore" held out his hand, "thank you."

Vadim, awkward and puzzled, took Andrey's hand.

"You were the first person I suggested setting up an organisation to several years ago. You have been a true comrade. We have come to a parting of the ways. Believe me, I am saying good-bye without any reproach on my part. I hope there will be none on yours."

This was said not without a touch of theatricality, though it would have only struck an outside observer as being so. One glance at Kolya the tenant, his lips trembling, his eyes wide and moist, would be enough to appreciate the special style of the friends' relationship, to believe the sincerity of what sounded like sheer pathos.

Vadim jerked away his hand. He almost shouted: "You can't just throw me out! I haven't refused . . . "

But the "comandore" didn't flinch: "Your option differs from mine."

"Andrey!" Vadim tried to interrupt him.

"That's right. They differ. Incompatible. You know me, I

never mince words. So leave now. Knowing too much is dangerous, especially for the odd man out."

"Me, the odd man out?" echoed Vadim almost tearfully.

"You've got your option, Vadik," Andrey spoke with sudden gentleness. "Try it. If it doesn't work, let me know."

He was silent, then added gruffly: "If I'm still going with my option by then."

Again he held out his hand to Vadim, but Vadim didn't budge. Andrey took his sleeve.

"I'll drop by in a couple of days. We'll talk then. Go now, Vadik."

Vadim shuddered.

"I'll go," he said, without looking at Andrey. "But you're doing wrong, because you're making me feel a traitor. And that's not true."

Andrey took his hand and squeezed it hard.

"It's not like that!" Then he added grudgingly: "If you really have found your option, believe me . . . I envy you."

Vadim pulled his hand free and left the room without another word. The friends heard him hurry down the stairs. The room was in silence for a little while, before there was a sudden, hasty knock. Kolya exchanged glances with Andrey and went to open it. Vadim stood on the threshold.

"God be with you," he whispered and dashed back down the stairs.

Kolya would have stood there with his mouth open had Andrey not shouted: "Door!"

"Well, well," exclaimed Pavel, drumming his fingers on the book.

Andrey carried Vadim's chair to his place and sat down. Kolya brought another chair and also sat at the table. They all felt sick at heart and sighed with relief when Andrey started to speak. Though he began uncertainly, searching for words, thinking about what he was saying. The friends didn't recognise their "comandore", but they listened carefully, perhaps to shake off their uneasiness after what had happened.

"I've already said messing around with leaflets and that kind of thing is useless. There's something we don't understand and we end up trying to force the situation . . . When it comes down to it, what do we know? That a system which claims to be ideal is criminal. We didn't find this out from secret documents, the information's there for anybody. But for some reason we're the only ones who react . . . And it doesn't look like we'll get to the bottom of that 'for some reason'. But we can't not react. We can't, am I right?"

"Get on with it," growled Pavel.

"There's a gulf between us and everybody else . . . In time or space, I don't know. The one thing I do know is that people were killed, and there are people who did the killing . . . "

Andrey stopped a moment. Konstantin stared at him.

Andrey stood up, paced the room, stopped in a corner. "So, I believe the one thing we have a right to do is punish the killers!"

"How punish! Kill them, you mean?!" gasped Pavel.

"No, not kill," Andrey answered firmly. "I said punish!"

"In the name of the people," muttered Konstantin, not without irony.

But Andrey strode across and leaned over him: "No, Kostya, that's precisely not what I mean! You remember Kipling. How does it go?"

Konstantin shrugged, trying to dredge the right passage from his memory. He recited two lines:

> If you can make one heap of all your winnings
> And risk it on one turn of pitch-and-toss . . .

"No, no," Andrey interrupted. "I mean, that's the poem, but a bit further on, though."

Konstantin thought some more and then continued confidently, as though listening carefully to the familiar words once more:

If you can talk with crowds and keep your virtue,
Or walk with Kings – nor lose the common touch,
If neither foes nor loving friends can hurt you . . .

"Right," Andrey crowed in triumph. "Right. Be your own man. We're neither with the kings nor part of the crowd. Tell the truth and be trampled by the crowd and be hounded by the kings. Everybody knows that. The two often came together. That's the kind of times we live in. And we can and must act in our name alone and be ready to answer for it with our heads. That's my option."

He sat down. But Pavel was on his feet. "Wait. I don't quite understand. How are you going to punish them?"

"The death penalty, Pavel," Konstantin grimly spelled out Andrey's intention.

"Kill?" Pavel exclaimed in horror.

"Some option," muttered Kolya, stunned.

Andrey watched in silence as Pavel strode about the room.

"And what are you going to use to carry out sentence?" Konstantin whispered semi-seriously.

"That's merely a detail," snapped Andrey.

"Too right," Konstantin agreed with a smile and began picking at the rim of his watch.

"Listen," begged Pavel, tugging at his flowing auburn curls, "think what you're saying."

He was appealing to both Andrey and Konstantin. Kolya didn't count. He had no part in it, apparently, and could only sit staring at first one, then the other.

"Leaflets, demonstrations, propaganda, that I understand! But killing! That's . . . "

"You kill people," Andrey snapped back coldly, almost aggressively. "But you punish killers."

"That's just words!"

"Keep it short," Andrey snarled.

Pavel stood right over him. "No, Andrey, I won't. You're not asking us to play forfeits!"

"You're wrong, Andrey," Konstantin said.

"In what way?" Andrey turned on him.

"How long have you been thinking about this option?"

"Two months," Andrey answered crisply.

"And you won't even give us five minutes?"

Andrey's cheekbones were working. "Very well. How long do you need to think?"

"Depends who," Konstantin answered calmly. "Ask each of us."

"I am asking. How long do *you* need to think?"

In the same even tone, still picking at his watch, Konstantin said: "I need as long as it takes you to ask the others."

Andrey studied him carefully, as if trying to catch something in his friend's intonation or behaviour. He turned to Pavel.

"How much time do you need?"

Pavel stood over him, bristling, determined.

"If you've already made up your mind and won't discuss it, I don't need any time. I will not kill!"

"Right."

They glared at each other. Andrey's look softened.

"I knew my option wouldn't suit everyone, Pavel. I even made allowance for it not suiting anybody."

The "comandore" was hardly sincere at that moment. But he went on: "Don't be angry! Each to his own. Thanks for everything!"

He held out his hand to Pavel, who immediately shrank back.

"Andrey, you've got to . . . "

Andrey cut him short.

"Don't worry. We're still friends. Sorry to have to remind you about our oath."

"Of course," muttered Pavel, unable to look him in the eye.

Arms folded, Andrey walked over to Kolya.

"What about you?"

It wasn't just that the question offered no hope, the question itself had a sarcastic ring.

Kolya shrugged, fidgeted, then to everyone's surprise blurted: "Same as you . . . I'm with you . . . "

Andrey couldn't conceal his astonishment.

"You seriously mean that?"

"Think what you're letting yourself in for, you fool," Pavel shouted.

Kolya glared at him. "Shut up if you're scared!"

"I'm scared . . . " Pavel hardly knew what he was saying. "I'm not scared. Anyway . . . that's not the point." He suddenly started to stammer. "Andrey, honestly, that isn't it. You have to believe me. I don't want to kill anybody. Anybody. Understand."

"I believe you," Andrey replied. "Word of honour, I believe you." He turned to Kolya and studied him curiously. "You're a funny one." Kolya stood there with a stupid, happy grin. "Completely unprogrammed. Give it some more thought."

"I've thought."

"Your lookout, then."

Andrey sat down at the table opposite Konstantin.

"What about you, Konstantin?"

Konstantin smiled.

"Like Kolya, of course!"

"Like me?" Kolya echoed in surprise. "I'm with Andrey!" Then he got the joke and laughed.

They all three of them now looked at Pavel, who was slumped on the couch with his head in his hands.

"No," he whispered. "I can't. If I give way now, I'll regret it later."

He stood up and walked over to Andrey. "I'm sorry, Andrey. This isn't for me."

"Good-bye." The "comandore" held out his hand.

When the sound of footsteps had died on the staircase, Andrey said: "So, there's the three of us. More than I expected, though."

"Three musketeers," Kolya quipped. "Andrey's got to be Athos, Kostya's Aramis. And me?"

"Yes," Konstantin nodded sympathetically, "there's not quite enough of you for Porthos!"

They roared with laughter, all three of them. It was an uneasy kind of laughter.

Andrey looked at his watch.

"Shall we make a start? Do you know a place called Lembolovo?"

They nodded. Andrey pulled an exercise book out of his inside jacket pocket.

"There's a man who lives there, Lieutenant-Colonel Mikhail Borisovich Kolganov. This is my dossier on him. Depositions from four witnesses. I took down the evidence myself. Fingers crushed, lips burnt with lighted matches, beatings, starvation, torture, dragging women by the hair and other such heroic behaviour. Now retired. Mad-keen gardener."

"Any family?" Konstantin asked cautiously.

"What if there is?" retorted Andrey. "They had families, too."

"Of course . . . I was only asking. I wondered whether he'd be leaving any heirs and what they'd be like."

"Don't know. I could make enquiries," Andrey suggested hesitantly.

"Forget it, to hell with them!"

"But how . . . ? What with?" Kolya asked.

"All we need is one pistol. And in . . . " Andrey checked his watch, "in four hours we'll have one!"

He fished in his pocket again, pulled out a piece of paper folded in four, opened it out and spread it on the table.

"Look. This is Suvorovsky Prospekt, this is Staro-Nevsky, and this Vtoraya Sovetskaya Street. Recognise it? Round about eleven a militiaman will leave this building here. He'll walk this way . . . See this corner here? We get him there."

"Get him?" Kolya asked, startled.

Andrey chuckled.

"Don't worry, we're not going to kill him. A punch in the solar plexus, then grab his gun . . . it's three minutes through the back yards to here . . . then split up. I'll have the gun and go to the bus stop. If one isn't coming, though there should be, I'll nip down the back of Staro-Nevsky. We meet back here tomorrow. That's all. Should go like clockwork. I've been staking it out for a month. So, let's give it a run-through . . . "

As they were leaving, Andrey stopped Konstantin in the entrance.

"Did you really think about it or just follow my lead? Be honest."

Konstantin sighed. "To be honest I . . . I just followed you."

Andrey looked disappointed.

"What could I do, Andrey. My dear papa, as you well know, is a Party boss, and he didn't get his job yesterday, either. So he was involved. And I'm a Komsomol activist . . . I've got to compensate for the family's record somehow."

"But you can always get out of it . . . They don't force you. I'm sorry, I trusted you, I never thought we needed to talk about this."

Konstantin leant against the wall and threw his head back.

"At university they say I'm an idealist. Ditching an ideal hurts, Andrey! All those fine words. They can't all be a lie. Hundreds of generations . . . millions of victims . . . Can evil really be so seductive? Look at history. Nothing but hatred and enmity. Communism is the idea of brotherhood, universal brotherhood . . . "

"And what's come of it?" Andrey interjected gloomily.

"Well maybe it simply isn't turning out that way. But if there's no dream, no ideal, what's the point in living? Vadim's found his answer. God! Does that say anything to you?"

Andrey gestured dismissively.

"Yes, I don't see it as anything more than a symbol of a failed ideal, either. Maybe there's something I don't know . . . Listen, let's get together one day and find an intelligent priest, hear how he explains it!"

"Is there such a thing?" snorted Andrey.

"Must be. There used to be."

"Let's see, maybe we will . . . To be honest, though, I don't relish the thought."

"I'd be curious, though . . . Me being a Komsomol activist," Konstantin went on sadly, "it means I could test the idea of thesis and antithesis . . . Don't be hard on me."

"I'm not."

"Great. I couldn't give a damn about the rest!"

Andrey suddenly slapped his friend on the shoulder, stepped aside, looked him up and down and laughed: "Dresses like a toff, in official life a Komsomol activist, unofficially an underground conspirator! The Holy Trinity, no kidding!"

Konstantin answered seriously: "Yeh, I realise there's something unnatural about all this, maybe even immoral . . . "

"Rubbish," Andrey stopped him. "I'm certain you're one hundred per cent reliable, and there's no more valuable human quality than that."

They shook hands and went their separate ways until evening.

II

The Hitch

At ten Andrey was sitting on a bench in a little park on Suvorovsky Prospekt. He had his arms stretched out along the back of the seat, looking just like a young loafer who finds even watching the world go by too much effort. He felt surprisingly calm. Not a hint of tension. For a month he'd been rehearsing in his mind what was going to happen in an hour's time and was absolutely certain of success. During the past three years he had carried out riskier operations.

It was a warm June evening. There was a cool breeze from the Neva. Somewhere a radio was softly playing an Italian melody.

A bohemian intellectual type came over, swaying on his feet. He looked at Andrey and flopped down next to him on the bench.

"Groovin'?" he asked.

"What?" Andrey failed to understand.

"You groovin', I said."

Andrey glared at him.

"Watching the girls?"

"Right," Andrey snapped, openly hostile.

"Keep cool," the "intellectual" parried reproachfully. "Watching the girls is the finest thing a man can do."

"The what?" Andrey was clearly spoiling for an argument.

"As long as you keep it clean," replied the "intellectual", ignoring Andrey's manner. "Woman is the wonder of the world. Its most profound mystery."

"*The* most?" asked Andrey, dropping his guard.

"Shh!" The "intellectual" bent and whispered in Andrey's ear. "Look! Look!"

A young couple strolled past.

"Look at her. Not at the stupid, smug oaf with her. Look at her!"

"I am looking," Andrey reassured him, for he really was looking at the girl. She was pretty and smiling, whispering something to the boy.

When the couple had passed, the "intellectual" leaned over to Andrey: "Well?"

"Well?" Andrey replied.

"What did you see?"

"You tell me."

The "intellectual" moved away from Andrey and looked at him with contempt.

"Dumbo!"

"I ought to thump him," Andrey thought, but didn't.

"You've just seen a happy woman smile," announced the stranger.

"So?"

"And do you know what a happy woman's smile is?"

Andrey shrugged.

Once again the "intellectual" moved close.

"Then listen here. A happy woman's smile is a revelation, an instant of universal harmony. Listen. People break their heads trying to define truth, justice . . . Do you know what 'truth' is?"

"No I don't," chuckled Andrey, intrigued now.

"But you want to know, don't you? I'll tell you." The "intellectual" was almost on top of Andrey. "Truth is a happy woman's smile."

"Is that all?" Andrey asked ironically.

"Yes!" The bohemian philosopher was triumphant. "A happy woman's smile is both truth and justice. It is the supreme meaning of existence! Do you know why the world is so sick?"

"No, I don't."

"Because," the philosopher's finger was hovering right in front of Andrey's eyes, "because men arrange the world for their own benefit. In fact, everything's simpler, but at the same time harder. The world must be arranged for the benefit of woman. And a happy woman's smile is the only, the supreme criterion!"

He bent and whispered in Andrey's ear.

"Nobody needs revolutions. Shh! Or any of this per capita production of this and that, either . . . !"

He giggled, coughed, then prodded Andrey in the chest.

"We men are beasts. We've lost the sense of what the world is about. Dropped out of it. By our own doing. Woman is right at the heart of it. Statistics? Useless rubbish! Who needs them? They do a survey, count the number of happy people, make comparisons. Is something bad? Is it good? What are all those philosophers and politicians on about? All you have to do is compare and choose. What to choose and compare, though?"

"Happy women's smiles," Andrey ventured.

"Right. Spot on."

"Well, there's one more option for you," chuckled Andrey

and spotted Konstantin approaching. "When the system crashes and asks you to help out, I'll come and give you a hand!"

"Cynic," the bohemian growled contemptuously as Andrey strode away.

He and Konstantin walked to the end of the square. Kolya was already waiting. Andrey checked his watch: "Fine. Let's go."

The arcade of the old Petersburg house projected over the pavement right up to the corner of the street, blanketing a crooked triangle of the crossroads in shadow. Between eleven and eleven thirty, ten people passed the corner. Not the one they were waiting for. Andrey stood absolutely still on the far side of the street in the light. He displayed no signs of nervousness. Then he gave the signal. He walked quickly back across the road and they took up position. When the militiaman drew level with them, Kolya and Konstantin grabbed his arms, while Andrey jabbed his fist into his solar plexus. The militiaman gasped and slumped against them. Andrey tore open his tunic, ripped his shirt to get at the pistol in a home-made holster under the armpit. Kolya and Konstantin let the militiaman go and he dropped to the pavement with a groan. Andrey had just stuffed the gun into an inside pocket when he was suddenly jerked flat on his back. The militiaman had grabbed hold of his leg and was wrenching it viciously. Andrey twisted, trying to break free or at least stop his leg from being broken.

"Don't just stand there," he shouted. His accomplices re-covered their wits and jumped on the militiaman, trying to drag him off Andrey. He wouldn't let go, though he was forced to relax his grip. Andrey half sat up. His hand found its way to the pistol. He grabbed it by the barrel, struck out hard and blindly and caught Kolya's arm. Kolya yelled and let go the militiaman, who saw his chance and head-butted Konstantin. The blow caught Konstantin on the chin. He staggered back off the pavement and collapsed. At this moment Andrey, almost unconscious from the pain in his leg, struck out again, blindly, at the militiaman. Andrey didn't just hear, he could feel the crunch. After that everything went according to plan.

*   *   *

They were supposed to meet at the flat at five. But during the break after the second lecture Andrey saw Kolya in the corridor opposite the lecture theatre. They quickly went downstairs. At the exit Andrey turned round unexpectedly, so that Kolya, who had hardly been able to keep up, almost fell over him. Andrey was furious.

"What are you doing here! Who said you could!"

Kolya looked at him in fright.

"Well," hissed Andrey.

Kolya could barely speak, he glanced around, swallowed hard: "You know you . . . we . . . we killed him . . . "

The fury on Andrey's face vanished. He looked gloomy. Facing Kolya squarely, he said wearily: "I know."

"How?" whispered Kolya.

"I found out yesterday."

Kolya's puffy lips began to tremble. He sniffed and looked away.

"It was me! Understand! You had nothing to do with it!"

"I didn't do . . . " Kolya began to justify himself.

"That'll do!" Andrey cut him short. "Phone Konstantin. Tell him tomorrow's off. Get your clothes cleaned up. I want no traces! If anything happens, make contact through Konstantin. No meetings!"

Then his voice softened as he added: "Try not to be miserable. Cheer up. There was a hitch. But we'll make it up, with interest! Right?"

Kolya nodded, without too much conviction.

"That's the way."

When Andrey shook his hand, Kolya winced.

"What's the matter?" Andrey frowned.

"My hand . . . You walloped me yesterday." Kolya sounded almost guilty. He pulled back the sleeve of his jacket and shirt to reveal a large bruise just below the elbow. "It's sore," he said ruefully.

"Go and see a doctor. It may be fractured."

"No, if it was I wouldn't be able to move my arm. Did something like it when I was a kid . . . " Kolya chattered happily.

"OK, OK, now scram. And keep out of trouble!"

Kolya ran off.

Andrey went back up the stairs to the lecture theatre for his exercise book. In the doorway he met the Dean, ignored him and walked straight past. The Dean turned in surprise to watch him go.

Out in the street he stopped to think. He got out what money he had and counted it, hailed a cab and climbed into the back seat. Paid off the cab at Narvskaya metro station. Found an empty telephone booth and dialled.

"Vadim, it's me. Anybody with you? Can we meet? You can spare the time? Great."

Vadim arrived in a state of great anxiety.

"Something happened?"

"No," Andrey replied calmly. "I just wanted to see you. We have to . . . talk . . . "

"Thank the Lord," Vadim sighed with relief. "I wasn't expecting you to call . . . not today, anyway. Wait here, I've got to dash back, there's something cooking on the stove. My father's asleep."

"I want to talk about your option," Andrey said when Vadim came back.

They walked down a lane away from the crowded street.

For a long time they walked in silence.

"Tell me, Vadim," Andrey said at last, "how is your option going to help you live in a world that's evil? If I understand rightly, it completely rules out active struggle? To maintain your righteousness you shut yourself off from an unrighteous

world, isn't that it? Anyway, tell me about your option."
Cautiously he added: "If you can, of course. And what you
can."

Vadim's reply was almost despairing: "I'm afraid to."

"What?"

"It's not me you should be talking to. It's more emotional
than anything with me still. I haven't begun to define it in
words yet . . . "

"But I'm not asking you to convert me," Andrey objected.
"I only want to understand you. Put it any way you can. If I
don't understand there's no harm done. I don't want to argue
with you. I just want to listen to what you have to say."

"I'll try," Vadim replied uncertainly.

They walked in silence for a little longer.

"Life is absurdly short . . . Right? But man has been given
the concept of eternity. Where did it come from? It's a paradox,
isn't it? . . . And what about infinity? Can you imagine infinity? It's way beyond the parameters of our existence!"

"Regurgitated Kant," snorted Andrey.

"Kant? No. I don't think so . . . Never read him. Too
boring . . . "

He spun towards Andrey: "And truth? You and I went on
and on about the truth. Yet nobody has any concrete idea what
it is."

"A happy woman's smile," murmured Andrey, grinning.

"What?"

"Sorry, nothing . . . Carry on."

"I mean, everybody searches for meaning, though they never
find any . . . But the concept of truth *is* in our consciousness,
it's there all right . . . In some ways it feels as though it isn't
actually in us, it's somewhere above us, and we crane our
necks, we stand on tiptoe . . . "

"You're a genius, Vadim," Andrey laughed happily. "You
haven't read Plato either, have you?"

Vadim looked glum and fell silent. Andrey took his elbow:
"Shan't do it again. It's interesting, honestly it is!"

He suddenly looked away.

"Hang on a second."

He approached another youth.

"Got a smoke?"

The young man reluctantly produced a packet of cigarettes and casually offered one to Andrey. Andrey asked for a light and without a word of thanks returned to Vadim. Vadim was almost speechless.

"Andrey, has something happened?"

"No," Andrey replied, inhaling deeply and with relish. "Don't I have the right to behave paradoxically?"

The joke didn't come off and it only made Vadim even more worried.

"Well, all right then," Andrey conceded, "eternity, infinity, truth, good, evil are parameters of something outside us. Let's call it God. How does that change our lives here?"

Vadim was on the point of attempting an explanation, when Andrey suddenly seized his shoulder and said loudly, viciously: "Try another philosophy. Have you got a cat? Come on, tell me."

"Yes, I have," replied Vadim in fright.

"Your cat's got one aim in life, to stay alive. When it's hungry, it miaows. When it's cold, it miaows. And what does it do when it's content? It purrs! And can you explain to me what purring is? Purring has no meaning. It's one of the prices of existence. So listen here, you cabbage-patch Plato, man's so-called intellectual life – and that includes religion – is a highly developed animal purring. Purring. Period. Nothing more."

"Andrey! What are you saying?" Vadim shouted so loud a woman laden with a string bag bulging with carrots turned to look. "What about reason!"

"Reason?" There was delight in Andrey's voice, as though this was the question he'd been waiting for. "Reason is the sixth sense, self-preservation. A cat's got five senses, a wolf's got five, but man has six. What you call reason developed in man when he moved on out of the general order of nature which only requires five senses. That sixth sense hypertrophied to give rise to so-called intellectual life, a bit like the way gluttony creates layers of fat. A fat man's all warm and cosy, but the fat can finish him off. Same with anything. Yes. Exactly the same. Reason preserves life, but it can be fatal. A loaf of bread and the atom bomb are both products of the rational mind. A cat can't control its purring, it's involuntary. Human creativity is the same. Ask me to define art and I'll point you towards your cat when she's playing with a mouse after her feed. You want a definition? Art is . . . "

"Andrey, that's enough!"

"Oh, no. You're afraid. Maybe I'm telling you the one truth which man isn't just afraid of, he doesn't even want to know it. Where was I? Ah, yes, here we are. Art is a by-product of a normally functioning living organism. This by-product is present in all living beings proportionately to their developmental level."

"And all the poets who died from consumption?"

Vadim had gone bright red.

"Like who?" Andrey asked spitefully.

Vadim was lost for words.

"Consumptives and people with ulcers, Vadim, engage in politics, the lowest form of purring. Or do I have to explain what an inferiority complex is before you remember Homer's blindness and Aesop's hunchback. Humanity lives by the same laws of eat and be eaten and self-preservation as the rest of the world. The idea of God, like all other ideas, is an attempt to impose collective self-control, an attempt to regulate the process of eat and be eaten!"

The cigarette had burnt right down. Andrey attempted one last drag, but it scorched his finger and he threw the butt away. It fell at the feet of an ice-cream vendor, who yelled at them both. Vadim hastily pulled Andrey round a corner. They turned under the arch of a large building, came out into the yard and stopped. The yard was deserted.

Andrey calmed down and returned to normal. The fever in his eyes died away. His movements became more restrained. His face moulded back into its usual mask of firm confidence. The way Vadim knew him. Or almost. There was something new in the "comandore's" eyes. Something new and disturbing. Not kindly. Otherwise his look would not have been so hypnotic . . .

"You understand, Vadim," Andrey spoke quietly now. "I can see no counter-arguments to what I was saying. I wanted to hear you out, but I've got a big mouth . . . This whole conversation was a complete waste of time."

Vadim answered him with melancholy certitude: "Something's happened to you. Is it serious? Don't tell me if you don't want to. Only . . . if it is what I think it is . . . "

"Go on."

"You're on your own? . . . I mean, your option . . . "

"No, I'm not on my own," said Andrey and his tone indicated that the subject was closed. "I'm going away. For a long time. One of the others may be going as well. Don't go and see any of them. It's very important."

Vadim asked timidly: "Anything I can do . . . to help?"

Andrey was silent.

"Yes. Have you got Olga's new number?"

Vadim searched hastily through his address book.

"Yes. Ready?"

"Out with it."

Vadim remembered that Andrey never wrote down telephone numbers. This was part of his system.

They each of them parted with the feeling they would never meet again.

Andrey stood outside the phone booth for about fifteen minutes, missing his turn five or six times. Then he went in. Dialled. Olga's number was engaged. He hung up and walked away.

III

Telephones

Five days went by. On the evening of the sixth the phone rang in Konstantin's flat. There was so much noise, nobody heard it at first, then a girl in a blue dress squealed: "Kostik, for goodness' sake, the phone!"

Konstantin went out into the corridor. Picked up the receiver. Answered limply.

"Konstantin! Hi! It's me!"

"Kolya?"

Pleased to be recognised, Kolya giggled. "Everything OK?"

"OK," Konstantin replied.

"Me, too . . . all quiet."

Kolya coughed into the receiver. The conversation was going nowhere.

"You know, I've been sitting in my room, just sitting, made me feel sick."

"Where are you calling from?"

"From a booth. On that corner. Am I interrupting something?"

"No, not really . . . "

Kolya sniffed loudly into the receiver.

"Listen, if I ask you something, will you give me a straight answer?"

"Ask away," said Konstantin with a sigh.

"You . . . well . . . you . . . you despise me, don't you? Right?"

"Wha-a-t?"

"Don't try to pretend, Konstantin! I know! And you've got a right to . . . "

Konstantin shouted down the receiver: "What the hell are you on about? Are you drunk?"

"No! Word of honour, I'm not," Kolya protested his innocence. "Wait, don't hang up on me. I wanted to say, wanted

to talk . . . I can only do it on the phone . . . And I haven't
been drinking, honest! I'm not allowed to, I've got an ulcer
. . . I'm only allowed a drop of pure alcohol. And that's not
easy to find . . . And it's expensive . . . Wine's out, stabs me
right in the gut . . . nothing spicy . . . cucumber brine is
something I really fancy, for example, but I can't."

Kolya was babbling.

"You've got an ulcer?" Konstantin asked, taken aback. "I
didn't know . . . "

Probably nobody knew.

"Listen, Konstantin," Kolya went on hurriedly, as though
afraid he wouldn't be able to finish what he had to say, he
wouldn't be heard out. "You know, I used to think I didn't
like you. It's the truth. I used to think that. But today I was
sitting and realised I was just jealous, jealous that's all . . .
Remember when we celebrated our anniversary and you
brought a sausage. I'd never seen anything like it . . . cervelat
or something, it was. I had bellyache all night after that, I had
a couple of drinks . . . to celebrate . . . And I was jealous of
you . . . Then you've got all those suits . . . I was jealous
of those, too. When I was on my own I used to practise talking
like you, all those wisecracks and stuff, but it always came out
feeble, so I was jealous again . . . You didn't know, but you
despised me . . . You were right. A stupid little shit . . . like
me . . . "

"Wait, Kolya, wait." Konstantin tried to stop him. He
wanted to suppress something troubling him deep down that
welled up inside, stifled, burned . . .

"No, no, I haven't finished . . . When Andrey told us his
option, I was scared but I agreed just to spite you . . . No,
not really . . . I thought you wouldn't do it. I said to myself:
'He won't, but I will.' But then you did . . . I'm ashamed of
myself, honest. Then you said the room was a pigsty . . . I
don't mean you're wrong. People should always be tidy, but
I've got to go to work, forty-eight hours a week in a stoke-hole.
When I drop that shovel and come home, I can't lift my arms,

but you've still got to get stuck into the books . . . No, I'm
not trying to make excuses . . . I mean, I am trying to make
excuses so you understand . . . You know, I've decided, if we
. . . well . . . if we get out of this, I'm going to change my
life. Can't tell how things 'll turn out now, so I've decided . . .
so I'll feel clean at heart . . . "

He sniffed loudly into the receiver again.

"You said everything?" There was a tremor in Konstantin's
voice. "Now it's my turn. Listen. You're a great guy, understand. And I'm just a prick. A smug prick! I didn't despise
you, but I acted like a slob. If we get out of this, we'll be
friends. Do you believe me? You still there?"

"What have we gone and done, eh?"

It was said in such a way it brought goose-pimples out on
Konstantin's back.

"Yeh," he replied dully. And suddenly the full realisation
of what had happened struck him for the first time. Also that
there was no way out. From that evening his life was divided
into two, and in the middle was an abyss. And there was no
way back. He also felt that someone very dear to him was on
the other end of the line, someone he needed very much . . .

"Listen, Kolya." There was haste and anxiety in Konstantin's voice. "Why don't you come over? Grab a cab and come
over. Have you got the money?"

Kolya sniffed.

"Mustn't."

"Why not? What's up?"

"Won't work. Better to talk on the phone."

"Don't be like that. I'll throw them all out and we can talk,
the two of us."

"Who've you got there?" Kolya asked with childish curiosity.

"Just a few people round . . . Three girls whose fathers are
something important, some up-and-coming postgrads and a
famous musician . . . "

"Not bad," whistled Kolya. Then he groaned. "See. Jealous
again! What are they doing? Tell me."

"At this moment? At this moment one of the girls is whispering Pasternak poems with her eyes closed."

"Is she decadent?" Kolya's question was deadly serious.

"No," Konstantin explained. "She needs a husband."

"Of course. What's the point in living on your own."

"Pardon?"

"I'm saying, it's understandable. Every woman wants children, a family . . . "

"Kolya, do you have any enemies?"

"What enemies? If . . . well, you know . . . "

"No, personal enemies, I mean. Is there anybody you hate?"

Kolya, puzzled, snorted. "Don't know . . . Nobody's done me any harm . . . Always been a case of me being stupid . . . "

"Have you got a girlfriend?"

Kolya was silent. Konstantin said sadly: "How come we've been friends three years and know hardly anything about each other?"

Kolya was silent. Then he said gravely: "Bye now, Konstantin."

Konstantin took fright.

"What's up, Kolya! I've not upset you . . . ?"

"No, no. I'm freezing, I came out in just a shirt. I'll phone again."

"You do that. You do that, don't forget, now."

"Right. Bye . . . "

The phone went dead. In the sitting room the famous musician was playing Chopin.

* * *

That same evening, at that very moment, another telephone conversation was taking place.

It took Vadim a long time to get through to Olga. Her number was always busy. At last she answered.

"Heartless, that's what you are," she said to him sadly.

"Olga!"

"Of course, I know. I always was an extension of Andrey as far as you were concerned. When I stopped being it, I ceased to exist. Why have you suddenly remembered me after six months?"

There was a horribly unpalatable truth to what she was saying.

"I haven't any excuses," he said with total honesty.

"Congratulate me, Vadim, I finished school."

"Congratulations!"

"Thanks. Congratulate me again."

"For?"

"For getting a place at the conservatoire."

"Good for you, Olga!"

"See how well things are working out for me. So, what have you phoned for? Not that you need to tell me, I know."

"You don't."

"Something's up with Andrey? Something's wrong? Right?"

Vadim was stunned. She laughed bitterly.

"You all think you're so deep and complicated, you parade it around as if . . . Lord! But it's always the same old thing, pure selfishness. So tell me, egotist, what's happened to your egotist friend with his king-size ego!"

She spoke calmly, or was trying to. All the same, Vadim sensed she was not wholly indifferent to the object of the conversation. Which was as it should be. After all, he knew quite a lot about it. But how to tell her and what to tell her?

"You're right, Olga. He is in a bad way. He doesn't know I'm phoning."

"Naturally. Andrey knows how to pick tactful friends."

"You shouldn't talk about him like this, Olga, you . . . "

"Oh, but I can," she interrupted. "Andrey's a lousy person. He is! You be quiet. I have the right to say that. Just think how many people there are around who are worth ten of him. How many good, fine people who could make you happy, truly, genuinely happy. Why does everything in life end up so idiotically? You're the brains, tell me, why? Come to think of it, better tell me what's up with Andrey."

"I can't tell you anything except he's in a bad way. Believe me, I don't know myself."

She answered bitterly: "Vadim, you never used to be a liar!"

"And I'm not lying now. I don't know what he's doing any more. Something's changed . . . "

"You haven't fallen out?"

There was a note of alarm in her voice.

"No. I can't explain, but we haven't fallen out. I saw him five days ago. He was in a bad way. He asked for your number. But you didn't phone me, so I knew he hadn't phoned you either."

"Why would I have phoned you?" she asked in surprise. "No, of course you're right. I'd have phoned you to find out what was really going on. He wouldn't have told me anything. 'Talk to a woman about love when you're in love, and about nothing at all when you're not. Never talk business!' Remind you of somebody? Rotten windbag! He really hurt me. Vadik, my dear, tell me why you're so devoted to him? After all, he doesn't love anybody. If he does stick with anybody, it's only for as long as that person feeds his wants."

"It's not like that," Vadim objected hotly. "I'll ask you the same question, why do you still love him even now?"

Vadim could see her face and the tears in her eyes as clearly as anything. He wasn't wrong. You could hear her fighting back the tears.

"I don't know. I don't know. He drove me to the end of my tether. I slapped his face so many times in my dreams. He tormented me even in my sleep. It was like banging my head against a brick wall. I never had a dream with him smiling or tender. You know, Vadim, I even thought it might be me being neurotic rather than love. I went to see a psychiatrist. And you know what? He laughed at me, the thick-skinned, insensitive bastard! So what do you want from me?" She was almost shouting. "You want me to go to him so he can get on his high horse and then ditch me? And you're no better. You just pretend to be nice. Don't you think it's pretty mean to phone when I might have only just got over it? To start the whole thing again? Don't you think it's pretty mean to set me up so I can be humiliated again? How can you? You're no better than him. Selfish swine!"

She threw the receiver down on the table. Vadim could hear her sobbing.

A minute or more passed. The receiver crackled.

"I'm sorry, Vadim. I've turned into a hysterical old bag." She sobbed, sniffled loudly.

"Olga, I understand, I do, but believe me I'm certain that sooner or later everything'll work out for you . . . "

She replied, still sobbing: "Things don't work out later! Later is too late . . . Things are just bad. I'm afraid it's way too late, anyway. I won't go to him, don't ask me to. Damn him!"

Vadim spoke quietly, but with conviction.

"Olga, there aren't many people like Andrey. I personally don't know anybody. Some day you'll understand. Another thing I know. He loves you."

"No, Vadim," she replied wearily. "He doesn't love anybody. Me included. I was useful to him . . . that's all. I won't go to him."

Vadim was silent a moment.

"OK, don't go. But promise me, if he does come to see you, you'll be patient. Believe me, I've known him a long time. I've never seen him like this before!"

"Him, him, him! You don't give a damn about me!"

"Don't be like that," he wheedled. "I think the world of you. And as for me not phoning, well, I didn't have anything to tell you."

"What?" She was angry now. "Nothing to tell me? At the very least you could have told me he was alive and well, he hadn't fallen under a tram or got into a fight with a militiaman, he hadn't been thrown out of college yet, he was still in this world, the rat! You wouldn't have had anything to tell me? You . . . !"

She slammed down the receiver.

*　　*　　*

They came for Konstantin the morning after Kolya's call. His father and mother had gone to work. On reflection, Konstantin thought that in this sense he was lucky. He wouldn't have to see their shock.

Five of them came. Plus official witnesses. They produced a search warrant and an arrest warrant. Konstantin acted calmly. It seemed he was inwardly prepared . . . It jarred, watching them rummage through his personal possessions, through his papers. He noticed one of them sneering as they went through the sideboard. He had to admit the justice of it. What need was there for a family of three to have seven sets of wine and liqueur glasses. And all the condiment sets and ludicrous quantity of china . . .

The contents of the well-stocked 'fridge also caused raised eyebrows. Half-turning to Konstantin, one of them asked: "What were you short of, eh?"

"Pigeon's milk," called another, rooting through the wardrobe.

At that moment Konstantin envied Kolya. During a search he could face all these people with a clear conscience. "How is Kolya?" he thought. "Have they got him as well?" He was surprised to find he was completely indifferent as to how they'd picked up his trail. It also seemed he'd never expected any other outcome to the story. In this sense it was even something of a relief.

He thought of his studies as of something in the distant past. It was as if the world had shrunk to this room where these hostile strangers were poking about. Beyond these walls was an emptiness that cut him off from everything else, dim, fleeting, alien. The sound of traffic drifted through the win-

dow, though it might have been a shooting star, so little relation
did it bear to him, Konstantin, who could have been half-alive,
or asleep, or hallucinating . . . He looked at his watch. He felt
like stopping it. But that would have been wrong. The spring
must be left to do its job to the end. Smash it? Pure bravado.
Remembered Kolya had no watch. He used to get on your
nerves, always asking the time. There was another watch in
the table drawer, a present from one of his father's colleagues.
He felt ashamed. Yes. He would have been perfectly calm
were it not for the feeling of shame which came with every
recollection. Had he been a rat? Not so much a rat, perhaps,
as utterly frivolous. A canary, more like.

"Answer when you're spoken to," a voice above his ear said
roughly.

"I'm listening," he replied calmly.

"Your papers? Passport?"

Konstantin tried to concentrate, remember where his passport might be.

"Under the vase, I think." He got up to fetch it.

"Sit down!"

He sat down. Smiled. "Why ask me, then? You're searching
the place, you find it!"

The senior of the five came over and said quietly: "You keep
your jokes to yourself. You familiar with the criminal code?"

"Why on earth 'criminal'?" Konstantin thought. "There
surely isn't any other."

"You can start giving testimony now. Write it yourself.
You'd be well advised to. In your own interest."

"Lord, how vulgar," he thought. He chuckled: "There's no
need."

"Up to you. Think of your parents. Your family's well-
known."

At that moment the phone rang.

Konstantin didn't turn a hair. The five, though, were staring
at him. The senior officer bounded across, grabbed him by the
shoulder and hissed: "This is your only chance, boy! There

won't be another. Murder carries the death penalty. It's your last chance! Pick it up. If it's one of your accomplices, get him here. Tell him it's urgent. Understand. Your only chance if you want to live! Well?"

He jerked Konstantin out of the chair and almost dragged him to the phone. Konstantin didn't resist. Somehow he couldn't grasp what they wanted of him, what he was supposed to do. Couldn't concentrate . . . He lifted the receiver, hoping it wasn't Andrey. But it was.

"Konstantin, hi!"

"Hello," he replied.

The officer was nose to nose with him. Eyes blazing, nostrils flared, licking his lips. Hissed: "Well? Well? Him? Yes? Get him here! Here!"

He squeezed Konstantin's shoulder so hard it hurt.

"Get him here, you sonofabitch!"

"Like a hawk with its prey," Konstantin thought, looking at him, and heard: "Everything OK?"

"OK," he replied mechanically and could feel himself going red.

"Kolya should have come, but he didn't make it. Do you know why?"

"No."

He suddenly felt he was choking. He was unbearably hot. Sweat beaded his forehead, his shirt stuck to his back.

"Were you asleep?"

Konstantin answered with another negative. All five officers were leaning over him.

"All right then," Andrey went on, "I'll phone you tonight. You'll be at home?"

"Yeh."

Recovering suddenly, he shouted unnaturally loudly: "Wait! . . . Listen! . . . I'm under arrest! I'm being searched!"

The receiver flew out of his hands. Handcuffs clicked around his wrists. They dragged him across the room and threw him in the armchair. He banged his ribs painfully against the arm.

"Puppy! Signed your own death warrant!" The senior man spoke without any particular ill-will, though not without irritation. Konstantin looked at him and felt no particular ill-will, either. A joy he had never experienced before entered his soul and swept everything out, all the nausea there. His head felt light and everything was somehow swimming, not receding, not vanishing, but as though displacing sideways, as if toppling onto its side, as though plunging down and at the same fixed, motionless, soundless and disembodied . . . Terrific! He fell in a faint.

IV

A *personal option*

Andrey spotted Pavel's auburn curls immediately, as soon as he turned from the staircase into the corridor. As he walked past, he nodded to him almost imperceptibly. Pavel hurried after him, unable to conceal his delight, yet still maintaining the proper conspiratorial distance. They went into a deserted lecture theatre. Pavel shook Andrey's hand excitedly. Andrey was to the point: "I've a favour to ask."

It was as though Pavel didn't hear.

"Am I glad to see you! This is great! I thought you'd pretty much . . . I kept thinking the last few days . . . I've thought of another option. It's really something. We won't have to kill. They'll start shooting each other themselves. Listen, I'll tell you all about it . . . "

Andrey frowned. "Hang on. We will discuss your option . . . Tomorrow . . . "

"Won't take long," enthused Pavel. He was flushed, his almost red curls danced across his forehead, he fidgeted, tugging at Andrey's sleeve.

"Pavel," Andrey was barely able to restrain himself, "I

haven't the time today. We'll meet and discuss it tomorrow. Tomorrow!"

Pavel, deflated, looked crestfallen.

"I've thought it through carefully . . . " he carried on by inertia.

"I've a favour to ask," Andrey repeated.

"Of course, of course," Pavel said hastily. "You know I'm always . . . Great to see you . . . "

"I need a typewriter. To type a statement. I need it now."

"I've got dialectical materialism next, I can't . . . " Pavel began, but then saw the look on Andrey's face.

"Oh, to hell with it. Let's go. We'll be at my place in twenty minutes! We'll have a cup of tea."

"Let's go," said Andrey. Then he added, "No talking on the way."

In the metro Andrey caught himself looking over his shoulder all the time. He felt dreadful. He took a grip on himself, but the tension remained. It was part of his life now. It'd be with him till the end! Till the end! The end! The end'd be soon! The words were spoken, and their meaning slipped away, caught on his skin and chilled him, then ricocheted away off the mind . . . Yet his thought processes were working smoothly, their clarity was extraordinary. He was calculating a hundred moves in advance. Never before had he been so certain everything would go exactly according to his plan. Even the end. Though he didn't yet know what that was going to be.

When they got there, Pavel was about to start fussing about in the kitchen when Andrey said firmly: "Pavel, go back to the institute. Now. You can still make second lecture. I'll slam the door behind me. I'll see you tomorrow."

Pavel's face fell. He looked pathetic. But though Andrey lied about meeting next day, he felt no pangs of conscience. He knew he would never see Pavel again. What the hell. There were a lot of people he'd never see again. They wouldn't be seeing him again, either. So they were all quits. If he wasted time and energy on sentiment he wouldn't execute his plan, he simply wouldn't be up to the job. Pavel had to go and be out of the way.

Andrey held out his hand. Said as gently as he could: "See you tomorrow. Cheer up! Till then!"

"Yeh, sure." Pavel was solemn. He had gone quite pale and the freckles stood out on his face, making him look a mere child. He wouldn't look at Andrey. For the first time ever he didn't believe Andrey. If only Andrey had been a fraction gentler, if only he hadn't been in his usual rush, he would have told him such a lot, poured his heart out to him. But Andrey didn't need him, Pavel, as a person. He only needed a favour. All right. So be it. He wouldn't impose on him. All the same, though. How could you sever the ties of several years of real friendship just like that?

He shook Andrey's hand warmly all the same.

"Forgive me, if there's anything . . . " he said.

It was the form of words people use when they are never going to meet again. Andrey understood. His response to the handshake was genuine.

He worked at the typewriter for about twenty minutes. The final draft read like this:

Sentence

Conscience dictates the sentencing of Mikhail Boris-ovich Kolganov, Colonel (retired) of the Committee of State Security, for crimes committed against humanity between the years 1932 and 1953, for acts of torture, violence and degradation, for outrages against human dignity, for abuse of rank and auth-ority, to the supreme penalty

death.

Sentence to be carried out by the signatory.

Andrey paused, then signed his own name beneath. He added the date and the time, the time fixed for the death of the pensioner Mikhail Borisovich Kolganov, faithful disciple of that russified Pole, Felix Dzerzhinsky, whose glory outshone that of all his heroic successors at the helm of the *Cheka*, OGPU, NKVD, MGB, KGB.

He had twenty minutes in hand. He strolled down Nevsky. The heavy militia service pistol weighed down his inner pocket. But it was more than just the weight of it he could feel. It weighed heavily on his heart.

He had felt something similar once before, ten years ago. The object in his pocket that time was his Komsomol card.

His mother, a village teacher, had brought him up an idealist, believing in everything he was supposed to. Faith was beautiful, it used such marvellous words, its deeds as described in schoolbooks and popular fiction were worthy of the heroes of the classical myths. The sense that you were living at a time when the entire historical development of the world was coming to fruition was intoxicating. It even made the future seem less interesting, because you thought of that more as being the end of history. The future looked grand, but a little dull, and Andrey was prepared to be generous and concede the right to live in that wonderful future to later generations. He reserved the present for himself, for it still presented ample opportunity for heroics, and he wasn't building himself up for less. Nor was his mother, she who had once been patted on the head by Kalinin, who had once seen Stalin in the flesh – "as close as I am to you now" – who had once been interviewed on national radio about the duty of a patriot to contribute to the State loan.

Having once felt part of the "great cause", she spent the rest of her life under its hypnotic spell. She left her husband when she discovered he lacked the necessary obsessiveness. Divorcing a petty-minded husband or petty-minded wife was at that time a highly laudable undertaking. She went even further – she almost broke with her parents, peasants from the

Urals, because they failed to appreciate the Leader's enormous wisdom on the peasant question.

Having been able to participate only on the fringes herself, she prepared her son for something much greater. The day he joined the Komsomol was marked by a ceremonial worthy of the most solemn family occasion. His grandfather and grandmother, duly coached in the behaviour expected of them, were invited, but failed to display the level of enthusiasm required. After that the boy was no longer sent to spend the summer months with them.

The grandson was hardly in a position to appreciate such niceties, since he was utterly absorbed by his own first encounter with the cause . . .

He felt the lack of an equivalent enthusiasm among his peers keenly. He dreamt of moving to Moscow or Leningrad, cities which he was sure were inhabited only by the politically conscious, cities which would never see a dimming of the revolutionary flame, because that was where the leaders lived. You could see and hear them in the flesh. Every stone, every building bore witness to the start and continuation . . .

He was not lacking self-assurance even then. And as he strode down the one paved street of the factory settlement, he was already utterly certain he would end up in Moscow or Leningrad. There life would begin for real, the key to it all being the little book that lay on his heart like a part of him . . .

Now he was walking down the main street of legendary Petrograd with a pistol next his heart. He had already killed once and was about to kill again, and by doing so put a full stop to his life, his absurd, unusual, but nevertheless consistent, life.

Whether he was right or wrong was not for him to judge. But he did have the feeling he was justified and that feeling turned every thought that threatened the onset of doubt into wild, unbridled spite.

He felt joy for Konstantin who had remained faithful to the last, and for the others, too, because he hadn't been mistaken in any of them. He felt pride as well. His friends were the work of his hands and his will. He could imagine each of their faces at the moment he had seen them for the last time, and the memory evoked tenderness and love. When he thought about the end, this was the only thing he regarded as a loss. But he tried not to think about the end. He didn't think about the militiaman, either. That mistake would have to be paid for with his life, the most valuable thing he had, and if that didn't make up for it, at least it cancelled it out.

Sometimes his hand automatically, or maybe deliberately, touched his jacket in the place where the pistol butt bulged slightly, and then he was conscious of the ease with which its ribbed contours would mould into his palm.

The people pushing past him knew nothing. If they had, they would have jumped aside, opening an area of dead space around him. To know their true worth, people have to have been in that situation, in a dead space. A cheap, petty truism. Here he was walking down a crowded street as if he was the invisible man . . . No, it wasn't obscurity bothered him. Simply invisibility was chilling, it made him feel alienated, isolated. It undermined the basis on which everything rested, a sense of purpose. It was what made the voice waver when it was supposed to be a clarion call, it was what lifted the finger from the trigger, it was this, this alone, that could turn a man's courage inside out and make him show his back instead of his chest.

There was something sad and even offensive about the indifference with which people passed him by. The thought occurred to him that if he spent the whole day walking a street like this, he might very well lose faith in his option by evening. The victor, in that case, would be weakness, not truth. Nobody is immune from weakness.

He still had one blatant point of weakness. Olga. No, that was taboo. Thank the Lord, he still had some control over his thoughts. His mind was an obedient, trained, intelligent dog. The result of yoga. He could lash an unwanted thought across the muzzle and it would slink whining back to the darkness of its kennel. One he wanted would work like a borzoi on the scent and he would often observe it with a certain self-satisfaction, almost as if watching from the outside . . .

During these final minutes of free time, he could permit himself a degree of sentimentality, though he shouldn't overdo it. This was why Olga didn't exist, though it was fine for her to get on with her own life somewhere out there, while his mother *did* exist, even though she was no longer alive.

This was a salutary moment for him to remember the day he rushed home after receiving the telegram to find his mother paralysed, motionless, unable to speak.

"You hear what Khrushchev said about Stalin?" The driver who fired the question bitterly at her in the street the day before had been a pupil of hers. He was drunk.

Andrey knew his mother. The man's attitude and tone of voice would have been enough to trigger a stroke.

"Lying through your teeth for years. Didn't do badly for yourself out of it, either. Nikita's gone and shoved your face in it now. It was you informed on Stepanych from the library, wasn't it? Never hurt a fly, Stepanych. Not like you. On and on like a broken gramophone!"

Mother died a week later. The driver who'd been her pupil tore at his shirt and rolled on the fresh soil of her grave while everybody looked on.

Andrey did not raise his hand against him. Though neither did he offer a crumb of comfort.

It was a changed Andrey that returned to Leningrad, as changed as anyone can be in a single instant.

It was then that the road opened before him that now led along Nevsky, down into the metro, then to the Finland Station, from there to Lembolovo, where the retired KGB Lieutenant-Colonel lived at his dacha.

Kolganov was a stickler for punctuality. He'd come out into the garden at six with his bright red watering can to sprinkle the flowers around the house, examining every individual bloom, tutting and muttering, shaking his head, frowning and stooping . . . Today he would water only three beds. When he started on the fourth, the one nearest the fence, he would fall, never to rise again. His last impressions in this life would be of pain and the scent of peonies. He didn't deserve the second! An intolerable luxury that, death coming to a man like that scented with peonies. But the most vicious brute still has the right to his dying wish. That was the ancient custom and there was no sense in dispensing with it. The peonies could be his last wish.

That's how it would be. And nobody would ever know what the man was thinking in the minute before his death, what he thought about his own life, whether he even thought about life at all. And if it was true a man sees his life pass before his eyes in the seconds before death, mightn't he die quicker than he ought because of what he saw? It was very important to find out whether he did or not. Maybe even more important than his actual death. But that was impossible. So he would collapse face down in the red peonies and death would blossom red as a peony across his white shirt.

At the sound of the shot a dumpy old woman would come running out of the dacha, see her husband and scream. But instead of rushing over to her husband, trying to lift him, stir him vainly back to life, she would yell for help and dash back inside, slamming the bolt to . . .

This last detail was the only point at which events deviated from what Andrey had calculated. Which was good. When everything goes absolutely to plan, it does wonders for your self-esteem, though it does make life a bit dull.

He had a sudden urge to take a pot shot at her, as if to say: "What are you frightened for, you old bag? Were you in it as well, if you're so scared for your own skin?"

No doubt there was utter panic soon afterwards. But Andrey wasn't around to see it. Seven minutes later he was on the platform, five minutes later he was on a train and forty minutes after that he was standing near the stone armoured car on top of which a sculpted Lenin had been making the same speech for the lasty forty years, a speech he would never finish, his arm frozen outstretched, words of stone trapped in his throat of stone . . .

Andrey had a question or two he would have liked to ask him. But a plan is a plan. He had no time for deviations. A large building on Kalayev Street was waiting for him, a monstrous concrete fortress, which he would have to walk into of his own free will, never to leave it again.

Fifty years ago at that spot a man his age, who may even have looked like him (stranger things have happened!), did what he had done – killed a man. Killed and was himself killed. The people who inherited his cause named the street after him. Today he, Andrey, had killed one of those heirs. They would kill him for that. But no street would be named after him. He had no heirs. The circle was closed. And at the same time opened. Dumb, senseless causality. He had slotted himself into it and by doing so left the last word to them, his enemies . . . Why on earth?

This thought stunned him at the very threshold of the big building. Why on earth serve himself up on a platter? Who was he trying to surprise by this gesture? But wait a second. His friends were in there. Konstantin, Kolya, perhaps Pavel and Vadim, too. He ought to be with them!

Too late. He had been tripped by doubt, he was already staggering, he couldn't keep his balance. He no longer had the strength that would carry him through the door. Another force, unfamiliar and oppressive, swept him on, did not allow him either to stop, look round or think. The same fever that had driven him through all the steps of his carefully laid plan, tore it to shreds at the last. Andrey suddenly felt himself wavering, he was disconcerted and disorientated. He had never known himself like this. He scared himself like this. He jumped on and off trams, hurried down metro escalators and inter-changes, twice bought ice-cream without thinking and had to throw it away. He'd never eaten the stuff, never.

But this was still not the full measure of the price to be paid

for doubt. Fear raised its ugly head. First came the words:
"Just let them try taking me!" Followed immediately by: "I
won't make it easy for them!" And then the fear came sliding
in like a snake. Fear of being caught stupidly, of giving
up easily. The city became his enemy then. Every passing
pedestrian was a potential enemy. And what could he do here,
in a tram or a metro train, among the crowds at the shop
windows and street crossings? In the city he was in a cage,
though the door was still open, for the time being.

He had to get out. As soon as possible and as far away as
possible. So he could be ready for them at any moment. Go
to the Urals, to his grandfather. They couldn't take him by
surprise there. He could give them a run for their money there.
To the Moscow Station. Now. Before they set up checkpoints.
Before they launched a manhunt. Maybe they already had.
How long could his friends hold out? They wouldn't stand up
to interrogation. How could they against real professionals?

He headed for the metro, then suddenly remembered. No
money. For a moment he was completely lost. Then his
memory began to function. Function creakily, evasively,
conscience-stricken, not firing on all cylinders. He had to dial
the number three times. Fumbled. Or muddled the digits.
Lord, what the hell was up with him!

*　　*　　*

Olga spent the half hour before Andrey arrived torturing the
piano. The ancient upright thundered inelegantly, managing
to sound somehow scared. The racket was audible several
floors above and below.

She was furious with herself. Fury clouded her mind, fury
boiled at her fingertips and spread to the keys. They ran amok,
chords growling, familiar harmonies disintegrating into a howl
of rage.

She hated herself. Despised herself. She was choking with
self-disgust. God! She'd waited so long for that call. She'd

prepared herself for it so carefully. Rehearsed her answers a thousand times, honed her tone of voice, even practised the expression on her face that he wouldn't see. She was ready for that call. There were plenty of calls, and every time she answered, she was primed and ready. So this long-awaited call was not unexpected. But all it took was a tremor in her hand, a noise in her head and a bad line, her having to ask him to repeat something and . . . she lost control!

She was all prepared to annihilate him, immolate him with contempt. She had dreamt of slamming the phone down and deafening him with the number unobtainable signal.

He asked was she going to be at home? She was so upset she hadn't understood. Had to ask him to say it again. He did so and said: "Be round in half an hour." Quite unexpectedly she murmured: "All right."

Arrogant swine! It was almost a year. She could have got married and had a baby. He tells her he's coming round as if he was last at her flat only yesterday. He was certain – would you believe it? – certain she was waiting for him and would keep on waiting. And he could phone when he felt like, one year, two years, ten years later . . . The rat! He was quite capable of phoning her in ten years' time as if nothing had happened and telling her he'd be round in half an hour!

Get out of there! Let him ring that bell till he dropped! She almost flew out of her chair. Mentally she flew out of it, threw on her coat, snapped off the light, slammed the door, dived into the lift, then out into the lobby and into the darkness of the street . . .

But the image of him standing humiliated, downcast at the silent door of the empty flat was too much. She could see him with his back towards her: tall and taciturn, pressing the doorbell . . . but that was all. Not his face, though . . . Doubtless still as brooding, hard and . . . imperious.

Ridiculous. Women have fought for equality, convinced it's as vital as the air they breathe. Then along comes some man (it wouldn't be so bad if it were, as often as not he's no more than a boy), furrows his brow – and breaks her heart.

She hadn't been able to cope with him on the phone. She didn't expect any good to come of their meeting and tried to shut it out of her mind. She felt twisted inside, despising herself, and she was bitter against the entire world, bitter about her own life, bitter about herself and bitter for herself.

The ring at the door sounded unnaturally harsh and loud. She let her head drop onto the keyboard and the piano gave a jangling sigh, reverberating in sympathy for as long as the ring drilled at the door. It stopped and she ran to the door, opened it without a second thought.

He stepped inside . . . the same and not the same . . . He had the same jacket, the same trousers on. She even recognised the shirt. His clothes were clean and ironed, as if he was trying to prove he didn't need a woman. And yet he was changed. In the first few moments she couldn't understand how, precisely. Because she couldn't look him in the eye. When she did, her heart shrank.

His eyes always had been hard, cold and penetrating, a combination that is usually considered a sign of masculinity. She knew Vadim and some others ran after him like puppies. She knew the village wenches always fancied him, as well as city girls jaded with bohemian lovers and out for new kicks.

She would never have fallen in love with him if that had been all she'd ever seen in his eyes. But she was able to catch, she always loved it when she could, a rare, fleeting longing in those demonstratively cold eyes. In a way it was like a new and incoherent tune can sometimes throw up one chord or even one sound, an undertone which suddenly reveals the secret of the melody. And starting from this hint, you gradually begin to sense how the melody harmonises with some no less indefinable mood of your own. You begin to need this music. You want to hear it again and again, because it tells you something about yourself, something you had only the vaguest inkling of. In human relationships it's known as kindred spirits. Kindred does not imply similarity. Similarity grates and repels. This is a contiguity of spirits, contact perhaps not even at the most important points, but certainly on something deeply intimate. And then the miracle happens: two beings as different as heaven and earth are joined forever.

This didn't happen to them. Because only one of them looked into the other's eyes: Olga. And what was even more hurtful, he looked as superficially and carelessly at himself as at other people. He only saw in himself what was obvious at first glance. Was he aware, for example, that when he frowned as per usual, when he was certain that at that particular moment anger was at the heart of his mood, his eyes were often, though not always, sad and did not match his behaviour, his words and gestures? It was as though they were watching everything from the outside, as something irrelevant, alien to them.

And then there was a hunger in his eyes. At those times she felt afraid for him. Or was afraid of him. This fear was undefined, there were no words for it, you couldn't explain it. At moments like that she forgave him everything, taking it all back later when she had forgotten that look of his, forgotten because it was impossible to fix in the memory, because it was only the merest hint of something in this man that was out of her reach and consequently beyond her understanding forever.

He said hello, quietly, drily. He walked in and sat down.

"Coffee?" Olga asked. She needed to gather her thoughts and weigh up the impression he made on her.

"May as well," Andrey answered indifferently.

She went out into the kitchen and watched him as she fussed over the stove. She wasn't afraid he'd catch her at it, because he was sitting in his favourite pose, sprawled in the armchair, staring up into the shade of the table-lamp. He told her once that dark blue had a magical, pleasantly soothing and anaesthetic effect on him.

Though she couldn't see his eyes, she was certain her first impression was right. He had changed. Something had

changed in him. There was nothing to show he was in a bad
way. She didn't even know what "in a bad way" meant for
Andrey. Difficulties at the Institute? Things there didn't
seriously impinge on his life. He never fell out with anybody.
He simply broke with people, crossed them out of his mind.
And if it did upset him, then not very much.

He had been in a bad way once before, when his mother
died. That was a long time ago. Sometimes she felt that it had
become a permanent condition. But he had never, either before
or after her death, said anything except banalities about her.
She couldn't even detect any particular emotion towards her.
But he had been changed ever since. For the worse it seemed
to her. He had his minor troubles, probably. Probably had his
moments of happiness, too. But his outward behaviour was
constant, uniform.

Outwardly everything was as usual today. But she had sensed
right away: something had happened. She even felt that today
he would tell her everything he had been concealing about
himself, everything he had left unspoken. Today she felt their
relationship would take the turn towards mutual understanding
she had been waiting for in vain. Once again she was being
seduced by hope, as though her hatred, bitterness and fury
had never been . . . "Typical female," she sighed.

She poured the coffee and sat down opposite him. He took
a sip and frowned, as he always did when the coffee was too
hot for him. She almost smiled, that involuntary movement of
the brows was so familiar.

He put down his cup, leant back in the armchair and looked
at her for the first time. It would have been better if he hadn't.
That look boded no good. It was one of anxiety – though not
for her sake, alas! Essentially, he wasn't there. The glimmer
of hope died in her and turned into an icicle, into a tiny crystal
that chilled to the marrow.

"I've been a swine to you, I think." He spoke casually, as if
he was talking about the weather or some other such trifle.

"I think you have," she replied, matching his tone and

preparing herself for worse to come, for something really bad. And she had thought she was ready for anything.

"You'd be within your rights to loathe me."

He was giving her permission to hate him and she answered: "Thanks!"

He ignored her sarcasm.

"Still, I've nobody to turn to except you."

He was playing on her affection. A couple of words and again she was full of love and readiness. Even if only to be needed by him like this!

"I have to get away. Today. Only I'm broke."

"How much?" Her reaction was too hasty, but she didn't care, just as long as he didn't need more than she actually had.

He frowned and said nothing.

"How much money do you need?" she asked cautiously and with such sympathy he was actually touched. He even passed his hand across his forehead as if he wanted to check whether the frown had dissolved . . .

"Not a lot. But . . . That's not what bothers me most . . . "

He got up and paced the room. He was nervous, very nervous. She couldn't remember seeing him like that before. What had happened?

"I can't give it you back. Ever . . . "

She didn't understand. The thought flashed through her mind he was trying to cross the border. No, that wasn't like him.

"You're going away for good?" She couldn't conceal her dismay.

"Yes," he snapped, rudely for some reason.

She couldn't understand his tone of voice. She understood only that this was the end and that although she had written off her stupid love as a failure long ago, she turned out to be unprepared for the actual end.

"How much do you need?" she asked again.

He named the amount. She had it. She fetched her bag from

the window-ledge, found her money, counted it and gave it to him.

He muttered his thanks and she realised he was about to leave.

"Wait," she said, though Andrey had as yet done nothing to indicate he was going. She bit her lip. She couldn't let him go. No matter how bad things were with him, they were worse with her. This injustice made her want to share the pain . . . What she said was misjudged . . . "Vadim said you love me . . . "

Andrey started, she even caught a flash of fear in his eyes.

"Vadim? You've seen him? When?"

"He phoned yesterday. Said you'd asked for my number . . . I was waiting . . . "

She shouldn't have said any of this. She walked across and stood next to him. He hung his head. He was thinking about something . . . not her.

"Andrey," she said quietly, tenderly, "do you understand, you're no good?"

He was silent, then answered in a similar tone, without lifting his head. "I can accept that."

"You never loved me and you don't now. Isn't that right?"

He stood up, remote, a stranger. "Olga, that's all completely beside the point now."

"To you it may be. But how about me?"

The look he gave her! Another second and she wouldn't have been able to help herself. But he said: "I must go. I'd like us to part on good terms."

She recoiled. She felt dizzy.

"Don't you think you owe me some kind of explanation. Don't you think I deserve one?"

She didn't recognise her own voice. More of a whimper than anything . . .

"Things are bad? Right? So let's go away together. I can sell the flat. Get right away. Together, though. Wherever you want."

He gave a strange, unpleasant chuckle.

"Yeh, sure, that's one more option. Well, it's not a viable one now, even if before it just wouldn't have been acceptable."

"You know, I had an abortion, Andrey."

Only utter despair could have forced that admission out of her.

"An abortion?" He grabbed her by the shoulders and shook her. "An abortion! You killed my child! You . . . you . . . trash!"

He literally threw her on the floor. It looked as though he was about to start kicking her, but he just kept repeating: "You killed the child! I could have left a son . . . or a daughter . . . You killed it!"

He was looking at her with disgust. She lay there, too scared to move, not even feeling any pain from the blow.

There was such grief written on his face, such enormous grief, that she crawled to him and threw her arms around his legs. She stammered through her tears: "Andrey, I didn't know . . . how could I? . . . you'd gone . . . left me . . . never told me . . . not one word . . . oh, Andrey . . . "

He lifted her up and held her, but his eyes were even more terrible. They were the eyes of a dead man.

"Andrey, we can still have . . . "

"No!" He cut her short, looked at his watch. "I have fifteen minutes. I can't make babies in fifteen minutes!"

"What are you saying?" she screamed, tearing herself free.

"How could you?" His voice was flat.

"Me? How could I? Are you a child or something? You didn't know where children came from? Didn't you ever think that might happen? Did you ever think about me? You can still accuse me? How dare you?"

She collapsed into the armchair, sobbing. The occasional word broke through, but she didn't hear them herself. She was clutching her head, crushing her temples, she was practically beating her head against the arm of the chair, she was choking.

"Go away," she finally gasped. "Go away. I hope you'll be as wretched as you've made me. I do!"

She was blinded by tears and didn't see him come over to the chair on his knees. He kissed her hands, her wet hands and said: "I do love you. I'll come back. We'll start again. It'll be different next time. Forgive me!"

Later, several years later, she would probably think he hadn't been on his knees, hadn't kissed her hands, hadn't said those words, that it had never happened, that he'd left without saying good-bye, and that this final scene was the product of her hysterical imagination, because if it had not been that way, how would she have been able to carry on living.

V

Alone

Russia drifted, floated, flew past the train window and dissolved into the distances.

So resonant a name, resembling a ringing call to arms, seemed ill-suited to this grey and taciturn land. A name which had meant something in the past, meant only very little today and would mean nothing in the future.

Or it was as though two Russias existed. One was in the mind – beautiful and nebulous as a dream, the second was a prototype of a dream with all the attributes of a prototype. Settlements floated by, settlements inhabited by people you thought of almost as foreigners. Hard to believe they even spoke the same language . . . Even more frightening was imagining you were a foreigner yourself, more frightening because it wasn't far wrong.

All his past activities seemed so paltry and pathetic out here, all that heart-searching, all those arguments and principles which had been the cause of making and breaking friendships, of broken lives, for the sake of which lives had been taken.

The railway that runs to the Urals and beyond the Urals to Siberia and beyond Siberia (though it was hard to imagine anything further beyond), this railway seemed like a bottomless well diving into the depths of Russia in time as well as in space. It wasn't kilometres that the train measured out from the centre, it was years, years away from the present to some kind of temporal constant which encompasses before and now and always, but which people from the big cities turn their backs on, so alien is it to them.

In the darkness he had a very real sense he was in a bucket hurtling down a well-shaft, and the clatter of the wheels over the tracks was not what it seemed, but the noise of the crank overhead spooling out an endless rope that only yesterday had held him firm at the top, basking in the sun, and he'd seen himself as strong, useful and in the right, utterly certain he had no need to look down into the darkness of the shaft, because he was bathed in the aura of the significance of all that was below him.

No! That was all nonsense! He'd guessed earlier on there was no meaningful link between his life and the destiny of that entity called Russia. The only explanation for this was that the existence of one of those two was meaningless. But the consequence was the recognition that he'd been feverishly tilting at windmills and so lost the right to order not only his own life, but also his death . . . Because it meant one thing: he did not understand Russia. He'd been in a hurry, cobbled some wings together, turned into some kind of dinosaur capable of one thing only – biting, and dying to the sound of its own jaws snapping.

Outside the train window Russia flashed past, Russia – so diverse, yet monotonous to the point of despair. Russia, in which Tyutchev said one could "only believe" without wasting time on comprehending it rationally. But the only thing incomprehensible rationally is the irrational. There had to be some kind of meaning in the meaninglessness of the last fifty years. That called for real inspiration, though. After all, each of us has only one short life, which we cling to. And he, Andrey, had bartered it away for a folly to which nobody, alas, was likely to subscribe. On reflection, the folly of the brave was no more than the bravery of fools. And to be brutally honest, how could he fail to recognise that by rising with a pistol against the hundred-headed hydra, he displayed a bravery born of desperation, of powerlessness, of fear of his incapacity to achieve anything greater than folly?

All the same. He had chipped off a tiny, minuscule piece of the iniquity that cemented this society together and caused some, even if minimal, discomfiture to this hydra that purred with smugness. He had stirred one square centimetre at least of the surface of this infinite swamp, at the price of the thing he held most dear – his life. The scale of the wager justified the senselessness, did it not?

And so he wanted to shoot and keep on shooting, for the rattle of gunfire to go on and on, to see confusion and fear written on men's faces that had frozen into unthinking masks, that were blank with indifference. He wanted to see buses career across pavements in a spray of breaking glass, to see polished armoured limousines overturn and the passengers come crawling out, the men who a minute earlier had been keeping people down on their knees. He wanted city avenues to be turned into ear-splitting blind alleys and in one of those blind alleys he, Andrey, would be there, pistol in hand, supported on his right and left by his comrades, full of joy and passion, with their banner . . . a red banner . . .

Andrey couldn't think why it had to be red, but he couldn't see it any other way . . . and he groaned loudly in his sleep, so loudly his neighbour on the top bunk, a soldier on leave, gently shook his shoulder.

*　　　*　　　*

His seventy-year-old grandfather couldn't fathom what particular piece of good fortune had made God send him the grandson he had given up all hope of ever seeing. He fussed about the house, talking to himself, oohing and ahing, overcome with joy at the sight of the handsome boy who looked so like the fairhaired soldier in the photograph on the wall with a St George's Cross pinned to his tunic. That was him fifty years ago when the village girls used to fall at his feet like the grass at mowing. Educated young ladies, all lace and white skin, went weak at the knees if he as much as winked, and plump widows sighed, the regret plain in their eyes. And when General Brusilov, no less, was inspecting the regiment, he stopped opposite him and clapped him on the shoulder. Well, he might be wrong about Brusilov, but a general it was, that he was certain!

When they finally sat down at table on their own (Andrey asked him not to invite anybody in) and had drunk each other's health, the words didn't come. So they immediately poured another one. They drank to the dead, Andrey's mother and grandmother, who never saw her grandson grown to a man. The old man's eyes were glistening. Andrey's, too. After the third, it was a different matter. The old man mellowed, started reminiscing about the Civil War, about the storming of Buguruslan, how he was wounded, hospitals . . . Then how the peasants had been given the land, how they'd divided it up gingerly, it was other people's property, after all . . . The first harvest from that land! How they'd saddled the horses and gone to town on a spree, the village girls dressed to kill . . . And how their good fortune ebbed away as the 'twenties drew to a close, sailors and factory workers with guns in their belts started appearing in the countryside. Collectivisation. The earth wept, the cattle that had grown strong and multiplied wept . . . How their homes were gutted and stripped, carts of wailing women and babes creaking down the back roads, kulaks! And then they began building socialism, the dream of all mankind, of course, only it's built by the sweat of the peasant's brow. How nobody cared any more, and young people had no respect for the land, no sense of responsibility.

How could they have an interest in it if they'd never set eyes on money or an internal passport? People have been pushed here, pulled there, they've forgotten the land has to be cared for. Turned the churches into farm buildings – no such thing as God, they say, not according to science!

"Do you believe in God?" Andrey asked.

"I'm not so sure but that He is there, and I've got my reasons for thinking that. Not that you'd understand."

"What are your reasons?" Andrey persisted.

"For a start, who had it in for the kulaks most? There were two brothers. Sanka and Pashka Kryukov their names were. I'm talking about people from hereabouts, because the place was crawling with outsiders, I can tell you. They were wild, those two. Liked a scrap. Came back from the Civil War Party members. Strutted about the village, poking their noses into everybody's business. So what happened? Kuzma Bannikov put a bullet in Sanka, and Pashka's own people informed on him. They sent him north and he never came back. Now after Kuzma Bannikov did Sanka in, he slipped back home through the back gardens, his own back garden mark you, and went headfirst down an old well. Never felt a thing. Smashed his head in on a rock. See, wrongdoing gets paid back. And how can that be if there isn't a God? Don't tell me Kuzma didn't know his own garden. Killed one of his own and it clouded his mind."

"Yes, but the other man probably deserved it."

"Did he ever! He was as wild as they come. Nobody was sorry. But killing one of your own is all wrong. In the dark, like a poacher. Bang, and get out of there quick. Things were never like that here. And for somebody to end up at the bottom of his own well, that's never been heard of, either. So what I think, sonny, is that there is somebody up above watching our souls, and he'll take you by the scruff if need be . . . There's a limit to doing just as you please!"

"And is there a limit to infamy? What about that?" Andrey interjected sullenly.

"Takes all sorts to make a world," his grandfather reflected sadly. "There's sorrow, and suffering, and sickness . . . But man's been given a cure that's stronger than all of them – patience."

"I see," Andrey snapped, "God turns the other cheek and we're supposed to do the same."

"Let me give you a piece of advice, sonny. Handy advice." The grandfather shifted his chair closer to Andrey and poured out homebrew vodka from a flask. They'd finished Andrey's bottle. He leant sideways, balancing his glass. "Don't blaspheme. It gives you no pleasure. And you never know, maybe He is out there somewhere . . . "

He jabbed the glass upwards, splashing vodka. Andrey looked up at the ceiling.

"There's nobody up there. Dead, empty space."

"How do you know? Have to look inside, see right through if you . . . "

"What?" Andrey slurred uncomprehendingly.

"Inside, I said. You? What are you? A beast with two legs and two arms. And if you look inside?"

"Guts, grandad, that's what's inside!"

Andrey clinked glasses with his grandfather and drank. He pulled a face and chewed a piece of last season's salted cabbage. His grandfather looked at him, disappointed.

"Educated you may be, but you're still daft. Cut a man in half and you'll see his guts all right. But it's not those innards I mean. Inside you there's a soul, and there's no blade can touch that."

"And if you put a sword into a man's guts, what's left of his soul?"

Andrey winked cheerfully at his grandfather, steering him away from a tedious topic of conversation. That wasn't so easy.

"Let's say somebody gets on your nerves. You do him in. He's lying there in front of you, dead as a doornail. He's all yours. You've taken his strength. But what about his soul? Have you got his soul? Never."

"Potent stuff this, grandad."

The old man was delighted.

"Not bad, eh? Drip a bit more through tomorrow. Wasn't expecting company, was I?"

Suddenly the old man was tearful.

"Your mum, my little girl, God rest her soul . . . good as gold she was, but hard hearted. Who ever heard of hiding a grandchild from the old folk? She was ashamed of us, ashamed because we were ignorant. Didn't understand all our learning was in our hands. The old lady had a hard time bringing her into the world and God never sent us any more children. You might say we spent our whole lives without children. She sent news of herself with the money orders. She was always good with the money. Never missed. People used to envy us. The old lady, though, used to cry every time the money came . . . Soft, she was . . . "

He wiped his eyes on his sleeve. Andrey embraced him. "Don't judge your own daughter too harshly, grandad. She was unhappy."

The old man jerked upright, startled.

"I wasn't judging anybody. And was she so unhappy? Depends how you look at it. She had her faith, it was her whole life, and people with faith are never unhappy. God give you a faith like that."

"What faith?" Andrey yelled. "In what my mother believed in? In who she believed in? In that bandit?"

"Steady on, steady on," said his grandfather, bridling. "Watch what you're saying. He might have been many things, but things were tidy when he was around. People knew their place. People need a firm hand. We're without it now and there's nobody to work the land. Everyone's off on his own little . . . Do as they please!"

Andrey gritted his teeth, buried his head between his fists.

"Grandad, what are you saying? Tidy! Things were tidy when they were turning you upside down and inside out. You know about the prisons and the camps. A bandit was in power for thirty years. A bandit! A bandit who kept things tidy. And they were bandit laws. Grandad, you were stripped clean as a whistle. You were draught animals for him and his gang!"

"Cut that out!" Andrey's grandfather glared at him from under his brows. "Some folks may have been, but not us. We fed Russia. Things weren't perfect, but where are they ever? In America, maybe? Neither you nor I've ever been there, so we don't know what misfortunes they've got to put up with. A bandit, you say? And who was it denounced me as a kulak in 'thirty? Stalin? No, my neighbour. Proshka Fedotov. You know what for? Because I'd had a few and gave him a clip with some reins. What'd Stalin to do with it? And taking the geese and chickens. Was there a law about that? No. But our activists whipped my old lady's cockerel right from under her skirts. And who was it gave them what for? You know who? Nikita from the village Soviet. Took to drink, he did, died from it, and before that he'd go swaggering about the village, waving his gun and cursing between his teeth. I tell you: if every person held back from his own bit of wickedness, there'd be half the misfortunes there are now."

"Is that all you remember?" Andrey felt numb with despair.

His grandfather took offence.

"What I remember is more than'll fit in your head. They gave you freedom to talk, and there's nobody left to work the land. Nobody wants to dirty their hands."

He grumbled on. Andrey sat, his head wrapped in his arms, and rocked from side to side. He looked so miserable, it stopped his grandfather short. He blinked in confusion, fidgeted on his chair.

"Don't take on now. If I've said something I shouldn't, don't take it to heart. Don't be hard on me. My life's done with and we all think our own is something special . . . Come on, eh, sonny?"

He grabbed Andrey's glass, filled it, and gently tugged at his grandson's sleeve. "Let's have a drink, eh?"

Andrey raised his head and turned to his grandfather. He looked into the colourless, tearful eyes, tried to read something unwitting and unaffected in them, something he felt must be there. He saw only old age. That, and a craving for human affection. He remembered the look in Olga's eyes and was surprised that it could be the same in somebody young and somebody old . . .

He hugged his grandfather so tightly you could almost hear the bones snap. His grandfather appeared hardly to notice and sank onto his grandson's shoulder. The old man was too moved to speak. He picked at Andrey's sleeve and wheezed into his ear.

They drank what was left, and only then did they set to the food which the old man had hastily prepared – cabbage, potatoes, cucumbers and salt fish of an indeterminate type. Several times the grandfather tried to apologise for the meagreness of the fare, but Andrey's busy chewing was proof, to the old man's delight, of his genuine pleasure and of a healthy young appetite that required simple and abundant fare. Then, surrendering to the alcohol, they tried to sing, only Andrey couldn't follow his grandfather's lead in anything except "Over the Wild Steppes Beyond Baikal", and then only for one verse . . .

The grandfather was ready to let the meal run on indefinitely, but Andrey felt so wretched he was forced to disappoint the old man and asked to retire to the barn, even though a wonderful, luxurious night's rest had been made ready in the ancient marital feather bed.

*   *   *

It was still quite light, though the sun was down. A wonderful view over the expanses of the Urals opened up from the loft looking into the sunset. The road from town zigzagged towards the village, dropped down into the broad street, hugged the bank of a sluggish stream, looped through the sparse woodland alongside it before finally disappearing in the darkness of the distant forests.

After a few drinks, it was easy to imagine yourself flying low over the earth. Looking ahead into the glow of the setting sun, it seemed to be coming closer and closer and in a few moments you'd have caught it up and broken through into day . . . But the day was retreating westwards, to where Andrey was running from, from where he was expecting the final show-down. Why not reckon all that had happened so far to have been a dream and calculate his awakening from the moment he lay in his bed of hay and watched the sunset? . . . He had slept through an entire day . . . Think up a reason why . . . Because he'd spent the whole night with a girl. With Olga. Olga didn't live in the city, she lived in a wooden house with painted fretwork at the far end of the village. And she wasn't a pianist, she was . . . the village librarian. She could be a milkmaid, but better a librarian . . . There was no city. His mother was still alive. She was over in the house, cooking the evening meal and she'd call him in any moment now. And he wasn't a student. He drove a tractor or a truck. A few days ago Olga lent him out a historical novel about the People's Will organisation, about an attempt on the Tsar's life. Afterwards he'd had this dream in which he'd had the star part. A lifetime packed into a couple of hours, the mental anguish of a whole generation. He'd taken on the State and he was doomed to die in an unequal and senseless struggle. But he'd woken up. And though the nightmare still continued to trouble him, his mind was already clear and at ease.

He was no hero, no freedom fighter. He was an ordinary village lad whose days passed sensibly and happily. His entire life was indissolubly bound up with these woods, with this sunset and the soft, vibrant scents of the earth. He was a necessary part of the landscape, everything responded with understanding and familiarity, and when he woke in the morning he greeted the world, challenged it as a friend and equal with a wink and a flourish of fists. And his every movement and gesture had a meaning that harmonised with the meaning of the world.

Instead of walking down the steps from the loft, he jumped the three metres and ran to the well. Splashed himself with icy water, gasping for breath, his body suddenly taut. Wiped himself down with a shaggy towel, tossed it around his shoulders and strode into the house to be met by his mother, young, pretty and strict. She told him off for keeping irregular hours and shooed him away to get dressed. When he sat down at table, she came up behind him and threw her arms round his shoulders. Her hand suddenly encountered something hard on his chest. She looked at him in alarm and he, no less alarmed, pulled a gun from his jacket pocket . . . He saw the terror in her eyes, she fell sprawling to the ground. Andrey could tell it was a stroke . . .

*   *   *

It was around five a.m. of the third day after his arrival. Andrey was woken by an odd noise. He lifted his head and glanced at his watch, then slid to the edge of the loft. A car was turning off the street into a narrow lane between the back gardens. It crawled behind some tall fencing. Stopped. The engine died. Four men emerged and moved in single file in his direction. Two houses away they split up. Two came straight on, the two others ducked away through the gardens. They came in through the gate of the nearest house, then made a dash, hurdling over garden fences, towards his grandfather's house.

"Didn't take them long to catch up with me," mused Andrey, and that, seemingly, was his only thought. His mind was blank. He felt a deep melancholy. The gun was already in his hand. He had reached for it instinctively. The men coming straight for him were at the gates now. They were out of Andrey's sight. The latch was raised and hung in that position a second or two. There was a creak of hinges and the gate swung inwards. The two men came into the yard. He could have shot at them from above quite easily, but for some reason he decided against shattering the peace of the morning, as if to do so would have been the most hideous crime. Also he hadn't been discovered yet and he desperately wanted not to lose this doubtful advantage.

Then he imagined his grandfather's face as he was suddenly woken. The thought was like a slap in the face. Why had he come here? Another idiocy in the senseless chain of his activities. This one bordered on treachery. Now, even if a miracle did happen, he did not want to live.

The two were already knocking at the porch door. After all last night's drink, his grandfather was no doubt sound asleep. Andrey looked through a chink in the roof at the other end of the loft and saw the other men coming through the back garden. Saw them for an instant before they went behind the house, dodging the windows. He went back for his gun, slipped the safety catch, leant out of the loft and called loudly: "What do you want?"

His shout had the effect of a kick up the backside on the two men at the house. They spun round, guns at the ready. Smaller than his. One of them called his name.

"That's me."

"Drop your gun. You're surrounded. Come down."

The *Chekist* didn't sound too confident. He was the one Andrey was aiming at.

"I'll surrender on one condition," Andrey called calmly. "You go back to your vehicle quietly. I'll follow you!"

"Stop playing the fool," the second snarled. "Throw out the gun and come down!"

As he spoke he made an odd gesture with his left hand. Andrey understood what it meant a second later when he heard a rustle on the far side of the loft. They were coming at him from behind. The staircase was on that side. Andrey half turned and fired in its direction. He was deafened by the shot. It was so loud, sharp and sudden. The pair at the door ducked

behind the house and at the same time two shots forced Andrey
back into the darkness of the loft.

"If it's noise you want . . . " Andrey thought and shouted,
firing in both directions.

The shots didn't seem like thunder any more. He liked the
sound now. But he remembered he only had three rounds left
and there were four of them, and the awareness that he was
powerless against four brought a deep sadness and regret about
wasted ammunition . . . He became suddenly almost feline.
He slunk from one end of the barn to the other, trying to
glimpse his enemy through chinks in the roof, but without
success. However, he could see people crouched on the porch
of the house opposite, indeed in every part of the street that
was visible. Curiosity had got the better of sleep and fear. He
also saw his grandfather come running towards the house. He,
apparently, had been up some time and gone off somewhere,
and now he was running for home, his legs twisting and
stumbling.

When he reached the gateway one of the *Chekists* darted out
in front of him, grabbed his arms, and to make a pretence of
not using the old man purely for cover, dragged him away to
one side, waving his pistol in his free hand and shouting: "Get
inside. All of you. Inside. There's an armed criminal in there.
Back inside!"

He shot in the air above his hostage's ear. The old man's
legs buckled and he slumped back against the *Chekist*, who
dragged him off behind the house, still using his body as cover.

Andrey leant out and shouted: "Leave my grandad alone,
you bastard. Don't you dare."

His grandfather saw him. His jaw dropped and he stared in
disbelief. He suddenly made a grab for the hand holding the
pistol, and before he disappeared from view, Andrey saw his
grandfather double up from a blow in the stomach . . .

The bystanders did disperse, only to regroup here and there.
The ones who caught a glimpse of the fugitive pointed at him,
shouted, and darted for safety before coming back out again.

"This is your last chance. Surrender. We'll get you anyway!"

Andrey couldn't help himself. He shot at the voice. His fire was returned. Andrey shouted: "Listen, you swine. You're used to people crawling to you. You're used to trapping people like mice. You try taking me. I'm the first to start shooting. There'll be more. They'll blow you up, run you over, push you under trains. You're the criminals. They'll teach you what fear is, you bastards!"

While he was shouting, the thought of surrendering stole through his mind. There'd be a trial. They were bound to sentence him to death, but at the trial he'd tell them what he knew and thought of them. Somebody would be at the trial. Someone would remember what he said.

But then he remembered what he'd been told by a survivor, a man who had in his time been a client of the Lieutenant-Colonel from Lembolovo and been under sentence of death.

Andrey imagined the handcuffs being snapped on his wrists when sentence was pronounced and being taken to the death cells. They'd suggest he ask for clemency. What if he couldn't stand the fear of dying and broke? But even if he did hold out, he'd be brought out, they'd read him the sentence, maybe they wouldn't – just shoot him in the back of the head and then calmly put a second bullet through the temple to be certain, the doctor would pull back his eyelids and sign the death certificate.

No! He wouldn't give them the satisfaction. Andrey crawled to the edge of the loft. He had one spare bullet. At least take one of them with him. He was suddenly scared. There'd be one bullet left. What if he only wounded himself? No, he couldn't risk that. And what real difference would one swine less make? Out of so many. Senseless!

He began whispering the names of all those dear to him, fearful he would leave somebody out. Grandad, Olga, Kostya, Vadim, Pavel, Kolya, his mother . . . mother . . . Now his memory began to slip, and his mother's face blotted out all the other faces and he couldn't remember anybody else. And the word "mother" rang in his brain despite himself, his lips whispered it, echoing his thought over and over, he even saw the word written up in big letters on a school blackboard and on paper, and as separate letters, hanging in the air . . .

He put the pistol muzzle in his mouth, but it was repulsive – the taste of burnt gunpowder, the metal hot and sour. He felt sick. He spat out the barrel and put it to his temple, but the image of his smashed and disfigured skull made him heave. He was frightened he might lose consciousness. Then he pointed the pistol at himself, put it to where he could feel his heartbeat, leant his weight against the gun so it wouldn't jerk away when he fired. He held the gun in his left hand, put his finger on the trigger and stayed like that for a minute or more, his mind a blank, empty of thought. And only when he felt certain he was prepared for the void before him, pulled the trigger.

As he removed the spent round from the gun, the *Chekist* was surprised to see the remaining bullet. He turned to his colleague: "Why do you reckon he left one bullet?"

The other didn't even bother to look round.

"Forgot he had it, I suppose."

THE VISIT

A DOCUMENT CAME into my possession recently. Its author was reputedly a provincial priest who died only last year. The document is so extraordinary, I felt unable to pass it on to anybody else, but it was equally impossible to remain silent. I decided to be devious. I wrote a story. And by doing so relieved myself of all responsibility.

*   *   *

The service in the village church had finished an hour ago, but Father Venyamin had only just left for home. He'd been discussing an important matter with one of his parishioners – the rebuilding of the church fence. The existing one, which had been up for longer than anyone could remember and been patched and re-patched, was rotten beyond repair. The discussion had been about posts and palings, about paint, in other words which colour was fitting for God's house. Pale blue, of course. But the shops only stocked red and yellow. They would have to pay over the odds. Father Venyamin stroked his beard, the peasant scratched the back of his head. Finally, they struck the best possible bargain: the posts and such would come for nothing, while they'd have to allow a bit extra for the paint and the palings. It was a deal.

The bargaining over, Father Venyamin was still in no hurry to go home.

We all know how it is: you do something, then find more things to do, keep busy, knowing that once on your own you will be besieged by melancholy thoughts, thoughts that will nag you till cockcrow.

The priest, however, was in his seventies. He knew from experience that melancholy had to be properly identified if it was not to lurk as an ill-defined torment in the soul. Understanding melancholy meant finding its source, and the source was always a concrete instance of some kind and every such instance has its own little shelf where it can be tucked away forgotten.

As soon as he arrived home and studied the ikons, he recalled the source of his melancholy. It was the face of a young man who had come to the church today at the beginning of the service and stood by the door to the very end, without crossing himself once. Then left without crossing himself. What had he read in the young man's face? For Father Venyamin that face held a memory. Many years ago, in his younger days, he had known faces like that, Russian faces, with suffering in their eyes. Those faces then began to disappear from Russia. The ones which replaced them weren't necessarily beardless, beards were not the point, they were simply different faces and they spoke a different language, in which the words were either barbed or spoken through gritted teeth. And that was the end of the old Russia. It was like living under a foreign heel. There were good Christians who didn't abandon the faith, but the Russian radiance left their faces, too, and there was only fear, despair and the pain of the godforsaken written there.

Father Venyamin had passed through schism and prison and survived by a miracle. He had brought God's word to people, like the cross the priest holds up to the prisoner condemned to die.

The priest had grown used to the idea that Russia was finished. But now, fifty years on, after all that had happened, he suddenly began to recognise familiar faces here and there.

He studied them with surprise and anxiety. At first he had always felt let down, for they gave the impression of being a mask, Russian faces rented for the day, ignorant of everything truly Russian.

One day he saw two young men in town. Chestnut beards, blue eyes, sensitive hands, standing aside from the crowd, talking heatedly. Father Venyamin tried to guess what it was they were discussing. The meaning of life? God? The ideal woman, perhaps? He came closer, and it was as if they had spat on all that was sacred! They were talking about hockey. They had the faces of Alyosha Karamazov and were discussing hockey!

And yet. And yet it was a sign. Perhaps the Russian faces would come first, to be followed by Russian souls.

Today one of these new young men had stood through the entire service at Father Venyamin's church. He had taken a good look at him. There was no sign of faith in the boy's eyes, but there wasn't that militant emptiness, either. Which meant there was something there. And that "something" was the cause of Father Venyamin's melancholy. Those eyes, he reflected, really belonged to a man behind bars or the incurably sick or someone who has lost the thing he values most in life . . . He felt he ought to pray for those eyes, ask the Lord to deliver them from pain and sorrow, felt he ought to do something himself to help, to relieve, to alleviate. He knew he would spend the night in prayer and tears, and he had a conviction that his prayer would of a certainty be heard.

Father Venyamin prepared his supper mechanically, frying eggs and making a cup of tea, and when he was sitting at the table, about to say grace, he heard a knock at the door. He was surprised, he had not been expecting company. His surprise was the greater when, on opening the door, he saw the person who had been at the centre of his thoughts.

"May I? I haven't disturbed you?" The young man sounded uncertain, hesitated to cross the threshold.

"Certainly not," Father Venyamin replied. "I was about to

eat on my own. The Lord has sent me a guest and I am very glad. Come in."

The young man stepped through the lobby into the room. He didn't ask a blessing or cross himself in front of the ikons. It was as if he knew he ought to, but deliberately chose not to do so in order to stress his attitude and avoid any ambiguity. His manner was unaffected. He sat gladly to table, and while he refused any eggs, he drank tea with pleasure, out of a saucer, holding it in both hands like his host, as though re-enacting an ancient custom.

They sat opposite each other, looking at each other and smiling, each perhaps at his own thoughts, but an intimacy of some kind was undoubtedly born. At the same time, though, a vague sense of alarm crept into the priest's heart.

"My name is Aleksey," the visitor said at last. "I've known about you for a long time. My aunt told me a lot of good things about you. She lives in the next village and comes to your church."

Father Venyamin sat silent. He sipped his tea and looked at his visitor.

"I've come to you for help, Father . . . Though I'm almost certain it's not within your power to help me . . . All the same, I've come . . . I had to try, didn't I?"

"Of course," the priest agreed.

He could feel the young man was finding it hard to begin. It wasn't the words he was searching for, but the form of words, as if he wanted to say very little himself, yet obtain an answer to the most fundamental questions. Father Venyamin did not hurry him, nor did he encourage him to be frank. He knew that people open their hearts either out of need or out of faith. His guest was without faith. So it had to be need . . . He would open up.

"Probably I'll tell you everything," the visitor went on. "Probably. But not immediately. To begin with I'd like your answer to one question, one which is a very important one to me. And I beg you, don't hurry to answer. I have a training in philosophy and I am familiar with theology. The standard textbook answer won't do. I want to know what you think personally. You've been through a lot. I need an honest answer from a man who has seen life. Treat it as though my life depends on the sincerity of your reply."

Father Venyamin was much troubled. "You may be certain I won't lie to you, no matter what the question. And should you really let your life depend on the sincerity of any person, even a priest? It is so very hard, after all, for one person to understand another. And if I have understood you right, you want to ask me something it will not be easy to speak about?"

The young man was somewhat abashed. "Well, I was overdoing it, I suppose. Essentially, my question . . . I mean . . . I could ask any priest . . . but knowing you by reputation, I felt more like . . . "

He was suddenly tongue-tied.

"Well, when you do give me an answer, please bear in mind I'm not a believer and what I've already told you. It's very important to me."

He was silent, then fired his question: "What's a miracle, Father?"

The priest was taken aback.

"A miracle? But . . . You're placing me in an impossible situation. You ask what a miracle is and say you're not a believer. So how can I answer you? You see, to me a miracle is the manifestation of Our Lord's existence, a sign of His presence in the world . . . if we're talking about so-called supernatural phenomena . . . But to me, believe me, all God's creation is a miracle. You find that hard to understand, but look at the world through the eyes of a child or as an alien would, then every bug, all human life, it's all a miracle, and nothing can be explained without God . . . "

The priest watched the sparkle go out of the young man's eyes and stopped in full flow.

"No. That's not it. Not it at all," the visitor mumbled. Suddenly he jerked, his whole body convulsed in a kind of spasm. He saw the alarm on the priest's face and muttered, embarrassed.

"It's nothing . . . I'll explain later . . . it happens every so often . . . "

Only then did Father Venyamin notice there was something unusual about the young man's appearance, about his manner, his posture, the way he sat. Hard to define precisely what. Was he ill, perhaps?

Now the young man was sitting sideways, gripping the back of the chair, and the tension both in his hands and his face was palpable.

"That's not what I wanted to hear from you," the visitor said, pulling a face.

"What did you want?" asked the priest, thinking what a thorough waste of time this was.

"You must at some time, you personally, I mean, you've seen a lot in your lifetime, you must have witnessed a miracle yourself, surely? A genuine miracle."

"No," the priest replied.

"And yet you believe in miracles?"

"I find it hard to answer you, young man. If I were to tell you that the resurrection of Our Lord Jesus Christ, His life, His death, that this was the supreme miracle, testified to by the apostles, you would not be convinced by my answer. Maybe after this sublime moment people were utterly unworthy of God's attention, since there was now so much to bear witness to. But that is merely my own opinion, sinner that I am. The Lord is infinitely merciful. And the miracles which happen to people are the manifestations of the goodness, the mercy, the fullness of love of God's heart. And may the one who rejects it find forgiveness . . . " Here he stopped and looked uncomprehendingly at the young man. "But . . . if you do not believe in God, even miracles do not exist. So why . . . "

"I believe in miracles, Father. Or at least I admit the existence of miracles."

"Impossible! Without God, what kind of a miracle could it

be? If we are surrounded by matter, by matter and strict causality, where can a miracle spring from? If you recognise the existence of miracles, it presupposes the existence of at least some kind of power, some kind of origin for the miracle . . . "

"Meaning," the visitor interjected with a certain malice, "one must presuppose the miracle has a cause, yet what were you saying a moment ago about causality? Tell me."

"Don't try to trip me up. That's not good. You know what I mean, you understand my train of thought." Father Venyamin was not so much offended as disappointed.

"Of course I do. But the whole point is that certain phenomena are possible which violate causality. Is such a viewpoint tenable?"

"Certainly," the priest replied calmly. "But you will not find the answer to your question and you will not be satisfied. An answer of that sort does not solve the question, it raises endless new ones."

"But doesn't the hypothesis of God generate doubts and an endless number of questions?"

The priest was silent for a little while, and when he spoke again he chose his words carefully.

"To see God as a hypothesis is the lot of the stiff-necked and proud. It is not faith that gives birth to doubt, but our weakness, our sinfulness, our inability to follow the path of faith. But faith is tested by doubt. Tried and tested. The vanquishing of doubt is a great joy which the godless can never know . . . " Father Venyamin suddenly felt that he was growing tired, that his words were feeble and unconvincing. "Do you not think, Alyosha, that we are discussing a topic on which, as you said, your mind is made up. I cannot get to the heart of your question. I can only speak of miracles as a Divine Manifestation, and you do not believe in God. How can I help you? Try to find the answer in science . . . "

Aleksey snorted sarcastically: "Unfortunately science is even less help!"

As he spoke, he jerked again. His face contorted. It was a

grimace of annoyance, however, rather than pain . . . He stood up and staggered across to the window. He gripped the windowsill with his left hand and the window latch with his right, standing in profile to the priest.

"Nobody can help me," he whispered with a kind of melancholy despair.

"Are you ill?" Father Venyamin asked hesitantly.

"Ill? I wish I knew what was wrong with me myself."

"I don't understand . . . " the priest murmured. His attention was riveted by his visitor's face. He was obviously in despair, but he did not look sick in the usual sense. What then?

It was Aleksey who broke the silence: "Where were we? Ah, yes . . . God as hypothesis . . . So, you believe miracles are in all cases a manifestation of God?"

"That's right," the priest answered reluctantly.

"If that is the case, there is meaning of a sort in every miracle? A kind of intimation?"

"Precisely. Why should God manifest Himself, unless to give a sign? However, God manifests Himself without imposing His presence, without imposing His will."

"I don't understand." Aleksey spoke nervously, hastily.

"A person who is obstinate in his unbelief cannot be helped even by a miracle. That is what I believe."

"And what if he isn't obstinate? If he wants to believe?"

"He will believe," Father Venyamin answered with conviction.

Now the visitor was smiling. It was a smile partly of condescension, partly of regret.

"Well, Father, what if you saw a man walking on water? How would you react to that?"

"I would go down on my knees in joy and give thanks to the Lord God for His grace . . . "

He was cut short by laughter, rude, cynical laughter. But the priest did not even have time to take offence. His visitor suddenly lifted away from the window, just as he was, standing, upright, and slowly floated towards the ceiling. Now the laughter fell on the priest from above, words fell, interspersed with laughter: "Well now, Father, go down on your knees and give thanks!"

At this the visitor swivelled to a horizontal position, reached out his arms and with his fingers outspread floated at the priest, laughing wildly.

Father Venyamin came to on his bed in the corner, brought round by the touch of something cold on his forehead. Aleksey was holding a wet towel to his head. He looked scared and there were tears, yes, tears in his eyes. They were the first thing the priest saw.

"You're alive! Thank God. Forgive me, please, if you can bring yourself to. It was a rotten thing to do. Forgive me, I beg you. Do you feel better now?"

"What was that?" The priest's question was barely audible. He was white.

"I'll explain. I should have told you everything. But it all came out stupid and wrong . . . "

"Are you a hypnotist? Have you come to make fun of me?"

"No. Word of honour, no. I'll explain. Now. Believe me, I didn't want it to happen like that. You had me frightened, you went so pale . . . Water?"

"Please . . . "

Father Venyamin closed his eyes, but immediately seized Aleksey's arm.

"Was it a hallucination or were you really flying?"

"I'll fetch some water . . . "

The visitor still sounded rather scared and ashamed, but as he rushed out to fetch water, it seemed to the priest the young man's feet were not touching the floor. When Aleksey came back with a dipper of water, Father Venyamin was on the verge of passing out again. He gulped down the water, his eyes closed. Then he groaned: "What was it you were going to tell me? Please. I'll lie here . . . Draw up a chair and sit next to me . . . And tell me . . . "

It wasn't that easy to begin, apparently, and the first sentences came rather haltingly, but only the first few. After that the confession began to flow.

"I graduated in philosophy . . . I was about to carry on as a postgraduate . . . Do you have any idea how tempting philosophy is, Father? The word itself is full of mystery. And the names of the great exponents have a magnificent ring – Hegel, Kant, Plato, Fichte. They don't mean anything now . . . But there was a time the mere mention of those names made me go weak at the knees. And the excitement when you begin to get into the thinking of a great philosopher, as if you've had to go through the whole process with him! You feel so proud. But that's nothing. Now when you spot the first slip-up, the first tiny flaw in the logic of a great philosopher you've spent years trying to understand, that really does something for your ego. Later on, when you're able to form your own opinion of the greats, you don't even want to share it with anybody, you feel so pleased with yourself. A lot of people are perfectly satisfied with that and stop there. They go on to make a career as nit-picking commentators, but they never make philosophers. I didn't want to stop, only something else happened: I suddenly felt it was all a sham . . . There are as many philosophies as there are people. Every one of them is right in so far as that is how the world appears to that individual . . . You won't find truth in philosophy, only more or less talented insights, original constructs . . . nothing more. And that's it! How to put it? . . . just walls . . . partitions . . . labyrinths . . . but no roof . . . there's no actual building. In the sense of a truth . . . " He broke off. "I'm rambling, I know. But I have to say it, believe me . . . "

The priest seized his hand. "Speak. There's no need for explanations. Speak!"

"It was then I became interested in religion. It was fashionable to wear a crucifix, have ikons . . . I read the Gospels and told myself I'd found what it was I'd been looking for. Here was a wisdom I could feel, even though it was beyond my powers to grasp intellectually. It was beyond my capabilities.

I realised that for the rest of my life I could absorb this wisdom a bit at a time, more than enough for one lifetime. And if there is such a possibility – to comprehend the ultimate wisdom – does that leave room for anything else in your life? At that point I declared myself to be a believer."

"Declared?" Father Venyamin echoed in surprise. "Hadn't you actually found faith, since you had come to the understanding that there is no greater wisdom?"

Aleksey smiled involuntarily.

"I declared I had found faith. I thought that to recognise Christianity's truthfulness and to believe in God amounted to the same thing."

"But isn't that the case?" asked the priest in astonishment.

"Certainly. Yet on the other hand, you might see Christianity as no more than a coded philosophy for preserving the human race we acquired, for example, from intellectually superior aliens from outer space."

"Yes," the priest concurred sadly, "people are prepared to believe anything except the plain, obvious truth."

"The obvious is a subjective category . . . " the young man began, and then fell silent. A moment later he continued: "So I became a believer. Grew a beard, stopped smoking, stopped fornicating . . . With my philosophical baggage I became something of a guru in my circle of friends. I started going to church, of course, and even began observing the fasts . . . Then a month ago . . . "

"Please could you fetch me some more water." The priest drank. His hands were shaking visibly and the pallor seemed to have returned to his face. "Well . . . I'm listening. Carry on."

"You probably think it happened while I was praying or meditating or reading the Scriptures. Actually I was lying on the beach, my mind was a blank, no thoughts of any kind, sacred or profane . . . I went to stand up, pushed my hands into the sand and suddenly I felt I was suspended above it . . . four centimetres or so . . . I didn't dare breathe, just thought, and I lifted a bit more. I went dizzy, in other words roughly the same happened to me as happened to you half an hour ago. I passed out. Only for a second or two. And when I came round, I knew, I had this physical sense that I could rise in the air without the slightest effort. And God didn't even enter my mind, remember that, Father. It was incredible . . . I resisted the temptation to try it again, pulled on my clothes, jumped onto a bus . . . It was full but not packed, and I pressed my legs together and hung between the other passengers . . . I got back to my room, locked the door and never even glanced at the ikons. I took a deep breath, plucked up courage and levitated to the ceiling. I floated up, came down again, turned somersaults, all the junk fell out of my pockets . . . It was like a dream . . .

"You say all miracles are God's work . . . But if that's true, I would have felt something in my soul. But I felt nothing! You understand, there was nothing, except maybe a feeling I was a bit outlandish, a freak . . . It didn't feel like a miracle . . . Only a paradox of causality . . . And then came the blinding insight. I had never been a believer . . . More than that, I felt, well, how shall I put it? the emptiness of the universe, the godlessness of the world, I felt I was quite alone in the world . . . "

"How can this be?" exclaimed the priest. "You can fly! Fly! And yet you speak of the emptiness of the universe, of your being alone . . . Lord! What's wrong with people? They refuse to accept either reward or retribution!"

He got up from the bed, walked over to the ikonostasis and fell to his knees.

"Lord, be Thou not angry at the ignorance of Thy servants. Their minds are clouded and their souls defiled. Great is Thy patience and great Thy love, O Lord!"

Aleksey stood aside. He looked vexed, or sad, or perhaps both at once. When the priest had finished and went to bow, Aleksey's voice broke in harshly, jeeringly even. "I haven't told you everything yet, Father!"

The priest went back to his bed and covered his face with his hands. "Tell me. Tell me everything. Leave nothing hidden in your heart."

Aleksey walked over to the ikonostasis. "Symbols! The symbols of your God! And does God recognise these symbols as belonging to Him? Blasphemy? Right?" He sat down next to the old man. "That time in my room, after discovering I was a freak, right at the end, I ripped an ikon from the wall. I flew about with it and mocked God. Risky, wasn't it? But nothing happened, except the ikon shattered when I dropped it from the ceiling. A pity! Now if *I'd* gone smash onto the floor and broken my arms and legs . . . "

"You would have believed?"

" . . . Not half," laughed Aleksey.

"No, even then you would not have believed . . . But perhaps not, no, I don't know."

Father Venyamin was embarrassed somehow, regretting having said what he did.

Aleksey ignored it.

"And so I began a new life. Living with a miracle. I even forgot to think about God the first few days. Flying's quite something. Lord! Can you imagine the pleasure, the sheer pleasure of flying. At night, over the steppe or a lake. Spread your arms and cruise and dip and soar. You don't need anything else in life. It's so easy . . . "

He stood up, put his hands on his head and, smiling drunkenly, floated about the room in a semi-vertical position. Apparently he suddenly thought better of it, because he dropped quickly to the floor, almost as if he'd jumped down, and glanced anxiously at the priest. Father Venyamin stood there, pale and solemn.

"A miracle. A miracle," he whispered. He sounded so full of joy, the young man looked frankly jealous. "Now I can go to my grave!"

Father Venyamin suddenly frowned. He looked worried.

"Why did God permit me to witness a miracle?" he asked,

looking anxiously at Aleksey. "Why? Am I not burdened with sin more than others? Surely . . . "

He blenched, as if he was about to faint, and swayed. Aleksey hurried to help him, but was gently pushed aside and he retreated in surprise to a corner. The priest sank onto the bed and stared blankly past him.

"There was something else you wanted to tell me . . . "

"How are you feeling? Some water, perhaps? . . . "

"No," the priest replied. His tone was detached. "Speak. I know you still have something very important to tell me . . . "

Aleksey shrugged.

"I've told you the most important things. Strange . . . First you were happy when you found out . . . Now you look the most miserable person in the world . . . I had my suspicions, but now I know. My miracle will bring misery to everybody in the end . . . "

"Everybody?" Father Venyamin hastened. "Was there somebody else . . . ?"

"We didn't get round to that," Aleksey sniggered. "I'll start with me, though . . . What am I supposed to do with this miracle? Life has lost all meaning. I can't live amongst people any more because I can't control myself." He smiled. "Ah, if only you knew, Father, how many times I've had to resist temptation. More than Jesus, believe me! The number of times I've wanted to levitate in the middle of the street and enjoy watching the reactions of my fellow citizens, all of them permanently drunk on the determinism of the natural world. And don't you think I didn't want to liven things up a bit at your church today?"

"But you didn't," the priest said quietly.

"I didn't. But it wasn't out of a sense of decency. If I demonstrate it in public, they'll either turn me into a scientific guinea pig or I'll be exploited by the church. I have my vanity. I've no intention of becoming an object of study!"

"And until now nobody . . . "

"Regrettably . . . " Aleksey interrupted. "But you need to be in the right frame of mind before I tell you."

He was trying to be ironic . . . But that was not how it sounded and so the priest answered in all seriousness. "I'm ready."

"I cannot live among ordinary people. It's too boring. It's not that I feel I'm a superman. I simply want to fly. I've turned into a bird of the night, Father. I can't fly by day . . . I came to the country, dropped my studies and everything as if they were so much waste paper . . . I never wanted to drink . . . haven't a clue about drugs . . . and yet it seems I'm suffering the same kind of addiction. I sleep during the day, and I keep flying in my sleep . . . I always wake up frightened: perhaps it was all a dream? If I'm alone, I have to try and see if I can still do it. I literally go shooting up into the air. When I'm certain again it's not a dream, that I really can fly, I weep with joy. If I go somewhere where it's impossible, I get this nagging doubt that the miracle's over, so I rush off to try it out and make sure . . . The worst thing, Father, is that the time I can do without gets less and less . . . People irritate me just by being there . . . I've become rude . . . cruel . . . All I want to do is fly.

"But the story I wanted to tell you is this . . . One day I went off away into the trees and began chasing birds. The uproar! . . . Birds, Father, are determinists as well. They hate to see the laws of nature violated . . .

"Anyway, I was completely carried away, and then I suddenly looked down and saw a man . . . He was standing there gawping with his mouth wide open . . . I should have got out of there, but instead I flew down towards him . . . He never uttered a sound. He just fell flat on his back. By the time I reached him, it was all over . . . I've killed a man. That's what I've done. And you very nearly gave up the ghost . . . "

The priest leapt from his bed. His eyes were wide and staring, his hands shaking . . . Aleksey darted away from him.

"That's it," Father Venyamin shouted. "That's it. I, too. You, and the man, and me!" He clutched his head.

"This is all I need," muttered Aleksey, backing towards the door.

"Stop," shouted the priest. "Forgive me!"

He suddenly fell on his knees before Aleksey. "Forgive me! For the love of Christ, forgive me. I preached you a sermon about faith. Forgive me, I had no right to. I was myself deluded and so deluded you. And the Lord. And the Lord. You are honest . . . forthright . . . While all my life I . . . "

He fell to the ground, sobbing. Aleksey was in despair.

"Damn this miracle," he yelled. He knelt beside the priest. Father Venyamin looked up, struggled back to his knees and embraced Aleksey.

"No. You mustn't talk like that. You do not understand. We have all betrayed God. I am the first. By His miracle He has exposed my lie!"

The priest's voice sank to a whisper. "I was frightened, you see. Understand? I was frightened. Like that man who did not believe what he saw. And you are frightened, too, when confronted by a miracle because you are without faith. I am, too. O, Lord! Can I be forgiven? I have been a hypocrite and a Pharisee! Do you understand?"

Aleksey extricated himself carefully, straightened up, and lifted the priest to his feet.

"I'm terribly sorry," he said, and his voice was hard, "but subtleties like that are obviously beyond me. I can't think straight when it comes to my own problems . . . I'd better go . . . "

"Wait! Wait! I beg you!"

Father Venyamin urged him to the chair and sat on the bed next to him, never letting go of Aleksey's hand.

"We cannot, please understand, we cannot part like this. The Lord in His mercy has bound our lives together . . . "

"Mercy?" snorted Aleksey. "What do I need His mercy for? I have recognised Him of my own free will. That was how it all happened. With this miracle He challenged the freedom of my faith and destroyed it."

"No, no, no," Father Venyamin objected hotly. "It was you who admitted there was no faith in your heart, was it not? Do not be stiff-necked! You want to be more free than God, but to be free of God means to be a slave. Understand?" He was so agitated he could only whisper. He gripped Aleksey's hand hard, much harder than you would have thought possible for a man of his age. "You think of God. You thirst for faith. Overcome your arrogance, be like the infant who is just discovering the world, listen to the promptings of your own heart. That is where your truth lies."

Aleksey made a dismissive gesture, but the priest did not give him time to speak.

"You do not want to accept a miracle. But think, you would have been one of those who rejected Christ. You would have crucified Him!"

Aleksey looked at him attentively.

"There is a kind of logic in what you say . . . But has logic ever been a reason for anybody to have faith?"

"It's not because it's logical, it's because it's the truth. An age-old truth, which the whole world acknowledged at one time."

"The whole world acknowledged Ptolemy as the truth. So what?"

"Lord," Father Venyamin whispered, his eyes closed. There were tears on his cheeks. "Lord, give me reason. Give me words."

Aleksey tried to shake himself free. He had not found comfort and the discussion had become burdensome.

"Listen," the priest said with passion. "Today, now, go home, fall on your knees and compel yourself with all the strength of your heart, compel yourself to be utterly sincere. And pray. If you feel nothing, pray harder. Pray for one hour, two, three if you have to, until you hear. You will hear, because you will be heard. My dear boy, your life is at stake, and not just this life, so fleeting and false, but life eternal, which is real, and for which the Lord, with His special mercy, is preparing you."

He embraced the young man, and continued: "I, too . . . will pray all night. And the Lord will hear the two of us if we ask for the same thing. My years are thrice yours. And I have to pray for forgiveness for all of them. Will I have the strength? I beg you. Go home and pray. Promise me."

Aleksey finally freed himself. He stood up.

"I promise you, Father, that I will go home now . . . "

He stopped, his eyes glowing with a secret joy.

" . . . It's dark now, right? So I can fly. I'll think over what you said while I'm doing it. I can't promise more than that."

Hastily he said good-bye to the priest. Father Venyamin, on the verge of tears, said nothing. He merely made the sign of the cross and whispered something.

By the time the garden gate banged shut behind Aleksey, Father Venyamin was already on his knees.

*　　*　　*

The night was dark and warm. A man stood on a hill. Invisible to all except himself. Perhaps God saw him, too.

The night was still. All around men huddled asleep in their shelters, dreaming their sinful dreams. The past had seen it all. Abel murdered and Christ crucified, both murder and crucifixion forgotten by mankind, as a child's naughtiness is soon forgotten. And the man on the hill under the starry sky, the son of Adam, was only the image and the likeness of Adam – of Adam, not of God, because he knew nothing of God, and he would not believe the person who knew of Him by hearsay.

The night was dark and warm. Mankind yelped in its sleep, like a dog cheated of a bone. The man on the hill heard the yelping, but felt no sympathy. He no longer belonged among men, cut off from them as he was by the warmth and darkness of the night.

The man looked up into the depth of the stars and thought: "Suppose there is something that unites this infinity of matter and space, something which embodies a meaning for all the world's diversity. I might imagine it as some kind of immanent reason. I might call it God. But what contact can there be between me – dust created of dust – and what one might assume under the term God? How does this Something reduce and simplify itself in order to speak the same language as me with my puny concepts? It'd be easier for a human to make contact with an amoeba. At least there's the same general principle at work . . . cells, proteins and so forth. The very idea of God is absurd . . . and I can fly!

"That's enough. Why rack my brains any longer. That's for humanity at large. Tomorrow it will discover who I am. I'll spit in the eye of both science and religion at once. I'll show the creeps! I can fly. Fly!"

He moved back from the edge of the hill, took a run and lifted off, arms stretched forward. He was intoxicated by the sensation, his mind was drained of thoughts, cleared of problems and contradictions. He didn't feel his body, he was conscious only of himself, as if he was now what he ought always to have been since birth – an immortal free spirit, liberated from all the cares of the flesh. His life was flying, it had no other meaning.

He lost all sense of time. He flew and knew that he would never tire of it. He changed direction automatically, not thinking about where he was flying to, or how far.

Quite some time must have passed. Suddenly the stars vanished, covered by unseen clouds. He lost his bearings. He had lost his sense of horizon, his sense of spatial relationships had vanished. Earth and sky vanished. Climb and descent were indistinguishable. Yes, he was now upright, but where the ground was, above or below, to the right or left, there was no knowing. Fear, something he had not experienced before, gripped his heart. He hunted desperately from side to side, in all directions, but they were infinite, as many as there were facets to his imagination. He shouted, wildly, despairingly, but mankind, even if it was somewhere close at hand, slept on and did not hear his cry. He knew he had lost the earth. And without it, it seemed, life was impossible. God had given him wings and the earth had given up its gravitational force.

He screamed and hurled himself into headlong flight.

* * *

Father Venyamin spent the night in prayer. Towards morning he dozed, exhausted, on the floor in front of the ikonostasis. He was woken by the woman next door, who brought him his milk as usual at seven. Worried, she asked if he was feeling well. Then she told him about the accident in the village. A man had been killed during the night. The girls found him on their way to milking. A young man, good looking, too . . .

"Where is he?" shouted the priest, giving his neighbour a bad scare.

"The militia came from town and took the body away."

The villagers stared curiously as the priest hurried down the village street, hair and beard flying.

The village nurse was taken by surprise when the priest burst into her office.

"Tell me, did you see him?"

"Who?"

"The young man . . . who was killed . . ."

"Yes," she replied, not understanding what was required of her.

"What happened?"

"I don't know, he looked like he'd fallen out of a plane . . . all smashed up . . ."

Father Venyamin ran back to his lodgings. He didn't stop to shut the door, he collapsed in prayer in front of the ikons and burst into tears.